The Sweet Life

The Sweet Life

DEBBIE MASON

FOREVER

New York   Boston

Copyright © 2025 by Debbie Mazzuca

Cover design by Daniela Medina
Cover images © Shutterstock
Cover copyright © 2025 by Hachette Book Group, Inc.

Forever
Hachette Book Group
1290 Avenue of the Americas, New York, NY 10104
read-forever.com
@readforeverpub

First Edition: June 2025

Forever is an imprint of Grand Central Publishing. The Forever name and logo are registered trademarks of Hachette Book Group, Inc.

The publisher is not responsible for websites (or their content) that are not owned by the publisher.

The Hachette Speakers Bureau provides a wide range of authors for speaking events. To find out more, go to hachettespeakersbureau.com or email HachetteSpeakers@hbgusa.com.

Forever books may be purchased in bulk for business, educational, or promotional use. For information, please contact your local bookseller or the Hachette Book Group Special Markets Department at special.markets@hbgusa.com.

Library of Congress Cataloging-in-Publication Data

Names: Mason, Debbie (Novelist) author
Title: The sweet life / Debbie Mason.
Description: First edition. | New York, NY : Forever, 2025. | Series: Sunshine Bay ; 3 |
Identifiers: LCCN 2024059602 | ISBN 9781538768792 trade paperback | ISBN 9781538768815 ebook
Subjects: LCGFT: Fiction | Romance fiction | Novels
Classification: LCC PR9199.4.M3696 S94 2025 | DDC 813/.6—dc23/eng/20250131
LC record available at https://lccn.loc.gov/2024059602

ISBNs: 978-1-5387-6879-2 (Trade paperback); 978-1-5387-6881-5 (ebook)

Printed in the United States of America

LSC-H

Printing 1, 2025

In memory of Donna Norris, a wonderful woman who made the lives of everyone she touched sweeter. She was, and still is, a blessing to her family and to all of us who had the honor of knowing her.

The Sweet Life

Chapter One

The high-pitched wail of a phone alarm dragged attorney Sage Rosetti from her recurring nightmare—the one where she stood naked in the front of a packed courtroom as the judge ruled in favor of her client's ex.

Over the alarm, Sage heard her assistant Brenda's voice and realized that she had fallen asleep at her desk again.

"Trust me, Sage can sleep through almost anything. This is the third time this week she's pulled an all-nighter," Brenda said.

Sage didn't think her team finding her asleep at her desk was a good look and tried opening her eyes, but apparently her body wasn't taking orders from her brain.

"Doesn't she have a partner or friends?" asked another woman, whose voice was almost as annoying as the alarm that had gone blessedly silent.

"No. All she does is work."

Hey, she had friends...Family counted as friends, didn't they? Sage managed to pry one eyelid open. Hovering by her desk were the blurred faces of Brenda and the junior lawyer who'd been assigned to Sage's team yesterday afternoon.

"If that's what it takes to make partner at this firm, I'd better start applying elsewhere. Work-life balance is a priority for me."

Sage snorted at the idea of work-life balance—but she must have snorted in her head, because the two women kept talking as if she weren't lying with her face on her keyboard, eyeballing them.

"Sage is a *junior* partner," Brenda informed the newest member of their team. And given how the founding partners felt about her inability to toe the company line, she would remain so until the three octogenarians either retired or dropped dead.

"Really? I thought she's one of the most sought-after divorce attorneys in Boston and makes the big bucks."

"She is, and she does. It's just that the founding partners are—"

Brenda's intention to share their low opinion of the founding partners with a brand-new associate was the impetus Sage needed to lift her bowling-ball-heavy head off the desk. "What time is it?" she rasped, peeling the keyboard from her cheek.

"Time that you picked a new alarm for your phone. It's been proven that the Radar alarm ringtone elevates people's blood pressure and makes them grumpy," Brenda said, handing Sage her cell phone with a pointed look.

Sage ignored her assistant's insinuation that she was grumpy first thing in the morning. In her opinion, the morning didn't officially begin until she'd consumed at least one grande Americano.

Bleary-eyed, she held the screen to her face. Nothing happened.

"You might want to fix your hair and your, uh, face. You were drooling," Brenda added, a smile flirting with her lips.

Sage pushed to her feet, feeling every minute of the time she'd spent asleep at her desk. Her knees creaked as if she were eighty instead of thirty as she hobbled to the closet-size bathroom off her office. She might not be an equity partner, but that tiny sink, mirror, and toilet more than made up for the bonuses she missed out on.

Sage winced when she caught sight of herself in the mirror above the sink. No wonder her phone didn't recognize her face. Her hair looked like she'd had a good time in bed with the partner she didn't have and didn't want, if her clients' relationships were an example of the price you paid for love. Her smudged mascara made her look like a raccoon, and thanks to the drool, there was a streak of red lip stain dangling from the corner of her mouth to her chin. She couldn't decide whether she looked like a rabid raccoon or the bride of Frankenstein.

As she finished up in the bathroom and washed her hands, she heard Brenda say, "Forbes, Poole, and Russell...Oh, hi, Ms. Rosetti. Carmen, of course. I'll get Sage for you."

Sage darted from the bathroom waving her hands and mouthing, *I'm not here!*

Carmen Rosetti was her grandmother. Ninety percent of the time, Sage adored her, but the other ten percent of the time, her grandmother got on her last nerve. Lately, it had been closer to twenty percent of the time.

Sage hadn't visited her family on Sunshine Bay in months due to her heavy caseload, and there was no one who did guilt better than an Italian grandmother. Carmen knew every last one of Sage's buttons to push, and she pushed them like a gleeful toddler.

"Sage, do you—" the junior lawyer began, her overloud voice nearly drowning out Brenda, who was in the middle of covering for Sage.

"I'm sorry, Carmen. She left the—" Her assistant sighed. "Yes, I did hear that. She just returned to the office for her phone. Here she is."

Sorry, Brenda mouthed, handing the phone to Sage.

If the junior lawyer followed through with her plan to quit, Sage was requesting a low talker for her replacement. "You'll have to make it quick, Nonna. I'm due in court in an hour."

Three hours, actually, but she had to see how far she'd gotten on the briefs before she'd fallen asleep. They were due to opposing counsel this afternoon. She prayed she hadn't hit the Delete button with her cheek.

"Work, work, work, that's all you do. No time for your family. I'm not getting any younger, you know."

Sage tucked the office phone between her ear and shoulder and walked to her desk. After placing her own cell phone beside the keyboard, she woke up her computer. "You'll probably outlive us all. You're in better shape than I am."

Sadly, it was true, but it was also true that her grandmother at seventy-four wasn't getting any younger.

Bringing up her calendar on the screen, Sage continued, "I'll come this weekend. I can fit you in on Sunday from twelve to five."

"What? You're such a big shot now that we have to make an appointment to see you?"

Sage winced. "No, of course not. It's just that my caseload is heavy right now, and if I don't work on the weekend, I'll get behind."

Back in January, she'd represented a high-profile client whose divorce had received a lot of attention in the press, in part due to the exorbitant support payments Sage had demanded for her client, and subsequently received. The publicity from the case was the reason she'd been inundated with new clients...and made junior partner.

She glanced at her calendar, mentally moving things around. "How about I sleep over on Saturday? We can have a movie night with everyone at Zia Eva's." Her aunt Eva had a large oceanfront home and would happily host a family movie night. It would be nice to see everyone, Sage grudgingly admitted to herself, even if it required her to pull another all-nighter.

"Si, that's good. We need to talk about your mother."

Sage sighed. She was the Rosetti family's official problem solver. "Okay. We'll talk Saturday night. I have to go—"

"Come for a late lunch. We'll have time to talk before the movie then. I'll make gnocchi the way you like it."

Sage's stomach grumbled at the mention of food. She couldn't remember when she last ate, and there was nothing she liked to eat more than her grandmother's fried potato dumpling pasta with Gorgonzola cream sauce and fire-roasted tomatoes, which Carmen well knew. Her grandmother could offer master classes on the art of manipulation.

Sage could use a master class on the art of saying no, but she had been missing her family. At least she had been when she'd had a moment to think about anything besides work. She reminded herself that she loved her job, and she really did.

There was nothing more satisfying than ensuring that women were protected, financially as well as mentally, and sometimes physically, from the men who'd promised to love and cherish them but instead treated them so badly that they destroyed their confidence and stole their identity.

She'd been raised by three strong and loving single mothers who went out of their way to help other women. Sage had known from an early age that she wanted to do the same. Except she didn't provide a shoulder to cry on or an ear to listen or free meals and babysitting services. She went after the men where it hurt most, their bank accounts.

"Okay. Ciao, Nonna. I'll see you Sat—"

"Don't hang up! I didn't call to chat. I called to ask you about Alice Espinoza. She's missing."

Sage slowly lowered herself onto her chair. "What do you mean, she's missing?"

"What do you mean, what do I mean? She's missing. It says so on Facebook. No one has seen her since yesterday. You haven't heard from her, have you? She didn't come to the city to see you?"

As much as Sage's mother, aunt, and grandmother had been her role models, Alice Espinoza was the reason she'd become a lawyer. Alice had begun mentoring her at sixteen, and Sage had spent the majority of her weekends and school holidays with Alice at her home and law offices on Ocean View Drive.

"I haven't spoken to her since..." Sage racked her brain, trying to remember when they'd last talked. She was positive it had been within the past two months, but then it hit her.

". . . New Year's Eve." She briefly closed her eyes at the realization she hadn't spoken to Alice in five months.

She'd called Sage around nine o'clock on New Year's Eve. They'd laughed at their similar plans for the night, working at home while watching Anderson Cooper and Andy Cohen ring in the New Year. Then Alice had shared her surprising news. She was buying a lavender farm outside Sunshine Bay. She planned to relocate her law practice to the farm as well. Sage had promised to help her with the move, and Alice had texted her the date last month. Sage had meant to call her, but time had gotten away from her.

Sage grabbed her cell phone, opened it with her face, and went to Facebook. Her sister, Willow, had uploaded Facebook and Instagram onto Sage's phone two years ago in a futile attempt to convince Sage that some people actually had lives apart from their jobs. The only reason Sage hadn't deleted the apps was because her mother, aunt, and grandmother regularly posted videos on La Dolce Vita's account to promote the family's Italian restaurant. "Who posted about Alice?"

"Her assistant posted on the firm's account, and your sister posted twenty minutes ago on *Good Morning, Sunshine!* Willow asked anyone who's seen Alice recently to contact the police." Sage's sister hosted a morning talk show on Sunshine Bay's local television station. Sage heard clicking, and then her grandmother said, "Sunshine Bay Police Department just posted that someone saw Alice riding her bike around sunset yesterday on Route 6A."

Sage frowned. The route would take Alice to the farm,

and Sage knew from Alice's text last month that she had no plans to move in until the sale of her home on Ocean View Drive closed a few weeks from now. The farmhouse had needed a new roof and the plumbing and electrical systems updated.

Sage found the post and began scrolling through people's responses to the sighting. Several mentioned seeing Alice in town earlier in the week, and then SBPD posted a photo.

At the sight of the iridescent purple bike lying in a ditch, Sage covered her mouth. "That's Alice's bike."

She'd know it anywhere. Alice had been riding the same bike for as long as Sage had known her.

It took several shaky attempts before Sage got the bottom drawer of her desk unlocked. Once she did, she grabbed her purse, tossed her cell phone inside the oversize leather bag, and shot from the chair. It wasn't until she was halfway out the door that she remembered she had to be in court.

Looking as panicked as Sage felt, Brenda waved her off. "Go. We've got this. We'll ask for a postponement."

"But the briefs. I—"

"I'll call you if there's a problem, but I'm sure they're fine. Now go, and let us know if...*when* you find Alice," Brenda corrected herself, biting her bottom lip as she glanced at one of the photos on Sage's desk. It was of Alice and Sage on the day Sage had received her JD degree from Harvard.

"Are you sure? I haven't had a chance to review anything with..." She couldn't remember the junior lawyer's name. Sage hadn't been a part of the hiring process, even though she'd asked to be.

The one and only female senior partner at the firm, and the lawyer who'd hired Sage, had recently retired. She'd been an old friend of Alice's. She would have made sure Sage had been involved in the hiring process. She'd always had her back.

"That's why you have me. Now get out of here. Wait!" Brenda called.

Sage stopped and turned, sighing when Brenda motioned to the phone still clutched in Sage's hand. She brought it to her ear. "Nonna, I'll see you in a couple of hours. Call me with updates, okay?"

"Si, si, you drive carefully. Try not to worry. I'm sure Alice is fine," her grandmother said before disconnecting.

Carmen didn't sound like she believed that Alice was fine any more than Sage did.

⌒

"I'm about a mile out," Sage told her sister, who'd called with the latest update.

In the time it had taken Sage to get from downtown Boston to the outskirts of her hometown, SBPD had begun organizing a search party. They were doing a grid search from the farm to where Alice's bike had been located. They had at least five miles to cover.

The police were working on the theory that a driver, blinded by the setting sun, had accidentally hit Alice, panicked, and left the scene. They surmised that Alice had been hurt and wandered away from the accident site, either in search of help or in a state of confusion.

"Sorry! I'm going to join another search team with my sister," Willow called to someone.

"No, you go with them, Will. I want to talk to the police and the search coordinator. I'll catch up with you."

"Are you sure? You and Alice are so close. I don't want you searching for her with a bunch of strangers. What if—"

"Don't." She cut off her sister before she could voice Sage's own fears. "Alice probably went for a walk on one of the trails at the farm with her earbuds in, completely unaware of the fuss she's caused. She'll be mortified when she finds out."

Instead of turning right toward the ocean, Sage headed left. She had a general idea how to get to the farm. When she was younger, she'd accompany her mom to pick lavender every summer. Her mom was the crunchy granola type—low maintenance, into yoga, all-natural products, and reducing her carbon footprint. Sage wouldn't have been surprised if her mom bought the farm, but she'd been shocked Alice had. "I'm going to the farm."

"Sage, I don't think that's . . . Fine. We'll meet you there," her sister said, and began calling out the names of the Rosetti family and the Monroes, Willow's newfound family.

It sounded like everyone had turned out, including Sage's aunt Cami, who'd been estranged from the family for more than two decades. Last summer, they'd discovered she was Willow's biological mother. It didn't matter to Sage. Willow would always be her sister, even if she was technically her cousin.

The traffic was heavier than Sage expected as she got closer to the turnoff to the farm. Then she saw why. There were several police cars and emergency vehicles parked on the side of the road. She slowed her silver BMW and pulled off onto the gravel shoulder, noting a line of vehicles behind her doing the same.

Her stomach dropped when two German shepherds and their handlers walked over to the group of law enforcement officers. Somehow, seeing the search-and-rescue dogs hit harder than seeing the photo of Alice's bike in the ditch. It made it more real. Alice really was missing.

With every intention of joining the search, Sage reached over the red leather seat for a pair of white sneakers. She kept them in her car on the off chance she'd have time to get in a walk on her lunch hour. They'd never been worn.

She slipped off her sensible heels and then opened the car door. A warm breeze carrying the sweet scent of lavender filled the car. The day promised to be hot for late May. It was ten thirty and already seventy-two degrees without a cloud in the bright-blue sky.

She took off the cream linen blazer with the black tuxedo side stripes that she wore over a black etched floral blouse and a black skirt, laying it on the passenger seat before slipping on her sneakers. As she got out of the car and shut the door, locking it with the app on her phone, a man caught her attention.

He had his back to her, talking to a group of first responders. They seemed to be paying close attention to whatever he was saying. She didn't think he was law enforcement, though. He wore a white T-shirt, faded jeans, and a pair of scuffed brown leather motorcycle boots. This didn't rule out that he worked at SBPD, but she knew most of the members of the small force and didn't recall anyone with his longish, copper-streaked brown hair. Nor had there been anyone as tall or as muscularly built as this man the last time she'd been at the station to bail out her mother. Sage would have noticed him.

But he did have an air of confident authority about him, she thought as she crossed the road. The group started to disperse, and she hung back as he talked with one of the handlers, waiting to introduce herself. Then she saw him holding Alice's favorite blue plaid flannel shirt. "Where the hell did you get that?"

Chapter Two

When the man turned his familiar cool-blue gaze on Sage, she staggered back two steps. He reached out to steady her, his warm hand and strong fingers closing around her forearm.

"Give us a minute," Jake said to the dog's handler.

The dark-haired woman nodded while giving Sage a sympathetic smile.

It was the sympathy in the woman's expression that shook Sage from her shock. "I don't need a minute," she said, pulling her arm free.

Jake had always been bossy, as well as so ridiculously hot that being in the same room with him had left her tongue-tied and made her toes curl even though she'd pretty much despised the guy growing up. He'd been Sunshine Bay's resident bad boy: cool, popular, and always in trouble. If it hadn't been for Alice taking him under her wing when he was in tenth grade, he would have wound up in jail.

Her eyes narrowed on his too-handsome face. "What are you doing here?" As far as she knew, he didn't live in Sunshine Bay and hadn't visited in years.

It wasn't as if she kept tabs on him. Alice sometimes shared updates on his life, whether Sage wanted to hear them or not. He'd enlisted in the military not long after high school. He was married and lived in San Diego. Every winter, Alice took off a week to visit him there. His family, the Walkers, lived in Sunshine Bay. But they were bad news and the reason Alice had taken Jake into her home all those years ago.

Sage crossed her arms when he simply looked at her with an eyebrow raised. "What are you doing with Alice's jacket?" A hint of accusation had slid into her voice, unintentionally, of course.

He'd heard it too, she surmised when he gave his head a slight irritated shake and said, "You haven't changed, have you?"

She didn't cower under the weight of his intimidating stare. He'd have to do a lot better than that if he thought to unnerve her. She'd dealt with men far scarier than Jake Walker in the past five years. Men who were used to things going their way—men with the means to hire unsavory characters to do their dirty work otherwise—and not once had she backed down or given in to their threats.

One of the search coordinators began calling out instructions to the volunteers, waving them forward. They moved toward a trail leading up the hill and into the woods.

The dark-haired woman approached, offering them both an apologetic smile. "We're going to head out."

"Right." Jake handed Alice's jacket to the woman. "I'll catch up with you," he said, offering his thanks before returning his attention to Sage.

Sage's grip tightened on her cell phone as she watched the

woman hold the plaid flannel to the dogs' noses. She focused on the sound of Jake's voice, willing the weakness from her knees.

"I got in late last night and stayed at the inn. Alice and I had planned to meet up at the farmhouse this morning. She wanted me to get rid of a waterbed for her and to give her a hand organizing her office. When she didn't show at the farm or answer her cell phone, I went to the house. She wasn't there, so I called Kendra. Her assistant," he added at Sage's blank stare. "She couldn't reach Alice either. We walked through the house and the farmhouse, but there was no sign of her, and no sign she'd been in either place all night."

"What about Max?" Max was Alice's beloved Maine coon cat. He was a beautiful black tabby measuring four feet long with a tail like a raccoon, and he hated Sage. Alice thought it was hilarious. According to her, Max loved everyone, especially Jake.

"Max was at the house. He hadn't been fed."

"You can't go to the worst-case scenario just because of that, Jake. The police could be wrong."

He nodded. "I don't buy their theory that Alice was hit by a car, but she did take a fall, and she was hurt."

"How do you know she wasn't hit by a car?" Why was she being defensive? Alice not being hit by a car was the best-case scenario, and she'd just said the police could be wrong.

"Because I was the one who sent the photo of the bike to SBPD. The damage isn't consistent with being struck by a car. It looked like she'd veered into oncoming traffic and lost control of the bike and ended up in the ditch. Tire marks indicated a car had swerved, braking hard to avoid her."

She couldn't bear the thought of Alice out there alone and hurt, which was probably why she asked, again with a defensive edge in her voice, "How can you be sure she's hurt? Maybe—"

Jake cut her off with a frustrated sigh. They'd fallen back into their old patterns. She'd get defensive and snippy with him, and he'd get frustrated and annoyed with her.

"I had a chance to look around before anyone compromised the scene. Alice was . . . She's hurt, okay. She had to have been lying there for at least a couple of hours. The grass was still flattened, and from the blood splatter . . . Anyway, it looked to me like she sustained a head injury. If I'm right, she didn't regain consciousness until well after dark. It would explain why no one saw her on the road."

"Or stopped to help her," Sage murmured, turning her head. She sniffed, swiping a finger under her lashes to catch a wayward tear, grateful when Jake let the action pass without commenting on her inability to keep her emotions in check. "What about her cell phone?"

"I didn't find it at the farm or the house, and it wasn't at the scene." He held up his own. "I've being calling her every fifteen minutes. SBPD put in a request with her provider to trace her phone, but it could take hours . . . if her cell's even on." He glanced at the trail. "I need to join the search party. Will you be okay on your own?"

She didn't miss the way his gaze moved over her face, looking for any hint of weakness. She lifted her chin. "I'm fine," she said, and went to walk past him.

His fingers closed around her bicep, gentle but firm. "You're not joining the search."

She peeled his hand from her arm. "Yes, I am, and there's nothing you can say or do to stop me from looking for Alice, so get out of my way."

He raked his fingers through his hair. "Look, I'm not trying to tell you what to do. It's just . . . you're not dressed for it."

She might be wearing sneakers, but she couldn't dispute the fact that her skirt and blouse weren't suitable for searching the woods. "That's not what you were going to say, is it?"

"Of course it is. Why . . ." He shook his head when she crossed her arms and stared him down. "Fine. You want the truth? I don't want you there in case we find her. I don't want your last memory of—"

She reached up, placing her hand over his mouth, desperate to stop him from stealing her hope. "Don't say it. Please, don't say it."

His warm lips pressed what felt like a tender kiss to her palm, and her breath hitched in response. He lowered her hand from his mouth, the tension in his jaw suddenly relaxing as he looked past her. "Your family's here. Stay with them, okay?"

She nodded, too stunned by her reaction to the feel of his lips on her skin to do anything else.

He handed her his phone. "Put in your number. I'll text you updates when I have them."

She did as he said, hesitating before handing it back to him. She searched his face as he'd searched hers only moments before. "Maybe you shouldn't go either. It will be as hard on you as it would be on me if you, if they . . ." She still couldn't bring herself to say the words.

"I was special forces, Sage. I—" Someone yelled out, and his gaze shot to the woods. He took off at a run. "Keep Sage away," he ordered her family as he sprinted past them and up the hill, stopping when the two women and their dogs walked out of the woods, their expressions somber.

The dark-haired woman hugged Jake. He nodded at whatever she was saying to him. He took a moment before glancing back at Sage. He held her gaze and slowly shook his head and then disappeared into the trees.

She moved to run after him, but her sister and mother darted in front of her, each of them grabbing her by an arm. "Let me go! He shouldn't be doing this on his own."

"He doesn't want you there, honey. He's trying to protect you. Let him. Please," her mother begged before she and Sage's sister sandwiched her in a hug.

"We're here for you," Willow said, holding her tight. "You don't have to go through this on your own."

Sage's grandmother and aunt joined in the group hug. Sage, her head on her mother's shoulder, hadn't needed to see Cami to know she was there. She'd felt her mother stiffen.

Taking a steadying breath, Sage wiped her eyes and moved out of her family's comforting embrace. She didn't have the bandwidth to play intermediary today. "Thank you. I'll be okay. It's just..." She swallowed, barely managing to get the words out. "It's a shock."

She had to shut away thoughts about Alice and the accident, her guilt over not being there for her friend, her sorrow over losing her. When she was alone, curled up on her bed at her condo, Sage would let her feelings out.

The last members of the search party walked out of the woods and down the hill. Jake wasn't with them. She pressed her lips together to hold back a sob, unable to stop the tears from rolling down her cheeks.

Her mother slid an arm around Sage's waist when two paramedics walked up the hill carrying a stretcher between them. They were followed by three police officers, one holding a roll of yellow tape in his hand.

The sight of the police tape took Sage's breath away. The officers and the green of the trees merged as everything in front of her blurred and spun. She placed her hands on her knees and bent over, pushing her breath through her clenched teeth.

"You don't need to be here for this. Let me take you home," her mother said, rubbing Sage's back. "I'll make you a nice grilled eggplant caprese. You'll feel better once you eat."

The Rosettis' love language was food.

Sage waited for everything to stop spinning before slowly straightening. She glanced at her phone, wondering if she should text Jake or leave him alone to process his grief. It seemed important that she stayed, for him and for Alice. "I can't leave."

As she stood vigil with her family by her side, a crowd gathered behind them.

A woman's voice rose above the whispers. "Her poor family when they find out she died alone in the woods."

Sage's fingers tightened around her phone. Willow looked over her shoulder in an attempt, Sage imagined, to get the woman to stop talking. It didn't work.

"I don't think she had any family. I don't think she ever married," another woman said.

"Really? She must have had a partner at one time. She's . . . she was in her early seventies, wasn't she?"

"Yes, but she had a busy legal practice. It didn't leave her much time for anything else."

Carmen reached around Gia to tap Sage's back, which Sage's mother didn't miss. "Really, Ma? You think this is the time to get on Sage's case about how much she works?" Gia said in a heated whisper.

Obviously, the women behind them didn't realize their conversation was giving Sage's grandmother talking points as they continued. "That's so sad. There'll be hardly anyone at her funeral. We'll have to go."

As the women discussed what they'd wear to Alice's funeral, Gia moved to the other side of Sage. The better to hear Cami and Willow's conversation.

Sage looked at her grandmother, who'd lightly elbowed her in the ribs. "Don't even."

"I wasn't going to mention how you'll end up like Alice if you're not careful." She looked up as two officers started down the path from the woods. "But it won't surprise me if the coroner discovers she dropped dead from overwork."

"Nonna," Sage muttered.

"God rest her soul." Her grandmother made the sign of the cross. "She was a good woman even if she worked too hard and passed her work ethic on to you."

Before Sage could say anything, not that it would do her any good, her grandmother raised her chin at Sage's mother. "Do you see what I mean about your mother? She's not herself."

Sage glanced at Gia, who didn't look happy about whatever her sister and her daughter were discussing, but other

than that, Sage didn't have a clue what her grandmother was
talking about.

She whispered as much to Carmen, who threw up her
hands. "Look at her face, her hair. Look what she's wearing.
Did you see her new car?"

"She got a new car?" Sage asked under her breath as she
checked out what her mother had on. It wasn't her usual
casual boho chic, but she looked fantastic in a pink T-shirt
and tight white capri jeans, paired with cute pink high-tops
that might be a little young for a fifty-five-year-old woman,
but who cared. Her mother was gorgeous and rocked whatever
she wore.

Sage casually leaned forward to check out her mother's face.
Umm, okay, so her usually makeup-free mother had quite the
smoky eye going on, but she totally rocked it, which Sage had
planned to share with her grandmother until Gia stepped forward, turning her head in the direction Cami and Willow
were waving. Sage got a better look at her mother's long dark
hair.

Sage turned to her grandmother and lowered her voice. "Are
the purple streaks in Mom's hair permanent or do they wash
out?"

"I think they fade but she'll just get them again. She says
they're *cool*." Carmen rolled her eyes.

"It's not something I'd do, but hey, it's her hair."

"Bah, she's acting like a teenager. Look at her car." Carmen
pointed at a line of vehicles parked on the side of the road. At
the front of them was a red muscle car.

"Uh, Nonna, you're not pointing at the red car with the
racing stripes, are you?"

Her grandmother got a smug look on her face. "Pazza, si?"

Sage and her sister only knew a few words in Italian—the menu at La Dolce Vita and swear words—but since Carmen had been insinuating that Sage's mother was going crazy, Sage assumed that's what *pazza* meant. "I wouldn't call it a crazy choice. More like...an interesting one."

As interesting as a forty-year-old man buying a candy-apple-red convertible. Clearly, her grandmother hadn't been exaggerating, as she was prone to do. Something was definitely going on with Sage's mother.

"Interesting, my culo. You're here now. You talk to her."

Movement on the hill caught Sage's eye, and she looked toward the woods. She'd used the conversation with her grandmother to distract herself, but that would no longer work. Nothing would. "Not now, Nonna. I can't talk to her now."

Her grandmother followed her gaze. "Aw, bella." She took Sage's hand in hers and gave it a squeeze. "Sometimes life is unfair, but you have your family. Even if some of them are pazza. We're here for you."

Gia glanced from her mother to her daughter and then looked up the hill. "Oh, baby." She wrapped an arm around Sage.

The rest of her family formed a tight-knit circle, trying to protect her from the sight of the men carrying Alice's body from the woods. One of the men carrying her on the stretcher down the steep path was Jake.

It wasn't his job. But it didn't surprise Sage that he would take this last walk with Alice. He loved her as much as Sage did, maybe more. Alice was the only real family he had. The only one who'd cared enough to extend a helping hand. The two women gossiping about Alice didn't have a clue who she really was, or all the good that she'd quietly done for the people in Sunshine Bay.

Later, Sage would wonder what she'd been thinking. But in that moment, she needed to be with someone who loved Alice as much as she did.

"I'm okay," she assured her family, giving them each a hug before leaving them to watch her walk to where Jake helped the paramedics load the stretcher into the waiting ambulance.

She couldn't look at the body bag that held the woman she'd loved. Instead, she focused on Jake. He turned as if sensing the weight of her stare, and his gaze met hers, her sorrow reflected in his light-blue eyes.

"Sorry for your loss, man," one of the paramedics said to Jake, while another first responder patted his broad shoulder. Jake nodded. "Thanks. Thanks to everyone for coming out. We appreciate it," he said, speaking for both him and Sage.

Those women didn't think Alice had family, but she did. She had them.

Jake's gaze roamed her face as he walked toward her and opened his arms. She walked into his waiting arms and buried her face in his chest, taking comfort in their shared grief, in the strong arms that he wrapped around her, and the soothing murmur of his deep voice.

Chapter Three

Gia watched Jake gather her daughter into his arms and pressed the tips of her fingers to her lips, holding back a sob. Her heart ached for Sage. Her powerful, self-reliant daughter who rarely showed her soft, vulnerable side had let her guard down to find comfort from a man who'd been her nemesis growing up.

Sage had shouted more angry words and shed more angry tears over Jake Walker than any boy or man Gia could remember. At the time, she'd suspected that her teenage daughter had a crush on him. She hadn't shared her opinion with Sage. Gia had had enough experience with volatile teen emotions by then to know when to keep her opinions to herself.

She'd gotten through her daughters' teen years by fostering strong, trusting relationships with her girls—listening and comforting instead of punishing. She'd also swallowed angry words, gritted her teeth to keep in hard truths, and spent many a sleepless night wondering if she was doing anything right. She'd survived her daughters' teen years with the support and wisdom of her mother and her sister Eva. Wine, yoga, and prayer had helped too.

A heavy hand gave her shoulder a comforting squeeze. "How are you holding up?"

In reaction to that smooth, deep voice, butterflies danced in Gia's stomach, and her face became embarrassingly warm. It happened every time she was in the same room with Flynn Monroe. He didn't even have to touch her or speak to her. A simple look from across the room, and she reacted like a starry-eyed teenager in the throes of her first crush.

She glanced up, her eyes meeting his. The man was as breathtakingly beautiful as their daughter. She groaned inwardly. She had to stop thinking of Willow as *their* daughter. Gia might have raised Willow as her own, but Flynn and Cami were her biological parents. Cami was Gia's younger sister, which meant the man was off limits.

Completely off limits, even in your dreams, she reminded herself while trying, and failing, to draw her gaze from his. After learning the other night that he was coming home for the summer to help out his father, she'd dreamed that Willow was her and Flynn's daughter, instead of his and Cami's.

"Gia?" he said, his brow furrowed.

Luckily for her, her deeply tanned olive skin ensured her now-burning cheeks would be barely noticeable. "Sorry." She forced her gaze from his, nodding in her oldest daughter's direction. "I'm worried about Sage. She was close to Alice."

"Willow mentioned that when she called about the search. I was with a team near the beach when we got word they'd found Alice. I thought I'd check on all of you before heading to the hospital."

It wasn't fair that the man was as caring and thoughtful as he was gorgeous. "How is Amos? Willow said the surgery went well." Flynn's father had broken his hip in a fall earlier in the week.

"His surgery did go well. It's keeping him in the hospital, that's the problem. They want him to stay another two days, and he's threatening to sue if they don't release him."

"Are you going to give in and bring him home?" It's what she would do if it were her mother. Over the years, they'd discovered it was easier to give in to Carmen than to fight with her.

"No way. I'm going to enjoy the next couple of days without him." He grinned. "I've shocked you, haven't I?"

"No. I'm impressed. If Carmen ever breaks her hip, we'll call you when she tries to sign herself out, which would probably be five minutes after surgery."

"I think your mother might be a harder case than Amos."

Gia could almost guarantee that her mother would be putty in Flynn Monroe's hands. Carmen thought the man could do no wrong, which was high praise coming from a woman who had a low opinion of most men.

"You're probably right," Gia said. "Willow mentioned you were doing some work at Amos's to get the house ready to bring him home?" It was embarrassing how Gia's ears perked up at the mere mention of Flynn.

"She's ruining my reputation as the coldhearted son leaving his father to languish in the hospital while he's having a good time with the ladies in Sunshine Bay."

Gia laughed. "Is that what he's telling everyone at the hospital?"

"He is, and he's obviously convincing because I've been pulled aside by his—"

"Hey, Dad," Willow said, interrupting Flynn. "Thanks for coming."

It still surprised Gia to hear Willow call Flynn *Dad*. He hadn't pressured or cared what she'd called him. He'd been happy to play whatever role in her life Willow wanted him to. But it became apparent early on in their relationship that Flynn, who had two other daughters and a son, took his newly discovered responsibility to Willow seriously.

"No problem. I'm just sorry it didn't have a happy outcome."

Willow glanced in the direction of her sister, who'd stepped back from Jake, nodding at whatever he was saying to her. "Me too. Losing Alice, especially like this, will be really hard on Sage."

"Losing someone you love is never easy," Flynn said. He spoke from experience. He'd lost his wife five years ago.

Willow gave him a side hug. "I'm sure it's not, but Sage knows we're here for her, so hopefully that helps."

"I'm sure it will," Flynn said.

Gia hoped they were right. "I'm going to ask Sage to spend the night, honey. I thought we could have a family dinner at the restaurant, just us girls."

Her daughter wrinkled her nose. "I wish I could come, but I have a meeting with Cami and Hugh about the movie."

Gia's sister had sold her memoir for a substantial advance last fall and had completed the manuscript in early April. Cami's boyfriend Hugh, an Oscar-winning director, had optioned the movie rights.

"Surely they can move the meeting to a more convenient

time given the circumstances." Her tone was sharper than she'd intended. From her daughter's sigh, she'd picked up on it.

While everyone else had forgiven Cami and welcomed her back into the family fold, Gia hadn't been able to bring herself to forget the pain her sister had caused, especially to Willow and her. But her daughter was too young to remember. Willow was also kind and forgiving, never held a grudge, and found something good in everyone she met. Since those weren't typical Rosetti traits, Gia figured Willow must have inherited them from her father, who at that moment was glancing from Gia to his daughter with a frown on his handsome face.

"Your mother is right, Will. I'm sure Hugh and Cami would understand. It's a little early for promotional talks anyway, isn't it?"

Gia appreciated Flynn coming to her defense. She wondered if it had anything to do with his personal feelings about the book. He'd obviously play a starring role in her sister's memoir.

"It's not about Cami appearing on *Good Morning, Sunshine!* to promote the book. It's about me playing her in the movie." Willow's voice dropped to almost a whisper on the last five words, so Gia had to strain to hear them.

She wished she hadn't. She couldn't believe Cami would ask this of Willow or that Willow would agree without a word to her. Maybe she was overreacting, but Gia felt betrayed at the idea of the daughter she'd loved and raised since the day she was born portraying Cami, the mother who'd abandoned her. They hadn't announced that Flynn and Cami were Willow's biological parents, but word had gotten around Sunshine Bay, and it hadn't been easy for Gia. The release of the book and movie would make it so much worse. "Why? Why didn't you mention this to me?"

"Seriously? Do you even have to ask, Mom? It's not like you hide your feelings about Cami. I knew how you'd—"

Gia cut her off. "This isn't the time or the place."

She didn't need Willow talking about this with Cami standing only a few yards away. She didn't relish her daughter airing their dirty laundry in front of Flynn either. Then again, Cami intended to put it out there for all the world to see, so it was only a matter of time. It wasn't as if anyone asked how Gia felt about the unhappiest times of her life being shown on the big screen.

"You're right, it's not," Willow agreed. "And I wish I could cancel but I can't. Hugh has only a small window. I have to make a decision today, and he wants me to read for him."

Gia bit back a snarky comment about how many people were doing their meetings via Zoom these days when a puffy-eyed Sage approached with Jake at her side.

Gia immediately forgot her anger and walked to Jake. She hugged him. "I'm so sorry for your loss."

"Thanks, Ms. Rosetti."

"Gia, please," she said as she stepped back, reaching for Sage's hand. She gave it a comforting squeeze before reluctantly releasing it.

Willow introduced Flynn to Jake, and father and daughter offered him their condolences. "I'm sorry for your loss, Sage," Flynn added with a gentle smile.

"Thanks." Sage returned his smile with a small one of her own. She'd given her sister's father her stamp of approval when she'd met him last summer. It was a bigger deal than Carmen giving Flynn hers. These days, Sage's opinion of most men was even lower than her grandmother's.

"Why don't you come to the restaurant? I'll feed you. Both of you," Gia said. "You should stay the night, honey. I don't want you to be alone."

"Thanks, Mom, but Jake and I are going to stay at the farm tonight and go through the boxes Alice..." Sage shook her head, looking away as she sniffed back tears. Her daughter hated showing her emotions. Though she hadn't always been as closed off as she was now.

Gia thought it had something to do with her job. Sage had to listen without reacting when some of the women she represented recounted horrific stories of abuse. Her daughter didn't only represent the wives of Boston's rich and famous; she also did pro bono work for a women's shelter.

Gia reached for Sage's hand to comfort her, but Jake beat her to it. Wrapping an arm around her daughter's shoulders, he drew her against his side. "We appreciate the offer, Gia, but knowing Alice, she left detailed instructions for us to follow in the event of her death."

"Of course. I'll bring you a lasagna..." She caught Sage and Jake's shared glance and half smiles that seemed to be directed at her offer of a lasagna, so Gia added, "Pizza? Whatever you want."

"We appreciate the offer, Mom. But I don't think either of us feels like eating."

At the hint of a smile on her daughter's face, Gia said, "Oh, okay then."

"Really, Mom?"

"Well, what was I supposed to think?" Gia glanced at Flynn,

who'd tucked his hands in his jeans pockets and was grinning down at his sneakers.

"Not that," Sage said, narrowing her eyes at Jake, who'd made a low sound of amusement in his throat.

Sage elbowed him, and he lifted a shoulder at her before saying, "Don't worry about us, Gia. What your daughter and I really need is a good, stiff drink."

"A bottle would be better," Sage murmured.

"I've got you covered." One of SBPD's officers called his name, and Jake glanced over his shoulder. "Sorry. I need to get over there."

"I'll come with you." Sage gave Gia and Willow each a quick hug before walking away with Jake.

"Call me if you need anything," Gia called after her daughter, who raised her hand in acknowledgment. Gia's shoulders slumped as she watched the couple walk away.

"I should get going too." Willow hugged Gia and Flynn before turning away. She held up her phone. "Cami, we have to go."

It was all Gia could do to hold back tears.

"Why don't I walk you to your car?" Flynn offered, obviously picking up on how close Gia's emotions were to the surface.

"Thanks."

He reached for her hand. "It was easier when they were little and you could kiss their hurts better, wasn't it?"

"So much easier," she said, trying not to read too much into his holding her hand or how much she enjoyed the feel of his warm, strong fingers wrapped around hers. "I feel like I have no place in their lives anymore. They don't need me, and as you just saw, they don't want me around." She made a face, glancing at him from under her lashes. "That sounded melodramatic, didn't it? Just ignore me. According to my sister Eva and my mother, I'm having a midlife crisis." She nodded at her car and let go of his hand. "This is me."

"Sweet ride," he said, trying and failing to hide a grin.

"If you tell me you dreamed of having a red Camaro when you were sixteen, I'm not talking to you ever again." She was almost positive her recent car purchase was the reason her family thought she was going through a midlife crisis. Apparently, they forgot she was fifty-five and not forty.

"Lucky for me then that I didn't dream of having a red Camaro at sixteen. I owned one." He tilted his head to the side, holding her gaze. "Because I really like talking to you, Gia Rosetti."

"Really?" She shook her head, flustered. "I mean, I'm glad you like talking to me. I like talking to you too. But did you really own a red Camaro?"

"I did." He bent to look inside. "And if I'm not mistaken, this is my old car." He gestured to an initial carved on the console and then straightened. "Who did you buy it from? They did a great job refurbishing it."

"Ted Harris. He was our neighbor. He died recently. His wife hated to part with the car, but she needed the money." She shrugged. "I thought she'd feel better knowing it was me who bought it, and she can see the car all the time. I park it in her garage."

"So you're not having a midlife crisis. You're just a sweet woman who did a kind thing for a neighbor."

She was pretty sure she was having a crisis of some sort, just not a midlife one. "I don't know about that, but I really do like driving this car, even though I feel like I'm contributing to the climate crisis every time I do."

He laughed, opening the car door for her. "From what Willow tells me, you more than make up for it."

"I try," she said as she slid behind the wheel. "Thanks for being there when I needed someone to talk to, Flynn."

"Anytime. I—"

Cami, who was walking down the other side of the road with Willow, waved. "Flynn, do you have a minute?"

He nodded and then looked down at Gia. "It's probably not my place to say this, but I'm going to say it anyway. You're an incredible mother, and you've done an amazing job raising Willow and Sage. No one can take your place with your daughters, Gia."

She grabbed her sunglasses off the console and shoved them on before he saw the tears in her eyes. She cleared the emotion from her throat. "That's sweet of you to say, Flynn. Thank you."

"I'm not being sweet. I'm telling you the truth. And trust me, Cami loves you and would never do anything to intentionally hurt you."

"Yeah, well, we'll have to agree to disagree." When he opened his mouth as though to defend her baby sister, she said, "She's written a book that's as much about my life as it is hers. Yours too, Flynn. But did she ask how any of us felt about it? Of course not, because everything revolves around Cami and what's best for her." At her sister calling out for Flynn again, Gia raised an eyebrow and reached for the door. "Have a good visit with your dad."

As she drove off, she caught a glimpse of Flynn, Cami, and Willow in the rearview mirror. The three of them were tall, blond, and head-turningly gorgeous. Anyone who saw them together would guess they were a family. Gia wondered how long it would take before they officially became one.

She felt bad for Cami's boyfriend. Hugh was head over heels in love with her sister. Six months ago, Gia would have said Cami was head over heels in love with him too. But lately she'd sensed a distance growing between the couple. At least on her sister's part.

Gia still hadn't gotten over her mood when she arrived at La Dolce Vita half an hour before dinner service. She wore her usual uniform of a white shirt, black pencil skirt, and black heels, her long dark hair pulled up in a ponytail. She'd added a pair of locally made dangly earrings. They were purple and silver and made of jasper stone, which purportedly helped the wearer relax.

She joined Eva and their mother at the bar for a glass of wine before dinner service, a tradition spanning more than twenty-five years. The thought didn't bring Gia comfort. It just made her feel old. She really was in a mood.

"So, you and Flynn?" her sister asked the moment Gia's butt landed on the barstool.

"What do you mean, me and Flynn? I can't talk to my daughter's father without raising eyebrows?" She slid the fishbowl-size glass of red wine toward herself. She caught her mother and sister exchange a wide-eyed glance and raised her glass. "To Alice, may she rest in peace."

They lifted their glasses, joining her in the toast.

"I thought the girls would come for dinner, but Sage is staying with Jake at the farmhouse, and Willow had plans with Cami and Hugh." She narrowed her eyes at her mother and sister. "You two knew, didn't you? You knew that Cami was going to ask Willow to appear in the movie, and you didn't give me a heads-up?"

"You're overreacting, Gia. Willow might not even get the part. Hugh won't give her the role just because she's Cami's daughter." Her sister winced. "I'm sorry. I shouldn't—"

"You shouldn't what, Eva? Remind me that Willow isn't my daughter, that she's Cami's, and all Cami has to do is snap her fingers to get her to come running. Don't worry, I've seen that with my own eyes."

"You're acting pazza," her mother snapped, raising a warning finger. "If you're not careful, your jealousy will drive a wedge between you and your daughter."

"My jealousy? That's right. I forgot. Cami can do no wrong in your eyes, can she, Ma? It doesn't matter that she's got you and my daughter keeping secrets from me or that I barely get an hour a week with Willow because she's too busy working on Cami's book tour with her." Gia took a long swallow of the full-bodied Cabernet before setting the glass on the bar and sliding off the barstool. "Won't it be fun hearing our relationships dissected on the late-night talk-show circuit? I can't wait to hear what everyone thinks about Cami's poor, pathetic older sister whose husband left her for her gorgeous, glamorous baby sister."

Chapter Four

Gia glanced at the illuminated clock on her nightstand for what felt like the hundredth time since she'd crawled into bed two hours ago and kicked off her covers. It was one in the morning. She'd come to think of it as her witching hour. The time of night—morning—when she gave into the inevitable, got out of bed, and painted the town red. Or whatever color suited her mood or piece of art in that moment.

She was Sunshine Bay's answer to Banksy. Except her art lacked the political bent and satirical humor the famous British street artist's work displayed. And it wasn't like her paintings on garden sheds and alley walls would make her rich. But her anonymous late-night forays onto the streets of Sunshine Bay gave her something money couldn't buy, something that over the past few years she'd thought was lost to her. She'd found her love of painting again.

She got out of bed, pulled on a pair of faded denim shorts and an oversize shirt that had once been white but now bore a striking resemblance to abstract expressionist Jackson Pollock's *Shimmering Substance*, and headed down the hall. Several years ago, she'd converted her daughters' bedrooms into her studio.

The apartment had been her home for almost her entire life. For generations, the Rosetti family had owned all three apartments beside the restaurant. They were attached to La Dolce Vita's large beachfront deck by a wooden staircase that made it particularly convenient to get to work. Something she and her sisters had appreciated as teenagers when they'd basically roll out of bed and into the restaurant after a night of partying.

Carmen had given up the apartment where she'd raised them when Gia had moved home from New York with Sage and Willow. The girls had been toddlers at the time. Her mother had moved into the one-bedroom apartment between Gia's apartment and Eva's. Eva's apartment stood empty now that she and her husband had moved into a gorgeous oceanfront home three years ago. Gia had been after her mother to rent Eva's apartment, but Carmen clung to the hope that one of her granddaughters would eventually move in. Better yet, that Cami would.

Gia pushed thoughts of her youngest sister out of her head. She'd already robbed her of a peaceful night at work. Carmen and Eva had spent the entire dinner shift trying to make her see things from Cami's perspective, which had only served to validate Gia's belief that Cami was ruining her life.

For more than twenty-five years, Gia had been running La Dolce Vita with Carmen and Eva, and she'd bet the restaurant that no one had a better partnership than they did. She loved going to work as much as she loved her sister and her mother, but now, if this kept up... She glanced out the large picture window she'd had installed during the renovation of her studio. The incredible views of sky and sea made the costly makeover worth it.

Opening the right-hand side of the window, Gia breathed deeply of the warm sea air as it ruffled the drapes she rarely closed unless the heat got to be too much to bear. The sound of the waves rolling onto shore washed over her, and she imagined them carrying her anger out to sea. The imagery was powerful. The result? Not so much.

She'd begun using mental imagery to manage her stress in the lead-up to her wedding some thirty-one years ago and had become something of an expert. But over the past nine months, she'd given it up, the same as she had her yoga and meditation practices. She woke up every day determined to incorporate at least one of the practices back into her morning routine, but the desire fizzled out by the time she'd finished her shower.

She left the window open, crossing to the comfy oversize sea-green chair she curled into most afternoons for a nap before the dinner shift. If Eva knew about Gia's new afternoon routine, she'd be dragging her to the clinic. It's why Gia told her she was painting. The excuse worked like a charm. There was nothing that made her sister and mother happier than Gia putting paintbrushes to canvas. Although she imagined they wouldn't be particularly pleased to discover she was putting her paintbrushes to work on the streets of Sunshine Bay. Actually, she was positive her mother wouldn't be.

Carmen had recently called in a complaint to the mayor about the mural Gia had painted on Surfside, her family's favorite bar on Main Street. Gia had painted a surfing scene with the owner riding a wave that covered almost the entire lower half of the building. The wall was located in an alley, which was how she'd been able to paint the mural without being discovered—it had taken her more than a week.

Her mother might not be pleased with the mural, but Gia knew the owner was thrilled. In the local paper last week, there'd been a photo of him posing in front of it with a huge smile on his face. Gia had known he'd love the mural, which was why she'd painted it in the first place. An anonymous thank-you for all the good times they'd had at Surfside on the establishment's fortieth anniversary.

She grabbed the canvas bag filled with her art supplies and headed for the front door. Slipping on a pair of canvas sneakers that had seen better days, she eased the door open. The last thing she wanted was to get caught. She had a feeling Sage wouldn't be so quick to bail her out this time.

Back in October, Gia had been arrested for illegal trespassing. It had nothing to do with her Banksy phase. She and at least a hundred others had been protesting a nuclear power station on Cape Cod Bay. The station had closed four years ago—something Gia and her fellow protestors took credit for—but in the ongoing process of decommissioning the plant, the company was petitioning to dump one million gallons of radioactive wastewater into the bay.

Easing the door shut behind her, Gia glanced at her mother's apartment. The windows were dark but still she tiptoed to the stairs and down them, wincing at every creak and groan. She continued in the same manner across La Dolce Vita's well-lit deck and to the stairs leading to the white sand beach. The buttermilk half-moon shone brightly in the star-littered midnight-blue sky, lighting her way to the pink hydrangea bushes bordering the path to the Harrises' house. Off in the distance, a dog barked, a motor revved, and tires squealed, but the pounding of the surf was the only sound that broke the quiet of her neighborhood.

As Gia walked the path toward the front of the house, the light on the Harrises' back deck blinked on. She froze, listening for any sign she'd woken up Liz, Ted's wife, but the house remained silent and still. Gia continued to the front yard and the Harrises' prized garden. Every year for the past fifteen, the couple had taken first prize on the local garden tour.

Today was Liz's first wedding anniversary without Ted, and Gia wanted to do something special for her. In recent years, Ted had given his wife a new plant for their garden on their anniversary. Gia didn't know much about gardening, but she did know how to paint.

She eyed the path she'd mapped out for herself earlier in the week and decided it would be safer for the garden's plants if she were barefoot. She slipped off her shoes, tiptoeing her way to the large white rock that stood in the center of the garden, setting her canvas bag on top of it.

Once she'd nestled a small battery-operated lantern into the rich dark soil, she sketched Ted holding out an extravagant bouquet of flowers. Then, crouching in front of the rock, she placed her brushes between her teeth and squeezed tubes of acrylic paint onto the palette. It didn't take long for her to paint Ted. She did a funny caricature of him wearing his favorite gardening overalls that Liz had thrown out five years ago. Ted bemoaned the loss every year, and she knew it would give Liz a laugh seeing him in them. Or at the very least a smile.

The flowers would take her longer. She'd found a book in

the library about the language of flowers and had sketched the varieties she'd use in the bouquet. Reaching for her canvas bag, she pulled out the pad in which she'd sketched the flowers. Liz had to be able to recognize the irises' *a message for you*, red chrysanthemums' *I love you*, yellow pansies' *I'm thinking of you*, honeysuckle's *I'm devoted to you*, and yarrow's *our love is everlasting*.

A light breeze fanned the flowers Gia crouched among, their heavy floral heads bobbing in and out of the lantern's light. Absorbed in her painting, she barely noticed until the lantern tipped over on a sudden gust of warm, rose-scented air. She smiled. Roses signified love. She'd take it as a sign that Ted approved of her gift to his wife.

Dipping her brush in cadmium yellow, Gia delicately dotted the yarrow's flowers just below the irises' lush, amethyst petals. She leaned back to see if the bouquet was coming together as she'd envisioned. Pleased with how the flowers' colors flowed, she swirled a touch of titanium white through the cadmium yellow to complete the yarrow. Then she changed brushes, adding cobalt blue and cadmium yellow to her palette, mixing until she got the desired color to create wisps of stems and hints of leaves throughout the bouquet.

She went back with a clean, damp brush and faded out the greenery. Five minutes later, the painting was complete. She'd just sat on her heels to see if any touch-ups were required when there was a click, and a bright flash lit up the garden. She startled, the movement causing her to fall off her heels and onto her butt in a rosebush. She groaned at the thought of calling Sage to bail her out tonight of all nights and decided to brazen it out.

"I don't know what you think you're doing, Officer. But I have the owner's permission—" She cut herself off with an *ouch* when thorns embedded themselves in the palm of the hand she'd used to lever herself up and out of the bush.

"Hang on," said a familiar, deep voice.

She whipped her gaze to the lane. "Flynn? What are you doing here?" Her eyes widened when she saw what he was attempting. "No. Stay where you are. You'll"—she bowed her head—"crush the flowers."

"Don't worry. No one will know," he said before leaning over and scooping her into his arms.

"I'm pretty sure the flowers know that you killed them, but if you were talking about the owners of the garden, Liz will know too."

"I promise. She won't. 'Stella d'Oro' daylilies make up a third of my dad's garden. I'll go dig some up and have them replanted before sunrise."

She glanced from the trampled yellow and gold flowers to the stars glittering in the night sky. It had yet to lighten. "What time is it?"

"Two thirty. I have plenty of time." He glanced around. "Now let's get you out of here so no one discovers you're J.R." He looked down at her. "You are trying to keep your street-artist identity secret, aren't you?"

"I am, and I appreciate you..." She waved her hand, indicating him holding her in his arms. "Whatever this is you're doing."

His lips twitched. "I was attempting to rescue you from the rosebush, but..." He looked down and winced. "I seem to be making things worse."

"What flower did you just behead?"

He lifted his foot. "A gerbera daisy. Dad doesn't have any in his garden, so I might have to steal a couple from the neighbors."

"Put me down. I know a way out that won't endanger any more innocent flowers." He slowly lowered her to her feet, which left her pressed to his side and in danger of taking out more flowers if she moved left, right, or backward.

"Let's try it this way." She flattened herself against him, desperately trying to ignore the feel of his hard body pressed against her. The heat and sensual woodsy fragrance emanating off him left her slightly light-headed.

Off limits, she reminded herself as she wrapped her arms around his waist, realizing as she did so that it was a big mistake. She should have let the flowers fend for themselves.

"Are we dancing under the moonlight?" he asked, sounding amused.

"No, you're walking carefully backward toward the rock so I can get my things, and then I'm leading you out of here." She placed her bare feet on top of his sneakers.

Glancing up, she met his gaze. She recognized the desire in his eyes. It surprised her. She was six years older than him. She wasn't hard on the eyes, but she was nowhere near as beautiful as her sister. He rested his hands on her hips before taking a careful step backward. He was right. The slow and sensuous movement of her body against his made it feel like a dance.

He reached out and grabbed her canvas bag off the top of the rock, handing it to her. She looped it over her shoulder and moved to step off his sneakers, but he held her in place. "You forgot the lantern and a brush, and there's not enough room for both of us." He angled his head. "We don't have time to waste."

She was about to ask him what he meant when she heard the drone of voices down the lane. "Hurry!" she whispered.

He shuffled her into position.

Hooking the fingers of her left hand into his belt loop, she leaned backward, scooping up the brush and lantern. He groaned, and her gaze shot down the lane as she straightened. No one was there.

She met his eyes, a question in hers.

He cleared his throat. "You're, uh, very flexible."

"Yoga," she murmured, then quietly directed him onto the path she'd taken through the garden earlier. She barely had time to grab her sneakers and his hand before the two men walking down the lane appeared. Gia and Flynn flattened their backs against the house, hiding in the shadows.

"Hey, look at that," one of the men said, a beam of light illuminating the garden. "It's one of J.R.'s paintings."

"J.R.? Like the guy from *Dallas*?" the other man asked.

"Who?"

"You know, *Who shot J.R.*?"

"I have no idea what you're talking about. But I'm talking about the painting on the rock. Look. It's the same artist who painted the mural on Surfside. J.R."

Gia burrowed into Flynn.

"That's pretty cool," the other guy said. "Whoever the artist is, they've got talent. I wonder why they waste it painting for free?"

The light went out, the men's voices fading as they continued down the lane trying to guess her motivation for becoming a street artist.

Before stepping away from the side of the house, Gia leaned forward to make sure that no one else was coming down the lane. "I think it's safe," she told Flynn.

He nodded, then lifted his chin at the path. "I'll walk you home."

"You don't have to."

"I want to." He glanced at her. "Unless you'd prefer that I didn't."

"No, it's fine," she said as they walked down the path. "What were you doing down here anyway?"

He removed his phone from the pocket of his cargo shorts and held it up. "Photographing Sunshine Bay at night. It's a hobby of mine. Photography, not photographing Sunshine Bay at night," he said with a self-conscious smile.

"You won't share the photograph you took of me, will you? Even with Willow? I don't want anyone to know."

"Of course not. I'd like to keep it, but if you want me to, I'll delete it."

"I don't know why you took it of me in the first place."

"A gorgeous woman sitting among the flowers with the moon shining down on her? I don't know who could have resisted taking a photo of you in that moment. I am sorry I startled you, though. I should have realized I would have. You were completely absorbed in your painting." He held up his camera, the picture of her on the screen. "I don't think I did you justice. I took a couple without the flash." He swiped the screen. "And then I took this one."

She leaned in, viewing the photos objectively. "I like the

composition and contrast. You have a good eye." She swiped through the other photos. "This one's cool. I like how you captured the moon." She nudged him with a smile. "Imagine what you could do with an actual camera."

He laughed. "I have an actual camera. I recently retired my old Nikon and splurged on a Sony a7 IV." He nodded at the sand. "Do you want to sit for a minute?"

"Sure." She followed him to a spot just down from her apartment. The glow from the lamp she'd left on in her studio window cast a circle in the sand.

"The reason I didn't have my camera on me was because I hadn't planned on taking photos tonight." He leaned back on his hands, crossing his sneakered feet at the ankles.

"No?"

"No. I didn't like how we left things earlier. Willow had mentioned that you sometimes paint late at night so I walked down this way in the hope you might still be up. I wanted to apologize."

"You have nothing to apologize for, Flynn. It's me. I over-reacted with both you and Willow. I'm sorry."

"Do you want to talk about it?"

She laughed. "No, thanks. I've talked about my sister enough for one night."

"Okay. How about you tell me why you decided to become a street artist? Because, Gia, Willow has shown me some of your work, and you really are incredibly talented." He raised a hand when Gia opened her mouth. "Don't get me wrong, the mural on Surfside, the one you did on the public library, and this one tonight, they're amazing too, but those guys are right. You're giving away your talent for free."

"Maybe, but I haven't felt like this in years. I think it's the anonymity. It's freeing. No expectations, no pressure. I was blocked before, never satisfied with what I painted, and now..." She smiled. "I'm having fun again."

"I get that, I guess. But from what Willow said, you were on your way to quite a career before you gave it up for them."

Gia frowned. "Is that what Willow said?"

"Yeah. It sounded like she and Sage feel the same way."

At one point in her life, Gia had thought she could at least make a decent living from her art. She'd had a showing at an exclusive gallery in New York City. The gallery's owner had been vacationing in Sunshine Bay and had seen her work in one of the local galleries. Her future had seemed so bright and full of promise then.

"Well, they're wrong. It had nothing to do with them." And everything to do with her ex. "But my mom, my sister, and I are partners in La Dolce Vita. The restaurant is my main focus now. This"—she waved her hand at the Harrises' garden—"is for fun."

"You might be doing it for fun, but from what I've seen, you're bringing joy to the people lucky enough to receive the gift of one of your murals."

"Thank you," she said, touched. "Maybe you'd like to tell my mother that. She says the murals are an eyesore. She's on a campaign to have them removed."

"Seriously? No wonder you want to stay anonymous. Who is J.R., anyway?"

"Me, and yes, before you say it, *Gia* does begin with a *G*. But when I was younger, I hated my name as much as I hated the old-fashioned dresses our nonna insisted we wear to school. All I wanted was to fit in, so I called myself Jane and insisted everyone do the same. Not my nonna, bisnonna, or mother, obviously. But by sixth grade, I was ready to embrace my heritage and who I was and went back to Gia. It's so long ago I doubt anyone remembers so I felt safe signing my work as J.R."

"You are as beautiful as your name, Gia Rosetti." He reached for her hand, gently rubbing at the speckles of paint with his thumb. "Any chance you'd go out with me?"

"You want to go out with me? Like on a date?"

"Well, I did, but you sound horrified by the idea so maybe forget I said anything."

"No, not horrified, just...Flynn, I'm six years older than you."

He frowned. "So, what's that got to do with anything? You're a gorgeous, interesting woman I enjoy talking to, and I got the impression you enjoyed talking to me too."

"I do, very much. It's just that you're my sister's ex and my daughter's father." She lifted a shoulder.

"And?"

She stared at his strong features bathed in shadows and light and tried to force a *no* past her lips, but he was so gorgeous and sexy and interesting, and interested in her, that instead she said, "Yes. Okay. I'll go out with you. But no one can know. It has to be our secret, Flynn."

Chapter Five

Don't roll over," Jake warned, but it was Sage, so of course she did exactly what he'd asked her not to and ended up sprawled on top of him while they rode the waterbed's waves as if they were on a blow-up raft on a choppy sea.

Sage slapped a hand over her mouth, making gagging noises.

He appreciated the distraction. If she didn't sound like she was seconds from hurling, he might be focusing on how good her warm, curvy body felt lying half on top of him.

"Maybe next time you'll listen to me," he said, knowing hell would freeze over before the woman in bed with him would listen to a single word he said—but he needed to give it the old college try. The rolling mattress wasn't helping the pounding in his head. He had the mother of all hangovers. "Stay still, and the bed will stop rocking."

She lifted her head from his bare chest, removing her hand from her pouty lips and peeking at him through a heavy fall of auburn hair. Silky-soft auburn hair, he amended as her shoulder-length locks brushed across his chest.

"Please tell me we didn't do anything stupid last night," she said, her voice a husky rasp.

Some people were instantly attracted to a face, to a specific part of a person's body, or to their personality, but not him. At seventeen, he'd fallen hook, line, and sinker for Sage's voice. The attraction didn't last long, though. All it had taken was being on the receiving end of her eviscerating wit to dull the appeal.

As he knew from following her career online, time had only served to sharpen her cool, dispassionate insults to a razor's edge. The woman was a ball-breaker, something that made Alice inordinately proud.

Thinking of Alice hurt more than he'd thought possible. She'd been a mother to him, far better and more loving than his own. He wasn't ready to let her go. He didn't know what he'd do without her strong, guiding presence in his life.

He'd opened his eyes to the midmorning sunlight filling the spare bedroom at the farm, positive yesterday had been a bad dream. But reality hit him like a sucker punch in the chest when he saw Sage curled up beside him.

He brought his attention back to her. She pushed her hair from her face, looking at him through panicked, bloodshot eyes. He knew what she was asking, but even with his head feeling like it was about to blow off, he couldn't resist the urge to tease her just a little. Another distraction before they dealt with the reality of their mutual loss.

"I'm pretty sure drinking nearly a bottle of tequila qualifies as the epitome of stupidity."

She covered her mouth again, making more gagging sounds before getting them under control with a hard, desperate swallow. Then she said, her voice even huskier than before, "Don't ever say that word again in my presence."

Her voice was getting to him, probably because she hadn't insulted him yet. He needed to get on that. "Epitome or ... *tequila*," he said, knowing full well that the latter was the word she meant. Even he felt a little queasy saying it, and he'd been notorious with the guys in his unit for his cast-iron stomach.

Sage lost what little color she had left on her face, rolled off him with her hand covering her mouth, and kept on rolling thanks to the waves. If not for the bed's raised leather-wrapped frame, she would have rolled right off. As it was, she kicked her way out of the tangled sheets while trying and failing to push herself off the undulating mattress.

He reached over, half lifting, half pushing her off the bed. She landed on the hardwood floor with a *thunk*.

"Sorry." He felt bad not only for practically tossing her out of bed but also for teasing her. "You don't have to worry. We didn't have sex. We just passed out in bed together." She was already halfway down the hall, so he raised his voice, repeating what he'd just said in order for her to hear him.

Instead of calling out her thanks for alleviating her worry, he heard her say, "Hi, Mom. Yeah, just give me a second," she added before flying back into the room, skewering him to the bed with a glare. "Are you trying to embarrass me on purpose?"

"Come again?" he asked distractedly as he took in what she had on while at the same time trying to be respectful about it, which wasn't easy given that she was standing directly in line with the sunlight coming through the window while wearing his white T-shirt and . . . nothing else, apparently. Then again, his T-shirt hung almost to her knees. But that wasn't the point.

The point was, why was she wearing his T-shirt and nothing else? They hadn't had sex, had they? No way. It didn't matter how drunk he'd been, he'd remember having sex with Sage. Anybody, he'd remember having sex with anybody.

"I can't believe you just said that to me." She fisted her hands on her hips, looking like a woman ready to do battle in a T-shirt that all but guaranteed her male combatants would fall at her feet. "Grow up, Walker."

He dragged his gaze to her face. "What are you talking about?"

"Really." She raised her eyebrows. "*Come again?*"

"Seriously?" He shook his head as he levered himself up on his elbows, groaning at the blinding pain that accompanied the movement, and then flopped back onto the pillows, pressing his palm to his eyes. "*Come again*, as in 'repeat yourself.'" He spread his fingers to look at her from behind his hand. "We didn't have sex, did we?"

She made a frustrated sound in her throat, which was surprisingly sexy, and then grabbed the pillow from under his head and hit him with it. "You just said we didn't!"

"I know, but when I said it, I didn't notice you were wearing my T-shirt and no underwear."

The pillow came down on his face again. "I'm wearing underwear!"

"Good, that's good. Now stop with the yelling and the hitting." He reached up and grabbed the pillow from her. "I'm ninety-five percent sure we didn't do anything . . . Why are you making that face?"

"I think maybe we did ... something."

He was a little insulted with the face she was making at the thought of them doing ... something. "What do you think we did?" he asked while digging through his own alcohol-impaired memories of the night before.

She walked to a chair in the corner of the room and picked up her blouse and skirt. "I was eating ice cream and dropped some on my top." She held it up as evidence.

"I think I remember." He'd teased her about eating ice cream with tequila, laughing when she'd upended half of the bowl on herself while attempting to replicate Tom Cruise's *Risky Business* dance move across the linoleum-tiled floor wearing a pair of Alice's crocheted purple slippers.

He'd stopped laughing when Sage started taking off her top. Then he'd started taking off his T-shirt to cover up all her lush curves before he did something he'd regret. They'd regret.

Her eyes met his. "We kissed," they said at almost the same time.

"It was a short kiss and completely unmemorable," she added, with more emphasis on the *unmemorable* part than he thought was necessary.

"Completely," he said, refusing to be the one to concede that parts of the kiss were memorable now that he was more awake and the drunken haze was clearing from his brain. "Uh, now that I think about it, there might have been some ..." He cleared his throat. "Touching involved."

"It was the tequila." She looked up from the blouse clutched in her hand. "We will never talk about this again. Not a single word."

"Talk about what?"

Her lips twitched with an almost-smile as she headed toward the door with her clothes in her hand. Then she turned so fast, he felt like she'd not only given herself whiplash but given it to him too. "How can you be so blasé about this? We kissed, and we, uh, kissed, and you're married!"

"Wow, you really do have a low opinion of me if you think I'd kiss you if I was still married."

"It has nothing to do with my opinion of you. We were emotional and had too much to drink. Things happen."

"Trust me, if I was still married, it wouldn't matter how much I had to drink. I wouldn't have kissed you." *Or touched you*, he silently added. *Or been within five feet of you when you looked as heartbroken as I felt.* They'd needed each other. There was nothing more to it than that.

"So how not-married are you?" She sighed when he gave her a look. "You know what I mean, Jake. Are you on a break? Recently separated?"

"Our divorce was finalized fifteen months ago," he said as he moved to the side of the bed, still bitter at how his marriage had ended. He had a compulsive need to succeed but there had been nothing he could do or say to change his ex's mind. So he'd taken Alice's advice and let his wife go without a fight. In the end, he supposed it had worked out for the best. They still had a great relationship, and his ex had moved on with her work husband, who was now a stay-at-home dad to their nine-month-old son. "Happy now?"

"You don't have to be a jerk about it. I'd just remembered you were married and felt bad that we'd been—" She waved her hand at the bed and then apparently noticed he was about to get out of it, and her leaf-green eyes widened. "No. You stay right where you are. My mother is out there." She angled her head at the sound of cupboards opening and closing. "Mom, stop snooping."

"I wasn't snooping," Gia yelled back. "I'm setting the table. Hurry up. You too, Jake. Your breakfast is getting cold, and it'll soon be time for lunch."

"She totally came here to spy on us," Sage muttered. "She knows I don't eat breakfast."

"Well, I do, and whatever she brought smells great." He moved past her to grab his jeans, grinning at the way she tracked his every move. "See something you like?"

"I, uh..." She dragged her gaze to his face and tossed her hair, ruining what no doubt she'd meant to be a contemptuous act by making a pained groan while pressing her fingers to her temple. "You're not all that."

"I'm disappointed. You were famous for your put-downs, and that was just...lame."

"I'm sorry if I'm off my game. I'm having a hard time working up contempt when I'm this hungover..." She slowly lowered herself onto the bed. "And sad."

He joined her, cursing himself for being an idiot and then cursing the waterbed when she ended up on his lap. "I'm sorry. It was a stupid thing for me to say to you." He eased her off his lap while holding her upright with his hand. "I shouldn't have teased you, not now."

"No. I'd rather fight with you than think about Alice..." She turned her big, glassy eyes on him, and he drew her back onto his lap, holding her close. "I hadn't talked to her in months. I didn't get to say goodbye. I didn't get to tell her how much she meant to me."

He leaned back, reaching for the box of tissues on the nightstand as she sniffed into his chest. "Alice knew how much she meant to you, same as you knew how much you meant to her. She bragged about you constantly. It was annoying."

She lifted her head from his chest. "Yeah?"

"Yeah," he said, then teased her in the hope of lessening the sorrow in her eyes. "But she still loved me best."

He hadn't realized it back then, but they'd spent their teen years fighting for Alice's time and attention. He'd never understood why Sage seemed to need Alice's approval as much as he did. She had a big, loving family who were there for her no matter what. The only reason his family wanted him around was to earn money for their booze and drugs—or, if he couldn't earn it, to steal it. If Alice hadn't intervened when she had, he would've no doubt ended up in prison alongside his old man.

Sage surprised him by nodding instead of arguing with him like she used to. "She did. Alice adored you. You were her—"

"Don't. Don't say another word, Sage." His voice was rough, the backs of his eyes burning as he moved her away from him and got off the bed. "Sounds like Kendra's here. I need my T-shirt."

Sage raised an eyebrow, her struggle to get off the bed ruining the superior attitude she'd been going for, but it had the desired effect of making him smile. As hard as Sage had tried—and she'd tried really hard—she'd never quite managed to pull off the condescending-bitch act with him. She'd either start stammering or turn red in the face or get so angry that she'd looked like she might cry. She could pull it off with the mean girls at the high school, though. No one messed with her sister or her cousin when Sage was around.

Once she made it to her feet, Sage straightened, lifted her nose in the air, and brushed past him. As she reached the door, her back to him, she pulled off his T-shirt and tossed it over her shoulder before clasping her skirt and blouse to her chest and sashaying down the hall, wearing a pair of high-cut silk panties. Whoever thought beige panties weren't sexy hadn't seen them on Sage.

He drew the T-shirt off his shoulder, pulled it over his head, and then groaned. The fabric was still warm from her body and carried her seductive scent of vanilla and sandalwood. He frowned at himself and his reaction. Sage wouldn't thank him for fantasizing about what it would have been like to peel his T-shirt off her himself.

He dragged his hand down his face and then slapped his cheeks to snap himself out of it. As luck would have it, Sage walked back into the bedroom, looking remarkedly put together for a woman who'd walked into the bathroom less than three minutes ago. Unless he'd been stunned stupid for longer than he thought.

"Slapping yourself with cold water works better," she said as she bent to retrieve her sneakers.

"You slap yourself with cold water often?" he asked, fighting a smile as she slipped on her white sneakers with her sexy skirt and blouse. It shouldn't have been hot, but it was. He frowned, blaming the wayward thought on his hangover and lack of food.

"Pretty much a couple of times a day," she said, and it was obvious she was telling the truth.

So Alice hadn't been exaggerating. She'd shared her concerns about Sage with him. He couldn't believe it was two days ago. If he'd only known it was the last time he'd talk to her. "You work too hard," he said.

She snorted. "Says who, you? The guy who retired from the military at twenty-five?"

He smirked, deciding not to enlighten her just yet. She'd always believed, despite Alice's best efforts, he'd end up a criminal. In Sage's defense, he hadn't done anything to disabuse her of the idea. In fact, he'd done everything he could to make her believe he was destined for a life of crime. It made it easier for him being around a girl who believed the worst of him. It would have been too easy falling for the girl Sage used to be with Alice and her family: brilliant, beautiful, compassionate, and kind.

"Don't knock it until you try it," he said, following the scents of sweet pastries and strong coffee down the hall.

"Okay. I get why, after you and your wife separated, you'd stop working *part-time* as an investigator for her law firm." He heard the eye roll in her voice. "But you must need to work to make a living?"

He'd asked Alice not to mention to Sage what he'd been up to for the past five years. Even though Alice hadn't understood why at the time, she'd apparently done as he'd asked. If he'd failed, Alice knowing wouldn't have bothered him. Sage was another story.

"I don't need a lot to make me happy. This way, I can take

off whenever the spirit moves me," he said, holding back a grin at the disgusted expression that came over her face.

"On the same motorbike you've had since you were eighteen," she muttered. "That thing is not safe."

"Says the woman who drives an old lady's car," he said as they walked into the kitchen. He leaned into her. "Now, your mom, she has a sweet ride."

"For an eighteen-year-old guy." She glanced at her mother, who was getting a cup of coffee for Kendra, a young woman with dark shoulder-length spiral curls. "It's not normal for a fifty-five-year-old woman to be driving a red Camaro with racing stripes, is it?"

"Bet you wouldn't say that about a fifty-five-year-old man."

"You just answered my question," she said under her breath before walking to where Kendra leaned against the counter. She extended her hand. "Hi, I'm Sage."

"Kendra." She offered Sage and Jake a watery smile. "Alice talked about you all the time. Both of you."

Jake walked over and gave her a hug. He felt bad for her. She was twenty, not much older than he and Sage had been when Alice started mentoring them. "How are you holding up?"

"Not great." She lifted a shoulder and then nodded at a blue folder on the counter. "You mentioned you were looking for Alice's will. I found it in a box in the front hall closet."

Alice had wanted to get her office organized at the farmhouse before clearing out the rest of her house on Ocean View Drive. There were still a couple of weeks before the sale closed on her house, and she'd been taking her time. It was something that had been bugging Jake. He didn't understand why Alice had been heading for the farmhouse the day of the accident instead of her place on Ocean View Drive. Her home was less than a mile away from where her bike had been found.

"Thanks, Kendra. We could have waited, though," he said, reaching for the file.

"I didn't mind. It's better for me to keep busy." She looked from him to Sage, who was accepting a mug of coffee from her mom. "It'll be a lot for you guys now that you've inherited the farm, Alice's legal practice, and the house on Ocean View Drive. I'm happy to stay on." She glanced at Sage, who stood frozen with the mug halfway to her mouth. "I'm sorry. I guess I shouldn't have read the will. It's just that I was making sure it was her last—"

"Don't worry about it, Kendra. It's fine." Jake managed to get the words out despite his shock as he read the will.

"Did she just say Alice left everything to us, as in you and me?"

He nodded. "She left us Max too." He glanced to where the cat slept on the couch by the window. After Jake had gone out for tequila and food—including ice cream for Sage—he'd picked up Max. The cat had barely moved from the end of the couch where Jake had put him yesterday afternoon. It was as if Max somehow knew Alice was gone.

Sage slowly lowered her coffee mug onto the table. "I don't understand why she'd do that. She knows we can't be in the same room together without fighting."

"I'm sure Alice believed we were adult enough to deal with this, Sage. We're in our thirties, after all." He held her gaze. "We didn't fight last night."

She gave him a withering glare.

He rolled his eyes. It wasn't as if he'd said they'd made out last night with her mother and Kendra standing right there. He'd said they didn't fight.

But it looked like Sage had already moved on from worrying about him oversharing. She had her hands clasped to either side of her head, turning in a slow circle. "How are we going to deal with all of this? It's too much. We'll have to manage things at the farm until we can sell it, and who other than Alice wants to buy a lavender farm? It was on the market for more than a year before she bought it."

This was a side of Sage he'd never seen before. Even as a teenager, she'd been in control. Nothing threw her, and this was definitely throwing her. He opened his mouth to tell her to relax, then thought better of it and glanced at her mother for help.

Gia looked as surprised by her daughter's reaction as he was, but at least she knew what to do. She reached for Sage. "Just breathe, honey. It'll be fine. I know it's a lot, but you don't have to do this alone. We're all here for you. Aren't we, Jake?"

"Uh, yeah. Sure. Don't worry about anything, Sage. I'll handle everything."

Those big, leaf-green eyes narrowed at him. "What do you mean, you'll handle everything?"

Chapter Six

"Mommy's home..." Sage made a face as soon as the words came out of her mouth. What a ridiculous thing to say, she thought as she closed her apartment door behind her. Almost as ridiculous as the high-pitched voice she'd used.

It wasn't as if she could take Alice's place in Max's heart, or as if she even wanted to. She just wanted to give him a happy life. She owed that to Alice.

Slipping off her shoes, Sage shifted the bag from the pet store in her arms and placed her keys in the ceramic bowl on the console table. She called out again, this time using her normal voice while trying to sound cheerful and upbeat instead of exhausted and sad.

"Hi, Max. I'm home. I picked up some special food for you. The staff at the pet store said it's the best." It had better be for what she'd paid.

She walked from the white marble entryway into the open-concept space and froze. The couches' cushions and throw pillows had been tossed around like a mini-tornado had touched down in her living room, while books, paperwork, and a vase of fake flowers were strewn across the cream-colored area rug. Someone had ransacked her apartment.

At the thought of who that someone might be—a former client's ex who'd promised retaliation against Sage once he'd been released from prison—the bag slipped from her arms. She cringed as cans of cat food noisily rolled out of the bag and onto the hardwood floor, alerting whoever had broken in to her presence. Then again, she'd pretty much done that when she'd called out to Max. Heart pounding, she stood perfectly still with her palm covering her mouth, listening for sounds that she wasn't alone.

When all she heard was the galloping of her heart, she slowly lowered her hand, patting her blazer's pockets for her cell phone. Then she remembered that she'd forgotten it in her rush to get Max settled before heading to the office. It was somewhere in her apartment. She needed to find her phone, and she needed to find Max.

Running on tiptoes into the kitchen in search of a weapon, she slid on the paper towels covering the white-and-black-tiled floor. In an effort to stay upright, she grabbed the corner of the granite-topped breakfast bar, noticing as she did so that the paper toweling had been shredded, and not by her toenails. She straightened, surveying her tossed living room with another culprit in mind. Her gaze stalled on the side of her couch.

"Max," she muttered as she scooped the paper towels off the tile floor, placing them on the breakfast bar before heading to inspect the side of the cream-colored couch that Max had used as his personal scratch pad.

She got distracted by the distant ringing of her cell phone

and followed the sound down the short hall. She needn't have worried about Max being bored when she was at work, she decided while stepping around rolls of unraveled toilet paper. Clearly, he knew how to amuse himself.

She tracked the ringing phone to the cat bed at the foot of her bed, digging it out from under the fuzzy throw she'd added to make Max feel at home. The phone stopped ringing, and Max gave her the side-eye from where he lay curled in a comfy, cozy nest of bedding that he'd created for himself. Her comforter would never be the same.

Apparently ticked that she had the audacity to interrupt his sleep, Max growled at her.

"I'm not impressed with you at the moment either, buddy," she said, opening her phone with her face. She frowned as she scrolled through her missed calls and redialed Jake. "Hey, what's up? You've called like fifteen times."

"Yeah, because you never answered or called me back," he said, sounding as ticked at her as Max. "You weren't in a good place when you left. I was worried about you."

She sighed. He was right. She'd still been in shock about Alice, and then to learn she'd left everything to Jake and Sage . . . It had been a tough way to start the day. She ignored the thought that waking up in Jake's arms had not been a tough way to start the day, until it had gotten awkward.

"I'm sorry. I ended up leaving my phone here and didn't realize it until I got to work. By then it was too late to come back and get it." Robert, one of the founding partners at the firm, had made her day that much worse by insisting she return to work to argue a motion in court for one of his cases.

"Sage, it's eleven o'clock. I've called several times in the last few hours, and you still didn't answer. If this is some kind of passive-aggressive—"

"What do I have to be passive-aggressive about?" She pulled a face, glad that he couldn't see her. Taking Max home with her could be construed as a passive-aggressive move. She'd been upset Jake got to stay in Sunshine Bay, surrounded by memories of Alice and her things, while Sage had to come home alone. Not that she'd admit to Jake that she hadn't wanted to be alone. "Anyway, it wasn't like I was ignoring your calls. I just got home from work."

"It's eleven o'clock. At night."

"Yes, I think we've already established that. Now, I have some work to do before I go to bed, so could you get to the point of your call?"

"What do you mean, you have work to do? You just got home."

She wanted to say, *And your point is—?* This was actually an early night for her. But she didn't think hearing that would go over well with Jake, especially because Max had been home alone all day.

"I'd left a lot of things unfinished when I took off for Sunshine Bay yesterday morning, and I didn't get in today until one. I can't afford to get behind." She got indigestion just thinking what her schedule would look like if that happened.

"Sage, it's a little over twenty-four hours since we found out Alice died. The last place you need to be is at work."

"No, it's exactly where I need to be." It made it easier to pretend this was all a bad dream. In an effort not to disturb Max, she slowly lowered herself onto the end of the bed. She got a grumbled yowl for her effort.

At the frustrated sigh coming over the line, Sage pictured Jake dragging his fingers through his hair. He'd reacted the same way as a teenager when she'd frustrated him.

"Okay. Whatever. I'm not about to tell you how to live your life, Sage."

"Thanks. I really appreciate that," she said, her voice laced with sarcasm.

He snorted. "Give me a break, okay. I was worried about you."

Surprisingly, she understood how he felt. After being unable to reach Alice, and losing her the way that they had, Sage would feel the same way if she hadn't been able to reach Jake or her family.

"Even though there was absolutely no reason for you to be worried about me, I appreciate that you were, and I'm sorry you couldn't reach me. Next time, just call me at work. I'll text you my direct extension and my work email."

"Thanks, I appreciate it. There's quite a bit that we'll need to discuss over the next few weeks."

"Such as?" There was an edge in her voice that he'd no doubt picked up on. She hadn't meant for suspicion to creep into her tone. It was residue from her reaction to this morning's news. She'd responded badly to Jake offering to handle their joint inheritance. She wasn't the most trusting person on a good day, and today had been far from good.

"Okay. I let it go this morning, but I resent what you seem to be implying, Sage. It's not like I'm going to take off with your share of the inheritance."

"I'm not implying anything of the kind. Don't be so sensitive." She winced. Of course this would be a sore point for him. It had taken Jake a long time to live down his reputation and his family's in Sunshine Bay. "I'm sorry if it seemed that way. I know you're handling everything so I shouldn't complain, but it still feels like a lot."

"I know. Sorry if I overreacted. I'll do what I can to handle everything on my end, but I will need your opinion on things, as well as your signature."

"Sure. Whatever you need. Is that why you were trying to reach me? Has something come up?"

"Don't worry about it. We can talk when you get to town."

"I'm not coming home for the weekend, Jake. I have too much to do. I can maybe get away next Saturday for a few hours. Would that help? It shouldn't take us too long to pack up the house, should it?"

"I don't need your help packing up the house. I just wanted to talk to you about this in person."

"Talk about what? Does it have something to do with Alice?" There was a long pause. "Jake, what is it?"

"After you left this morning, I went back to the scene of Alice's accident and took the same path she would have taken to the trail. I found her phone."

"Did you give it to the police? What do they think?"

"I haven't given it to them yet. It's damaged, but I know a guy—"

"You know *a guy*? Jake, you have to give the phone to the police. It's evidence."

"I'll give them Alice's phone once he's taken a look at it. He's good, Sage. Way better than anyone they've got working at SBPD. He's fast too. He should have something for me at the beginning of next week."

"Are you worried that this was something other than an accident?"

"No. Not at all. Given the distance between Alice's bike and the tire tracks, with the dip in the road, the person driving the car likely had no idea she'd fallen. I just can't figure out why Alice went to the farm instead of her house. I'm hoping there's an explanation on her phone."

Even though Jake couldn't see her, Sage was nodding her agreement. She'd wondered the same thing. "If Alice had gone home instead of to the farm, she wouldn't have been on the road. She would have taken the bike path. She'd still be here."

"Yeah," he agreed, his voice gruff.

Sage got up slowly and then stretched out on the bed, curling herself carefully around Max so as not to disturb him. Talking about Alice made her sad, and she wanted the comfort of someone who loved and missed her too.

A heavy silence hung over the line until Jake cleared his throat. "How's Max doing? Did he settle in okay?"

"Yeah, he's good. Really good. He loves my place, especially my bed," she whispered while tentatively stroking Max's thick, silky coat. He lifted his head, let loose an offended yowl, and batted her hand away.

"Oh my gosh, okay, no petting," she said, holding up her hands. She realized she should have lowered her voice when Jake started laughing. But before she could come up with a cover story, Max growled again, batting at her like a boxer. She tried cajoling him into sharing the bed with her, but he didn't let up until she was an inch from falling off the mattress.

She got off the bed—glaring at Max, who snuggled into

the bedding with a smug yawn—grabbed a pillow, and said to the man who'd been laughing throughout her entire fight with the cat, "Good night, Jake." She ignored the thought that Jake made a much better bedmate than Max.

⌣

"Would someone please tell me why I agreed to take on her case? It's been two years. Two years, people, and she can't stop dragging that poor man back into court," Sage said as she strode into her office Tuesday afternoon.

It was the first time in her career that she wanted to offer her services to a client's ex. Of course it would be the one client she represented that the founding partners had wholeheartedly approved. The woman's parents came from old money and were only too happy to bankroll their daughter's divorce, which was why Sage found herself in court with her every few months.

Sage's assistant and her associate didn't bother looking up or answering her. They sat huddled behind her desk, smiling at something on the computer. "Hello? What's so interesting..." she began, rounding her desk. She got a look at the familiar face on the screen and frowned. "What's going on?" she asked Jake.

Brenda and Renata swiveled on the office chairs, fluttering their eyelashes. In case their reaction to the man on the screen wasn't clear enough, Renata mouthed, *He's hot.*

"You weren't answering your phone, so I called your office," Jake said, oblivious to the reaction of his fan club.

"You called once. I was in court. I would have called you back." She should have called him back as soon as she'd left the courthouse, she realized, casting a furtive glance around the office for Max.

It was his second day coming to work with her, and he already had more friends at the firm than she did. Except he was supposed to visit with them in her office. The last thing she needed was Max wandering the halls of Forbes, Poole, and Russell and ticking off the founding partners. She managed to do that all by herself.

"He wanted to see Max, so we set up a Zoom call," Renata informed her while sharing a conspirator's grin with Jake. Brenda was doing the same until she noticed Sage eyeing her.

Her assistant shrugged. "You can't blame him for wanting proof of life, Sage. You haven't had fur kids before."

"And we know why," Renata said, rolling her eyes.

"Hey, I'm a good cat mom. I brought Max to work with me, didn't I?" She put her hands on her hips. "And I sent you a picture of Max on Sunday." Granted, it was a picture of Max's tail. The cat had a thing about getting his photo taken. "He's fine."

She hoped. She still didn't see any sign of him, and it wasn't as if she could ask Renata or Brenda where he was with Jake looking on. "Now, if that's all you wanted, I'd better get to work. Ladies." She raised her eyebrows, indicating she'd like her desk back.

"Actually, I need to talk to you, Sage. It won't take long," he said, then offered Brenda and Renata one of his heart-stopping smiles as they got up from their chairs. "Nice meeting you both. Thanks for the update on Max and Sage."

"Wait. You asked for an update on me?"

Brenda took Renata by the arm. "Maybe we should give Jake and Sage some privacy."

"No. I think I should stay in case Jake needs corroborating evidence," Renata said.

"What evidence are you corroborating?" Sage asked.

Renata held up a hand as if she was about to tick off the evidence against Sage, but Brenda intervened. "Would you look at that? We're going to miss our break if we don't take it now, Renata. I know how important it is for you to have time communing with nature. We'll join Bill and Max on the rooftop garden."

Bill from security had gotten a glimpse of Max yesterday morning when Sage had unsuccessfully tried sneaking him onto the elevator at seven o'clock in the morning. Max hadn't appreciated her carrying him. Luckily for Sage, Bill was a big cat lover, and Max seemed to like him much better than he did her. Bill had gotten him on the elevator and into her office with no problems whatsoever.

"If you need daily progress reports, I'm your person, Jake. Just email me. Anytime," Renata said, placing a finger under each eye and then pointing them at Sage, in the universal sign for *I'm watching you*.

Brenda hustled Renata out of the office before Sage got to say anything, at least anything to her associate.

Sage sat in her chair, pushing her hair back from her face. "I don't believe you, Jake. You're asking for progress reports about Max and me?"

"No, and before you get upset with Renata, she has your best interests at heart. Yours and Max's." His lips twitched.

"Max is fine, and I'm growing on him. He only growled at me once today."

"You still sleeping on the couch?"

She sighed. "Yes, but only because I have a very comfortable couch." She leaned over to put her purse in the drawer. "So what was it you wanted to talk to me about?"

"My guy came through." His gaze roamed her face. "You were the last person Alice called, Sage."

"No." She shook her head. "I checked. I checked the day she went missing." She'd checked obsessively, even after learning Alice had died.

"It was an audio message. She didn't get a chance to send it."

"She was dictating it when she went off the road, wasn't she? It's the reason she got distracted."

"We don't know that."

Sage pushed the words past the emotion tightening her throat. "What did she say?"

"I'll send you the audio file if you'd like, but she said *Sage, call me as soon as*, and then it cut off. I think she wanted you to call her about some guy she was talking to at the Smoke Shack just before she headed for the farm."

The Smoke Shack was known for having the best BBQ brisket on Cape Cod. The food truck had been a fixture in Sunshine Bay for the past thirty years. They had a patio and an outdoor bar with live music on the weekends and a great location on the beach. Alice loved it. She used to take Sage and Jake there at least a few times every summer. Usually when they had something to celebrate.

"A guy? What guy?" Sage asked.

"From what I could piece together, there was a guy asking about your family. They said Alice overheard him and approached him. The conversation got heated on Alice's end, according to the staff. They said she seemed upset."

"And they didn't think this is something the police should know?"

"They'd taken a couple of days off to go camping and just got back today. They had no idea Alice had died until they went to work this morning. They were pretty cut up about it."

"Do you think this guy could have something to do with Alice's death?"

"Other than upsetting her? No. It was an accident, Sage. Plus he spent the night at the Smoke Shack. Closed the place down, according to the staff. I talked to SBPD an hour ago. They mentioned that your mom, aunt, and grandmother have had issues with obsessive fans in the past. So it's possible Alice was being protective of your family. The police have his description. They'll keep an eye out. Might be a good idea for your family to do the same."

"Okay, I'll let them know. What did he look like?"

"In his fifties, good shape, about six feet tall, well dressed, and he wore Tex Aviator sunglasses. They didn't get a hair color. He wore a black ball cap. They also didn't see what he was driving or which way he went when he left. They were anxious to close down for the night."

"Did your guy find anything else? A reason why Alice would have gone to the farm instead of going home?"

"No. Nothing. The phone was damaged, and he couldn't retrieve everything. He'll keep trying, but he doesn't hold out much hope."

"So we'll never know why she was heading to the farm that night."

There was a knock on her office door, and one of the mailroom staff entered. "Urgent memo from the founding partners," he said, rolling his eyes. No one understood why they insisted on sending hard copies instead of sending an email.

"Thanks," she said, accepting the memo. She scanned it. There'd been a cat sighting at the firm, and Forbes, Poole, and Russell were not happy. "Uh, Jake, I have to go."

Chapter Seven

Sage had managed to keep Max's existence from the founding partners at Forbes, Poole, and Russell for almost two weeks. It played in her favor that none of the managing partners or their teams ventured farther than their offices on the top floor. But now she sat in the wood-paneled executive suite of Robert Forbes, waiting to face the music.

Robert waved an impatient hand at his personal assistant as she placed cookies on the plate in front of him. "How many times must I tell you, Emilia? The iced cookies are not to touch the plain cookies."

"I'm so sorry. I forgot," his assistant said, carefully rearranging the cookies to his specifications.

Robert pursed his lips. "No, that won't do. Take them away and bring me a new plate and fresh cookies."

Sage glanced at Nina from human resources, who'd accompanied her to the meeting. Robert didn't seem to care that Sage was to meet with a new client in fifteen minutes, something she'd told Emilia when she'd tried rescheduling until later in the day. But Robert's assistant had seemed personally affronted that Sage didn't immediately clear her schedule for the man now taking a delicate sip of his tea with his pinkie raised.

Returning the teacup carefully to the saucer, Robert folded his hands on his chest and peered at Sage over the top of his glasses. Apart from the bifocals, he reminded her of Mr. Burns from *The Simpsons*.

"As you know, Ms. Rosetti, we at Forbes, Poole, and Russell were deeply saddened to learn of Ms. Espinoza's passing. We're also aware of your personal relationship with Ms. Espinoza and are sympathetic to your loss. But as sympathetic as we are, the cat must go."

Sage had seen no signs of the founding partners' sadness or sympathy for her loss. She wasn't surprised or offended by their lack of empathy or understanding, but she didn't appreciate Robert lying about it to her face.

"Max is a support cat, Mr. Forbes," she said, repeating what Nina had told her to say, including quoting the clause in her contract that could be massaged to fit the situation.

Robert's lips folded inward, looking at Nina as if he blamed her for the addition of the clause in the contract. Nina didn't bat an eyelash. As intimidating as the man could be—and he was, even at eighty-three—he didn't intimidate Nina. Probably because she was his third wife's daughter and knew where the skeletons were buried.

Nina leaned forward to place a file on Robert's desk, pushing it toward him with the tip of her finger. "This is the supporting documentation for Sage's request that Max, as a working support animal, be allowed to remain with her in her office. I've also included a petition signed by eighty-five percent of the employees at Forbes, Poole, and Russell requesting that Max be allowed to continue in his role as support cat at the firm."

Everyone, other than the founding partners, loved Max. Sage's colleagues regularly stopped by to pet him and pour out their troubles into his nonjudgmental ears. They spoiled him with toys and treats. So much so that her office felt more like Max's space than hers. Cat climbing shelves now decorated the wall across from her desk, a cat castle sat in a corner, and a cat lounge chair took up the other corner.

If Sage was being honest, she'd admit she found her new office décor almost as annoying as she found her revolving office door. She didn't have time to socialize with her colleagues. Before Max, she knew less than one percent of their names. In her defense, it was a big firm. Now, not only did she know eighty-five percent of her colleagues' names, but she also knew their romantic and childhood histories.

Robert flicked through the file before returning it to his desk with a loud *thwack*. It was the most animated Sage had seen him in years. "We'll allow the cat to remain with the option to revisit the situation three weeks from now," he said, turning his attention to the plate of fresh cookies Emilia had placed on his desk.

"Great, thank you," Sage said, coming to her feet.

"I didn't give you permission to leave, Ms. Rosetti." He pointed his cookie at the chair she'd just vacated.

She widened her eyes at Nina, indicating the time on her phone with her chin. Nina knew about her meeting. She was a big fan of Sage's new client, who would no longer be her client if Sage was late for their meeting.

"Mr. Forbes, Sage has a meeting with a rather important client that she can't be late for."

His milky-blue eyes narrowed behind his bifocals. "Are you insinuating that Ms. Rosetti's meeting with her client is more important than her meeting with me, Nina?"

"Of course not. I—"

"I thought not." He took another delicate sip from his tea-cup and wrinkled his nose, calling for Emilia to warm it up.

Placing her phone at thigh level, Sage texted Brenda, letting her know she'd be late, only to discover her client had already arrived, and said client was allergic to cats. Sage asked Brenda to check if any of the conference rooms were available. They were all booked. She then asked Brenda to arrange for her to switch offices with one of her colleagues.

"Am I keeping you from something, Ms. Rosetti?"

"Sorry." She stuffed her phone in the pocket of her blazer. "What can I do for you, Mr. Forbes?"

"Stay out of the news, for one." This time his pursed-lipped attention was directed at her. "Our clients choose Forbes, Poole, and Russell because of our high moral and ethical standards, Ms. Rosetti. They also choose us because they know that their affairs will be handled with the utmost care and privacy."

"Mr. Forbes, my client and I had nothing to do with the media circus her ex-husband orchestrated. He was angry the judge awarded full custody of their son to his wife and supervised visitation until a court-appointed psychologist deems otherwise." Something Sage doubted would happen anytime soon.

"The same man whom you refused to represent in his divorce

proceedings, even when we requested you do so for the good of the firm."

It had been a risky move. The ink had barely dried on her diploma. But she'd crossed paths with Chad a time or two, and she refused to represent a misogynistic narcissist. If not for the senior partner who'd hired Sage backing her decision, she probably would have been fired. The Winthrops were among the elite of Boston's elite.

"Yes, and I stand by my refusal to represent him in the divorce proceedings against his first wife. Monica is his second wife," she added in case Robert had misremembered the details of the case.

"I'm aware, just as I'm aware that this is not the first time one of your cases has shined an unflattering spotlight on this firm, Ms. Rosetti. Attention seeking is not a trait we at Forbes, Poole, and Russell approve of in our employees."

She didn't understand how winning her cases shined an unflattering light on the firm...unless you counted the fact that one or more of the founding partners typically had a connection to her clients' high-profile soon-to-be exes.

"Good thing I'm not an attention seeker then. But Chad Winthrop is, so if you want the firm out of the spotlight, I suggest you call your best friend the congressman and tell him to rein his son in." Sage rose from the chair. "And while you're at it, tell him that if Junior sends me any more threatening emails, I'm going to the police." Robert's upraised voice and Nina's placating one followed Sage out of the office. She closed the door behind her.

At her desk in the outer office, Emilia swiveled in her chair to face Sage. "I swear, you're going to give poor Robert a heart attack one of these days. I don't understand why he lets you speak to him that way."

"It's called billable hours."

The door to Robert's office opened and Nina walked out while, behind her, Robert yelled from his desk, "Where's my hot tea, girl? And while you're at it, bring me more of those iced cookies."

"What I don't understand, Emilia, is why you let him speak to you that way." Robert's assistant ignored her as she hurried off to do her boss's bidding.

Sage said to Nina, "You should be writing him up for how he treats her."

"I have, and I will again. But right now, I want to talk about the emails Chad Winthrop has been sending you. How bad are they? Should I talk to security?"

"They're no worse than usual. I'm also surmising they're from Winthrop. He's smart enough not to give himself away." Unlike some of the men who'd threatened her in the past. "It's only been a couple of days since the judgment came down. Let's give it a few more days."

"Okay. But I want to see the emails. Have Brenda forward them to me, and I'll pass them on to security. Like you should have."

"I have a lot on my plate right now, and they honestly slipped my mind."

As they walked out of Robert's reception area—which was bigger than Sage's and Nina's offices combined—they heard Emilia pick up the ringing phone. "One moment please, Mr. Winthrop. Mr. Winthrop returning your call, sir. Should I put him through?"

Nina gave her a smug smile. "You see, he does take my warnings seriously." She nudged Sage. "And you need to take these threats seriously. I know you've had more than your fair share of hate mail over the years, and nothing has ever come of it, but all it takes is one time."

And that one time came quicker than Sage could have imagined.

After a productive two-hour meeting with her new client in her colleague's office, Sage walked back to her own office.

She frowned down the hall at Brenda and Renata. The two women looked frazzled as they knocked on office doors. "What's going on?"

Ignoring her question, they poked their heads in the respective offices, asking if the occupants had seen Max.

Sage wasn't alarmed. It wasn't unusual for Max to disappear for an hour or two. If one of her colleagues was having a stressful day, they'd commandeer the cat. Sage glanced at her watch. "Try Roland in personal injury. His client's condition has improved."

"I did," Brenda said, fast-walking to the next door. "We've almost finished checking all the offices on this floor."

When both women received negative responses at the last of the offices on the floor, they headed for the bank of elevators. "Maybe Bill took him up to the roof," Sage suggested. The rooftop gardens had become Max's personal playground.

Bill, who was trying to quit smoking, credited petting Max with helping him deal with the cravings. To hear some of her colleagues talk, you'd think Max was the Dalai Lama of cats.

Her phone buzzed in her pocket. She pulled it out and glanced at the screen. Jake was FaceTiming her. They talked every day, mostly to ensure that he wasn't having Zoom calls with her team. No one seemed to think Sage was cat-mommy material. Annoyingly, they were probably right.

She knew she should have left Max with him at the farm as Jake had initially suggested. She felt petty about her decision to take him with her, petty and selfish, but she couldn't bring herself to return Max to Jake. Not yet at least. Jake brought out the worst in her. She'd been just as petty when he'd offered to take care of everything. She'd reacted like she didn't trust him not to steal away in the night with the proceeds from their joint inheritance. In her defense, it wasn't outside the realm of possibility. The guy didn't have a job or a steady income. And come on, he had a criminal history.

She'd also been hungover, sleep-deprived, and still reeling from Alice's death. She still was, but work helped. She could pretend Alice was walking the trails on the farm without a care in the world. She debated whether to take Jake's call. Yesterday, he'd been making noises about them planning Alice's memorial service. Sage didn't want to. She wouldn't be able to pretend Alice was still here if they did.

Her phone stopped buzzing, and she was relieved Jake had given up. But then her cell pinged with an incoming text. She glanced at the screen. *Crap.* Jake was here, in the building, with the paperwork she had to sign. She'd been positive he'd said Friday. She glanced at her phone and groaned. It was Friday.

She shot off a text—I'll meet you down there—and walked toward the elevators while calling Brenda. "Please tell me you've found Max," she said as soon as her assistant picked up.

"No, and he's not on the roof with Bill. He said Max wasn't in the office when he went on his break."

"Dammit."

"I know. I'm beginning to worry he got out of the building too."

"Don't say that!"

"Isn't that why you said *dammit*?"

"No. I said it because Jake is here, and he'll want to see Max, and if I've lost him, he'll know I'm a horrible cat mother and take him back to the farm, and then I'll be all—"

Another text came in, presumably from Jake, cutting off her emotional diatribe. Had she really been going to confess to Brenda how lonely she'd be without Max for company? How pathetic was that? The cat hated her, and she didn't care, as long as she wasn't by herself. Something was seriously wrong with her. She loved living on her own with no one to answer to.

She glanced at the screen as she went to press the Down button for the elevator, sucking in a panicked breath just as the doors slid open and Jake walked out.

He frowned. "What's wrong?"

She didn't want to tell him, but she had to. There was no way she could keep this from him. She turned her phone, showing him the photo of a tattooed arm holding Alice's beloved cat against a muscular chest. "Max has been catnapped."

Chapter Eight

Word had spread quickly throughout the firm that Max had been catnapped. Sage's anxious colleagues were now packed into her office, sharing what they'd seen with Jake, who'd taken charge of the investigation. No one had questioned his authority to do so, including Forbes, Poole, and Russell's head of security and their lead investigator.

It was a little weird seeing Jake seated behind her desk, questioning her colleagues, while Brenda and Renata looked on, taking notes. It was also a little annoying how they hung on his every word, acting as if he were some investigative savant. Was he an excellent interviewer who had her colleagues opening up to him with incredible ease, latching on to the smallest of details that might have escaped even her? Yes, he was, and admittedly she'd been a little surprised how good he was at this, but he had been an investigator for a legal firm for years, even if it was on a part-time basis.

They couldn't fool her, though. Brenda and Renata were like thirty-five percent of their coworkers. While genuinely worried about Max, they were equally entranced with the man behind her desk. She supposed she couldn't blame them. She wasn't as indifferent as she pretended. Even in her initial panic—she might have had a mini-meltdown—at seeing the photo of Max in the tattooed arms of the catnapper, she hadn't missed that Jake had somehow gotten even more muscly and gorgeous. She put it down to his deep-golden tan and not his confidence and authoritative air.

She caught her reflection in the computer screen. She didn't look that pale and haggard, did she? She leaned closer. She needed to stop pushing her fingers through her hair.

Jake cocked his head. "What are you doing?"

She hadn't realized how close she'd gotten to the computer, or to him. Why did he have to smell so good?

She took a step back and waved her hand at the screen. "I was reading emails. The font seems smaller than usual." It actually did. She squinted until the words came into sharper focus. Then wished she hadn't when she read one of the most recent threatening emails she'd received. Jake had been going through them over the last two hours while questioning her colleagues.

Every so often, he'd send her a raised-eyebrow glance. She hadn't been sure what it meant, but just then, he decided to enlighten her. "The entire team of lawyers I worked with didn't receive this many death threats the entire time I was there."

"It must have been a small firm," she said while surreptitiously glancing at her hair on the screen, finger-combing it into place.

"It wasn't. You need your own security team."

"She does," Brenda agreed. "She also needs to have her eyes checked."

"No. What she needs to do is stop working until all hours of the night and go home at a decent hour," Renata said. An opinion she shared with Sage on a daily basis, and one she'd no doubt shared with Jake.

Several of their colleagues snorted their amusement. "I know, right?" Sage said.

"We were agreeing with Renata. You make all of us look like slackers, Sage. Don't you want to have a life apart from work?" asked Roland, the personal injury lawyer, and he was serious.

Sage looked at her colleagues, the majority of whom were nodding in agreement with Roland. She was genuinely shocked. She'd thought Renata was the anomaly, but apparently it had been her all along. She opened her mouth, then closed it. Whatever defense she went with wouldn't endear her to her colleagues. And when had that become an issue for her?

Jake, who'd been texting with someone, pocketed his phone and then leaned back in her chair and cracked his knuckles, ensuring he had everyone's attention. Although, let's be honest, he'd had it all along. "Thanks for your help. Now, if you don't mind." He lifted his bearded chin at the door.

A few of her colleagues dragged their feet, clearly hoping to be in on the action, while others wished them good luck, asking Jake to let them know when Max had been found. Not her, Jake.

Once Brenda had ushered the last of their coworkers out the door, Jake turned to Sage. "How do you want to do this?"

"Do what?" She glanced at the screen, noting that the threatening emails had been replaced with a street map. "Wait. I recognize that address."

"I thought you might."

Renata and Brenda leaned in to look at the map. Sage refrained from giving them a dig about their eyesight. She was trying to find a way not to embarrass Jake in front of his fan club, but she didn't have a choice. There was no way, given Robert's connection to the Winthrops, that she could accuse Chad of being the catnapper without hard evidence. As far as she could tell, Jake didn't have any.

"I understand why you think Chad is involved, but trust me, he's not." She lowered the map and brought up the threatening emails from three years ago. They were from the ex on one of her pro bono cases. "I'm pretty sure it's this guy. Look at his build and tattoos. They're very similar. In his email, he also says no one close to me, including my dog, would be safe when he gets out of prison. He was scheduled for release two weeks ago." Despite what everyone seemed to think, she did pay attention to the threats, especially when they were directed at her family.

"You don't have a dog," Jake pointed out.

"No, but..." She scrolled down to the pictures he'd taken of her playing on the beach with a black Newfoundlander. "Admiral is my cousin's dog. He must have thought he was mine."

Jake blinked and then gave his head a slight shake. "I, uh, already ruled him out. They added another year to his sent—"

Pointing at the photo on the screen, Renata, appearing to be in complete and utter shock, interrupted Jake. "Wow, you look...happy." She frowned. "And hot." Then she moved her hand up and down in front of Sage. "Why, when you have a body like that, do you hide it under boxy blazers and—?"

Jake stabbed the keyboard, replacing the photo of her at the beach with the one she'd received of Max on her phone. "You can't always go by a photo. They can be Photoshopped."

"Excuse me. Are you saying you think my body has been Photoshopped?"

"No, and I can share why I know that it hasn't been, if you'd like me to." He lifted his gaze to hers. "No?"

Ignoring Brenda and Renata's curious glances, she gave him a death glare. His lips twitched before he continued. "See here." He pointed to an area just above Max's head. "Also here, and here." He ran his finger along the man's forearm and then pointed at a spot between the catnapper's waist and Max's tail. "But sometimes you get lucky." He tapped the screen on what looked like a window to the left of the man.

"What am I looking at?" she asked.

He enlarged the window. "The car parked alongside the curb."

"Chad drives a silver Jag."

Jake nodded. "And lucky for us, the owner of the blue Volvo keeps it clean and shiny because right here"—he pointed at the car door—"is the reflection of a silver Jag."

"Oh my gosh, you're right."

"Yeah, but that's not how I know it's Chad."

"It's not?" Sage, Brenda, and Renata asked at the same time. She hoped she didn't sound as breathless as they did.

"No. Chad did an okay job concealing his identity in the photo, although he forgot to remove his MIT class ring, but—"

"I totally missed that." She stabbed her finger at the screen. "We got you now, loser."

Jake's eyes crinkled at the corners. "We do. But the silver

Jag and the MIT ring probably won't be enough to convince your bosses, so we went a few steps further."

Jake had asked her if anyone at the firm had an issue with Max. Sage didn't think it was relevant, but she'd told him about her earlier meeting with Robert. Now she was glad that she had, because Jake knew what they were up against. Thinking back to what he said, she frowned. "Who's *we?*"

"A friend who owes me a favor."

She narrowed her eyes at him. "That sounds sketchy."

"Sometimes you have to walk a fine line between legal and illegal to catch a thief," he said, a hint of challenge in his voice, as if he expected her to share his past with Brenda and Renata. It hurt a little that he believed she'd embarrass him like that.

She crossed her arms. "I trust you."

He held her gaze as though waiting for the punch line. When it didn't come, he nodded. "Thanks."

Something about the way he looked at her reminded her of the morning they'd woken up together in the waterbed, and she quickly looked away. She was not thinking about that now. "So, what evidence do you have that will convince the founding partners?"

"Because an app was used to manipulate the photo, my guy was able to get a location from the text. It was sent from Winthrop's address." Leaning back in the chair, Jake crossed his arms behind his head. "And the only person Bill and Roland remembered seeing near your office around the time Max disappeared was Robert Forbes's personal assistant."

"Wait, you're insinuating that Emilia is in on this?"

"Nope. I'm insinuating that your boss is." He raised a hand when Sage and Brenda opened their mouths to protest. "Hear me out. Emilia doesn't have the background to disable the security cameras and isn't involved with anyone who does, including the security team at the firm. But your boss could have the cameras taken offline anytime with no questions asked, and the person who did it isn't about to tell us, if they value their job."

Renata flipped through her notebook, waving it at them. "Look." She tapped on the statement under one of their coworkers' names. "She said she saw Mr. Forbes's personal assistant carrying a large box off the elevator. The timeline fits. It was just before Brenda and I came back from lunch and you got out of your client meeting, Sage."

"I can't believe Robert would do something like this," Sage said, lowering herself onto Max's lounge chair as the implications hit her, which might have been why she'd thought sitting on Max's chair was a good idea. It wasn't. It was a lot farther down than she'd anticipated. "I can't go to him with this, Jake. He'll fire me."

"Personally, I don't know why you'd want to work for someone who'd do this, but if you're worried about losing your job, you can sue him for wrongful dismissal. Or you can threaten to go to the press if he threatens to fire you." He got up from the chair. "But you don't have to confront him. I'll go get Max now."

"Jake, Chad's not just going to hand him over. He wouldn't go to this trouble for no reason," she said while struggling to get up and off the lounge chair, wishing she'd worn pants instead of a skirt.

Jake helped her up before she embarrassed herself. Only she kind of did that when she placed a hand on his very muscular chest for balance, was enveloped in his heady masculine scent, and silently muttered, "Why do you have to smell so good?" Except the way the three of them were looking at her suggested that she must have said it out loud instead of in her head.

She blamed it on the terrifying thought that she was seconds away from possibly putting the job she loved at risk. It didn't matter that Jake was right. If Robert was behind Max's catnapping, the last thing she should want was to work for him, but Jake didn't understand how important her job was to her. It wasn't just about the money either.

Brenda bit her lip, no doubt trying not to laugh at Sage's inane remark, before she asked, "But what if what Chad wanted was Max?"

Renata nodded. "Brenda's right. Everyone in this building has been talking about Max. His reputation is spreading far and wide. It's not out of the realm of possibilities that Chad has heard about him and wants some of Max's nonjudgmental love for himself while getting back at you for taking his son from him. And the way the guy acted after the judge ruled against him, he needs all the comfort and support he can get." She held up her hands. "I'm not defending him. He deserved what he got. I'm just stating a fact."

"I know, and you're right. It's just that there's no way Chad would have heard about . . ." Sage trailed off and then argued against her own argument. "Unless Robert shared how he felt about Max at the charity event Chad's father hosted last weekend. They were both there."

She knew this because there had been a photo of them together in the society pages of the newspaper she'd used to line Max's litter box.

"Okay, so the three of you are right. It looks like Robert

might be behind this—and I stress *might be* because until we get proof that he set up the catnapping for himself or on Chad's behalf, we can't rule out that Emilia took it upon herself to get rid of Max for Robert, and that she approached Chad."

"Actually, we can. In the past week, there has been no communication between Chad and Robert's PA."

"And you know this how?" Sage asked, hoping Jake hadn't taken a walk on the criminal side. Because accessing information on Chad's or Emilia's phone was illegal.

"Plausible deniability is a thing."

She groaned. "Jake!"

"On that note, I'm off to rescue Max."

"You didn't let me finish! What I was going to say before you told me you leaped over that fine line is that Chad isn't simply going to hand over Max when you knock on his door and ask for him back."

"I didn't plan on knocking on his door or asking for him back." He winked, then gave Brenda and Renata one of his heart-stopping smiles and sauntered out the door.

They stared after him, Renata releasing a lovelorn sigh, Brenda patting her chest while saying, "That man. He's so—"

"Annoyingly obnoxious with a superhero complex? Yeah, I know," she said, grabbing her purse.

"Where are you going?" they called after her.

"To make sure he doesn't end up in jail."

~

At least that had been the plan, but now there was a good chance Brenda would have to bail them both out. "You don't know him like I do, Jake. If I knock on his door, he's just as likely to punch me in the face as he is talk to me, and then I'll have to punch him back," Sage said from behind the wheel of her BMW, eyeing Chad's McMansion through the rearview mirror while arguing with Jake. "I have a better idea. Why don't you go knock on his door and distract him, and I'll rescue Max?"

He turned his phone, showing her the layout of Chad's house that he'd been studying on the way over. "Right, because somehow in the past decade you've become an expert at breaking and entering." He pointed at the screen. "My gut says he'll be keeping Max close by. Either here, here, or here," he said, indicating the family room, den, and kitchen. "It'll be a quick in and out. But if you're not comfortable distracting Winthrop, don't worry about it. Drive to the rendezvous point, and I'll meet you there with Max."

"No, you can't do this on your own. You need me to distract him. I'll just stay an arm's length away and pretend I'm there to help him earn back his visitation rights with his son or something."

"You don't feel guilty about him losing his custodial rights, do you?"

"No. Chad hasn't had any involvement in his son's day-to-day care, and he's just a baby. He needs his mom, who is a wonderful hands-on mother. But as unprepared as Chad is to parent, and as horrible a husband as he is, it was obvious he loves his little boy, and he's only allowed supervised visitation twice a month."

"It's not your fault. You did your job and protected your client and the baby. Chad's a big boy with plenty of resources.

Just because he provided the sperm doesn't make him a father." He glanced at her. "Don't worry, you don't have to do anything. I've got a plan to distract him."

"In case you forgot, we have joint custody." She sighed. "And Max got catnapped on my watch."

"It could have just as easily happened on mine, Sage."

"It wouldn't have, and you know it." She twisted her hands on the steering wheel. "I should have left him with you, Jake. I'm sorry. I wasn't being fair to either of you, especially Max. No wonder he hates me. I took him from the people and places he knows and loves and dumped him in my office while I work."

"I don't know. It looked to me like he has a pretty sweet setup, and your colleagues love him. The change of scenery has probably been good for him."

"You really think so?"

"I do." He smiled. "Now, am I doing this on my own or are we doing this together?"

"Together," she said, thinking for the first time it felt like she and Jake were a team instead of adversaries. She couldn't help but wonder if that was good or bad, because now that she sat with it for a moment, it felt dangerous. Or maybe the nervous flutter in her stomach had more to do with the situation they were walking into than her evolving relationship with Jake.

Chapter Nine

Sage listened to the hollow ring of Chad's door chimes for the third time as she once again stepped off the front porch and onto the walkway, ensuring she was well out of his reach. She had little doubt he'd be unhappy finding her on his front doorstep. She just wasn't sure if he'd try to hit her or call the police, the latter being the worst-case scenario. The last thing she needed was for the cops to show up.

Which was why Jake suggested that, instead of pretending that Robert had sent her to help Chad come up with a winning custody strategy as she had planned, she'd go on the attack and accuse Chad of catnapping Max. It would put him on the defensive, trying to prove his innocence while making it less likely he'd want to involve law enforcement.

When Chad didn't come to the door, Sage texted Jake. **Are you sure he's home?**

Yeah. He has a doorbell camera and knows it's you. He's trying to put Max in the pantry but he isn't cooperating. Dots came and went, and then... **Max is in the pantry and**

Chad is on his way to you. I'll be in and out in under two minutes. Don't drag it out.

Sage smiled and pocketed her phone, so relieved that Max was minutes away from being safe and in Jake's arms that she barely resisted the urge to pump her fist. Now it was her turn to ensure everything went smoothly, and she knew exactly what to do. She'd accuse Chad and then pretend to fall for his innocent act and get out of there ASAP. She'd talk with Jake about what to do about Robert's presumed involvement on the way back to the office.

She couldn't bail on her clients. They needed her. And sadly, she needed the resources and the connections the firm provided to support the women's shelter she partnered with. As she considered using Robert's involvement in Max's catnapping to get the firm to write a check with a lot of zeros for Chrysalis House, the front door opened.

Chad, his white-blond hair slicked back from his sleekly handsome face, wore a pink rugby shirt with a pair of white chinos. Sage didn't know why, but she didn't trust a man who wore white pants. Then again, she could count on one hand the number of men she trusted.

She also didn't trust the smug grin on Chad's face as he crossed his arms over his chest and his bare feet at the ankles while leaning against the doorframe. Not only did he look smug, he looked camera-ready, which should have been her first red flag but wasn't, because Chad opened his mouth.

"Well, if it isn't Boston's answer to Gloria Allred. To what do I owe the pleasure?" Then he brought three fingers to his lips like a tween fangirling over Taylor Swift. "Wait, it wouldn't have anything to do with my cat, Maxamillion, would it?"

Sage's carefully rehearsed lines dried up in her throat.

He drew a checkmark in the air. "I win." He laughed. "Too bad the press wasn't here to capture the moment I rendered Sage Rosetti speechless." He made an exaggerated O with his mouth and then bent to eye level to what she assumed was his doorbell camera. "Say cheese."

She rolled her eyes but appreciated the reminder that he'd have a digital record of her visit. She had to tread carefully. She wondered if two minutes had passed but didn't want to push their luck by leaving too soon. She couldn't risk Chad catching Jake in the act.

Just as she opened her mouth to keep Chad from closing the door, he turned his phone toward her. There was a photo of him with Max on the screen. "Which pic do you think I should have enlarged? This one..." He swiped to another photo. "...or this one? I think this one. It radiates with his love for his new daddy, don't you think?"

Her temper obliterated not only her ability to tread carefully but also her guilt about Chad's restrictive visitation schedule. "Look, I understand that you're upset you lost custody of your son and only have supervised visitation with him twice a month," she said to ensure he wouldn't play the recording for anyone else. His divorce and custody agreement were sealed, as per his father's demand. "But we both know it's not me who's to blame. It's your anger issues, your cocaine addiction, and your inability to keep your dick in your pants."

A haze came over his eyes, exactly like her client had described, and he stepped toward her, his fist drawn back. Then a car horn blasted, and he gave his head a slight shake as he lowered his hand, taking two steps backward.

"Get me my cat or I'll call the police," she said, because that's what he'd expect of her. She just prayed he didn't do as she asked or this had the potential to go sideways.

"Please do. You'll save me the trouble." He shook his shoulders playfully, becoming the Chad Winthrop that social media knew and loved, and tapped his chin. "Now, what shall I have you charged with? Harassment? Trespassing?" He wrinkled his nose. "I'm sure my father and I can come up with something that ensures you lose your license to practice law. Or maybe we'll just tell Robert to fire you. He'll do what he's told this time. After all, if he wants to ensure his grandson's bid for—" Once again he made an exaggerated O with his mouth before pressing his fingers to his lips.

Right before her eyes, Sage saw everything she'd worked for destroyed because an entitled narcissist thought the rules didn't apply to him. She disagreed with many of the things the founding partners stood for, but she hadn't wanted to believe that Robert would be involved in catnapping Max, and now it looked like he had been, but not by choice. And the Winthrops had something else to hold over his head.

She didn't know if there was a way to save her job, but she had to try. She glanced at her phone, surreptitiously pressing Record before returning it to her pocket. She ignored Chad's self-satisfied smile when she didn't call the police.

"You blackmailed Robert into handing over Max, didn't you?"

"*Blackmail* is such a strong word. Besides, I'm sure you've already checked the security footage from the lobby, so you know it was Emilia leaving with a very large box. A little pressure, and I'm sure you can get her to admit to removing my

Max from your office. But it would be a shame, wouldn't it, for her to be deported just when her family has arrived here?"

At the thought of how far Chad was willing to go to get what he wanted, his lack of remorse or empathy for Emilia and her family, Sage saw red and raised her fist. "You son of a—"

Chad leaned forward, a manic smile on his face as he patted his cheek. "Right here. They'll get my best side."

The words pierced her anger, and her fist stalled midair as she followed his gaze and glanced over her shoulder. Two men were leaning against a blue Volvo with cameras in their hands, the long-range lens pointed at her. Chad took advantage of her distraction. She felt the graze of skin against her knuckles, turning her head to see Chad stagger back from her, clutching his jaw.

"She punched me. Call the police!" he yelled.

As if on cue, she heard the sound of sirens.

Chad smiled behind his hand. "You can make it all go away by testifying before the judge that my wife lied to you. I'll give you back your cat, and I won't press charges."

"You set me up," she whispered, stunned that she'd made it so easy for him.

"I did." He grinned. "You're not the only who graduated with a perfect grade point average."

"Yeah, but I'm not a psychopath," she said under her breath while removing her phone from her blazer pocket. She played back the recording for him, smiling as he realized she'd gotten everything on tape. She made a checkmark in the air. "I win."

She got to enjoy her victory for less than a minute before Chad did exactly as she'd predicted. He punched her in the face.

⌒

Jake scowled at Sage from where he sat behind the wheel of her BMW. He'd gotten worried when she hadn't shown up at the car and didn't respond to his texts and calls, only to hear the sirens. By the time he'd finally made it to her, the street was crawling with cops and press. Chad must have called them at the same time he'd called the cops. Something else Jake had missed in his bid to get to Max sooner rather than later.

The only positive out of the situation was the expression on Winthrop's face when he caught a glimpse of Max in Jake's arms. Seeing Winthrop in the back of the cop car had been a positive too, but Sage had come into view at the same time, negating the pleasure Jake had taken in the sight. If it weren't for two cops standing nearby, Jake would have planted his fist in Winthrop's face.

"How in the hell do you think it's a win when you can't see out of your left eye and your cheek is swollen?"

"It's nothing a bag of ice and some ibuprofen won't fix, and look, we got Max back." She reached over the seat to pet the cat, who was sprawled in the back, sighing when Max rolled away from her hand. "I was in on your rescue too, you know. You could at least pretend to be a little grateful."

Jake might be in a foul mood, but Max's reaction to Sage never failed to make him laugh. The cat really didn't like her, and he couldn't figure out why.

"I'm glad you think it's funny," she muttered at him. "I knew I should have been the one to rescue him instead of you playing hero. Maybe then I'd get some love too."

"Trust me, if for one minute I'd thought he'd punch you

in the face, I would have traded places with you. But the last thing we needed was for you to get caught breaking into his house."

"Oh, come on. How hard could it have been? It's the middle of the afternoon. His patio door must have been open, and you knew where he'd put Max."

"First off, I had to climb a ten-foot-high fence. Second, his patio door was locked. And third, he has an alarm, and it was armed," he said as he merged with traffic. It reminded him why he loved his motorbike and why he hated city living. He loved being back in Sunshine Bay. He just wished Alice were still there.

"Why would he have his alarm armed when he was home?"

"Oh, I don't know. Maybe because he had Max, and he knew the probability of you coming for him was high."

"I can't believe he set me up like that." She made a face, then winced, which she tried to hide from him but failed.

He strangled the steering wheel. "I can't believe I missed it."

As furious as he was at Chad, he was equally furious at himself. He used to be better at this. Lifting his hand from the steering wheel, he gently traced the edge of the bruise with the tips of his fingers. "I'm sorry. It's my fault he was able to pull this off. I should have taken more time to think it through, and I should have gone on my own."

"Hey, you don't get to take this on. It's on Chad...and a little on me, I guess. I shouldn't have provoked him with the whole checkmark thing. But I'd do it again if we got the same results. I'd be the one in the back seat of a patrol car if the cops hadn't witnessed him punching me."

"You realize, due to who his old man is, he's got a get-out-of-jail-free card, right? The most he'll get is a slap on the wrist."

"It doesn't matter." She held up her phone. "I recorded everything."

"And you know as well as I do that Massachusetts is a two-party consent state. You can't use it."

"Of course I know that, and it's not like I'd give it to the press or to the police anyway. It would put Emilia, Robert, and the firm at risk, which would negatively impact my colleagues. I don't want anyone to suffer because of Chad's revenge plot against me."

"You're a lot more forgiving than me."

"Let's hope the other founding partners are as forgiving when it comes to the negative publicity. They share the same feelings as Robert about my 'media stunts,'" she said, making air quotes.

"I don't know how you work for these guys, Sage." Admittedly, he was disappointed that she could. It wasn't a firm the girl he used to know would have worked for. He got that the money was good, but Sage was the last person he thought would sell her soul for the almighty dollar.

"Sometimes I don't know how I do either, to be honest. But there are benefits working for a firm as well connected and respected as Forbes, Poole, and Russell."

"I have a hard time respecting a man who would put not only his personal assistant but also one of his junior partners at risk the way Forbes did."

"I know. I can't believe he'd do that to Emilia. The woman dotes on him. But it's gotten worse since several of the senior partners who held the founding partners in check have retired." She glanced at him. "It's not just about the money for me, Jake. I'm given the freedom to take on pro bono cases that matter to me. The firm has also contributed tens of thousands of dollars to the women's shelter I work with. If not for their connections and contributions, Chrysalis House would have been forced to shut their doors by now."

And there she was, the girl he remembered. He should have known she wouldn't abandon her principles for a six-figure paycheck. But he was worried that she was too close to the situation to see it clearly. "And no doubt got a nice tax break for their charitable contribution and some good publicity for the firm."

She frowned at him. "When did you get so cynical?"

"I've always been cynical." He'd grown up not believing a single word out of anyone's mouth. Everyone had an agenda. It was the one lesson his parents, if you could call them parents, had taught him. And they'd taught him really well.

"I just want you to be prepared for..." He was afraid that Forbes was going to fire Sage, but he couldn't say it. He'd seen how she'd reacted earlier at the thought she'd lose her job. As he'd discovered, he didn't know how to handle a distraught woman, especially when that woman was Sage. "Anything."

"Anything as in you think he's going to fire me." She held up her phone. "Trust me, I might not be willing to hand this over to the press or the police, but I'm more than happy to use it as leverage against Robert. I'm thinking it's time they made another donation to Chrysalis House."

He glanced at her as he pulled into her space in the underground parking lot. "I see you've developed flexible morals since you started working at Forbes, Poole, and Russell."

She made a face and brought her hand to her cheek.

"Okay, ice and ibuprofen before your meeting with Forbes." Brenda had texted as they'd gotten into Sage's BMW. The press had begun calling for a comment about Sage's run-in with Winthrop, and Robert was reportedly livid.

"You won't get an argument from me." She glanced at Max in the back. "Would you mind sticking around? I'd feel better if Max was at the farm with you, at least until I know Chad won't make another move on him. I'll drive him to the farm after I'm done here."

He hadn't been sure how to broach the subject, so he was glad she'd brought it up. But he wasn't only worried about Max. "Sure. You should stay too. I mean, not with me obviously, but with your family." He caught the look on her face and added, "Just until things settle down here."

"I can't. I have too much on my plate," she said as she got out of the car and closed the passenger-side door.

"You do remember the weekend comes after Friday, right? In case you don't remember, it's when most people who work during the week take off."

"Says the guy who doesn't work."

"Who do you think has been clearing out Alice's place, taking care of the farm and the paperwork?" He didn't know why he got defensive. It was his own fault she thought he was a slacker. "Which reminds me, you have to sign off on the papers I brought to you."

He could have simply emailed them, but he'd wanted to see how she and Max were doing, and there was also the news about Alice that he wanted to give her face-to-face.

"You're right. I'm sorry." She held open the door to the

building, and he carried Max inside. "Now that we're here, I'm not as confident about my meeting with Robert." She reached out to pet Max, blowing out a frustrated breath when the cat moved out of range of her hand. "He really does hate me, doesn't he?"

Jake bit back a laugh as they took the stairs to the door that opened onto the lobby. "He's not your number one fan." He opened the door for her and then put his arm around her shoulders.

"What are you doing?"

"I have a theory," he said as they reached the bank of elevators in the lobby.

"What's your theory?"

"Okay. You can tell Max loves me, right? Other than Alice, I'm his favorite human."

She rolled her eyes and then brought her hand to the side of her face. "Dammit, that hurts."

"Sorry. Bad time to tease you. But the point is, I lived with Alice and Max. I'm like his family, and you were mean to me when we were growing up, and I think he remembers that."

"I was not mean..." She trailed off when Brenda, Renata, and a third woman walked off the elevator. Brenda and Renata were carrying boxes and looked like they'd been crying. The other woman looked like she wanted to be anywhere other than there.

Jake swore under his breath, tightening his arm around Sage's shoulders. "Just breathe," he said, hoping it worked as well as it had when Sage's mom said it.

Sage was shaking her head from side to side while trying to back away from the women. "No," she said. "He can't do this. They can't do this."

"I know," the third woman said. "It's BS, and I'll do everything in my power to reverse their decision. But for now, you're on leave, Sage."

"I can't go on leave, Nina. Ask Brenda. Ask Renata. They know what my caseload is like. Besides, this isn't my fault. Chad..." She trailed off when a silver-haired man walked through the building's front doors with his entourage. Jake recognized him. It was Congressman Winthrop.

Jake tightened his hold on Sage as she tried to wriggle free. "Trust me, Sage. This isn't the time. You've gotta be strategic, think this through."

"He's right, Sage," Brenda said, moving to stand between Sage and her view of the congressman. Renata and Nina did the same.

"How long? How long am I on leave," Sage rasped.

Nina bit her lip before admitting, "Indefinitely." Her eyes went wide. "Sage, what's wrong?"

Jake shoved Max at Nina with one hand, holding tight to Sage with other. He turned her to face him. She was ghost white and rubbing her chest. "I...I think I'm having a heart att—"

Brenda and Renata dropped the boxes and rushed to her side at the same time Sage collapsed in his arms.

Nina screamed at the security guard heading their way, "Call nine one one!"

Chapter Ten

This is a really bad idea," Gia told herself as she stood outside the Monroes' side door, balancing a care package on one arm while holding a container of chicken soup in her other hand. It made knocking on the door precarious, almost as precarious as visiting Flynn at his dad's house.

She knocked anyway. She missed Flynn. She hadn't seen him in four days, unless she counted their FaceTime calls. It was ridiculous that she missed him. It wasn't like they'd been dating for that long. Two weeks, and they'd gone out together six of the fourteen days.

Geesh, next she knew, she'd be counting the hours. Her brain flashed the number of hours they'd been apart, and she shut it out of her mind with a sigh. It didn't matter. The evidence was there for anyone to see if they bothered looking hard enough. She was a fifty-five-year-old desperate divorcée. At least that's how she assumed it would look to everyone, including Flynn. She turned and headed for her car, wincing when she heard the side door creak open.

"Hey, where are you going?"

That voice, she thought as she turned around. *That face*. Of course she'd be stupid over this man. He was beautiful, and not just on the outside, on the inside too, which made it so much worse.

"I brought you and your dad some chicken soup, and I picked up a few things I thought you might need from the drugstore." She held them out to him. She'd also changed three times before deciding what to wear, only to end up choosing an outfit that didn't look like she was trying too hard.

She should have tried harder, she decided, glancing at the white sneakers tied with chartreuse laces that she'd paired with a denim skirt and a white cotton shirt she wore tied at the waist. Flynn didn't seem to care what she had on, though. His gaze hadn't strayed from her face.

The man had gorgeous eyes. The azure cotton shirt he wore untucked over his tan cargo shorts highlighting just how blue they were.

She shook her head at herself. Her mother would say she was smitten, and she'd be right. Thinking back, Gia realized she'd probably been smitten with Flynn Monroe for the past six months. They just hadn't had this much one-on-one time together. He was an architect of some renown and owned his own design consultancy firm, which took him all over the world. If they continued the way they were going, she didn't want to think what it would be like when he was gone months at a time. It had been hard enough not seeing him for the past four days.

Amos had come down with the flu. Flynn hadn't felt comfortable leaving him on his own. He'd invited her over, of course. But hanging out at his place with his dad didn't match her idea of keeping their relationship secret. Flynn didn't feel the same and hadn't been happy about her moratorium on daytime dating. Then again, he hadn't been happy she'd only date him secretly.

"Tell me the truth," he said as he walked to her. Instead of taking the proffered container of soup and care package, he put his hands on her hips. "You were going to take off without seeing me, weren't you?"

"I was thinking about it," she admitted, glancing down the driveway while trying to ignore the feel of his warm hands on her.

"No one can see us, Gia," he said, drawing her closer.

"Flynn," she protested even as she held the container of soup and the care package out from her body to accommodate his tall, rangy frame.

He bent his head. "I've missed you," he murmured against her lips before deepening his kiss.

It took every ounce of self-control for her to pull back, breaking the kiss. "Someone will see us."

"And?"

She blew out a frustrated breath. "I know you don't care, Flynn, but I do." She could tell he was disappointed by her answer and went up on her toes, kissing the underside of his jaw. "I've missed you too."

"Good." He stepped back, taking the container of soup and care package from her. "You can rescue me from another game of chess."

"I don't want to interrupt your game with your dad. Maybe I should just—"

"Trust me, my dad has had four uninterrupted days with

me. He'll be just as happy to see you as I am." He smiled. "Maybe not quite as happy as I am." He put the care package on top of the soup container and opened the door, leaning back against it to make room for her to get by.

She looked around as she walked into the kitchen, pressing her lips together to hold back a laugh. With its avocado-green-wallpapered walls and harvest-gold appliances, it was like she'd stepped into the 1970s. "Have you and your dad had lunch?" she asked when he deposited the containers on the counter.

Flynn's arms came around her waist from behind, and he nudged her hair over her shoulder with his chin, pressing his lips to the side of her neck before bringing his mouth to her ear, nibbling on the lobe. "Are you laughing at my father's slightly outdated kitchen?"

"No, and you need to stop doing that," she said, her breathy voice giving her away.

"Are you sure you want me to stop?" he asked, his voice low and deep as he moved his hands slowly from her waist, mapping her body with the tips of his fingers.

She arched her back, needy for more of his touch. "Flynn."

He turned her around, lifting her easily into his arms. "Let me show you the project I've been working on," he murmured, moving to the other side of the kitchen. He opened a pantry door and then walked inside, closing the door behind them, shutting them in the dark.

"We can't do this. Your dad—"

"Is at this moment sitting in the living room watching Gotham, a YouTube chess channel on his iPad, in the hope of discovering a strategy to beat me. And before you ask, he won't hear us because he'll have his headset on, pretending he's watching the PGA Tour on YouTube instead of Gotham." He brushed his lips across hers. "Okay?"

She wrapped her legs around his waist. "Okay."

"Gia Rosetti, have I told you lately how much I like you?"

She smiled against his mouth. "You did. Last night when we were having phone sex."

He drew his head back. "Is that what we were doing?"

"I think so. I've never had phone sex before." Their eyes met, and she saw something in his gaze that made her groan. "If you're going to tell me you had phone sex with Cami when you were seventee—"

He shut her up with a kiss. At first, she was annoyed, but she thought that had more to do with the idea of him having phone sex with her sister than with him cutting her off with a kiss—because Flynn Monroe kissed better than any man she knew.

"Dad, answer the side door. I have my hands full!" Willow yelled from outside the house.

Gia sucked in a shocked gasp. The dad in question stumbled, slamming Gia's back and head into the pantry's shelves. "Ow," she cried, covering her head with her arms as boxes rained down around her.

"Hang on to your horses," Amos yelled, sounding much closer than the living room. "Your dad's got his hands full too. I'll be there in a minute."

"Madonna santa! You said he had his headphones on and was watching chess on YouTube!" Gia whisper-shouted at Flynn, who was trying not to laugh.

Close to tears, she swatted him. "It's not funny," she said, then began frantically brushing fiber cereal from her hair.

"I know." He helped her rid herself of the crumbs before taking her hand in his and bringing it to his lips. He kissed it. "I'm sorry, honey. I had no idea Willow was coming over."

The door opened, and Flynn's father stood there, leaning on his walker. "You should have asked me. I could have told you she was coming over."

"Don't worry, Gramps. Cami just pulled in. She'll let me in," Willow yelled through the side door.

Gia made a pained sound in her throat, and both Monroe men looked at her quizzically.

"Why don't you sit in the living room and visit with my dad?" Flynn guided her from the pantry as though he wasn't sure if she was about to explode or break down.

"I told you this was a bad idea, but did you listen to me? Oh no, you——" He kissed her to shut her up again. She pushed at his chest. "Flynn, you can't keep doing that, and your father is standing right there." Her cheeks heated, and she gave Amos a small, embarrassed smile. "Hi, Mr. Monroe. I'm glad to see you're feeling better. I, uh, brought you some chicken soup. I'm sure your son"—she gave Flynn a look—"can heat it up for you."

"You're not going anywhere," Flynn said, taking her by the hand and walking her into the living room. He gently pushed her into a comfortable armchair.

"Hey, Gramps. You're looking much better today."

Gia briefly closed her eyes and sank down in the chair.

"Have I told you lately how beautiful you are?"

"Don't even." Gia shook her head. "Compliments aren't getting you out of this one."

"I love your face."

Unexpected tears welled in her eyes. "Flynn, don't."

"It's true, and I don't care who knows. And that includes our daughter," he said, moving to the ottoman across from her when Willow walked out of the kitchen. "Hey, kiddo. Look who stopped by."

"What are you doing here, Mom?" Willow said, smiling as she walked over to give her a hug.

"I made a batch of chicken soup and brought some over for your grandfather." She stood. "I should probably get going, though. Let all of you have a visit."

"I insist you stay and have some soup with us, Gia. You just got here," Flynn said. He was an easygoing man but far from a pushover, and she saw signs of that in the firm set of his jaw. Admittedly, she found Flynn's alpha-male persona attractive when it periodically made an appearance. There were times when it even made her pulse race. This was not one of those times.

"Dad's right. Stay and have a bowl of soup with us, Mom. I feel like I haven't seen you in weeks."

Probably because you haven't, Gia thought as she lowered herself onto the chair. As uncomfortable as this would be, she wouldn't pass up an opportunity to spend time with her daughter. Even if Cami was here.

She forced a smile for her sister, who walked into the living room, looking gorgeous in a gauzy white sundress. "Hello, Cami."

"Gia, what are you doing here?"

Amos stopped pushing his walker, looking from Gia to Cami. "Thought you two were thick as thieves growing up. You used to brag about Gia all the time. Now it's as if you can't stand being in the same room together."

"Dad," Flynn said, a warning in his voice.

"What? It's my house. I can say whatever I want. I call it as I see it. And you know what I call this..." he said, letting go of his walker to fall backward into his chair.

Gia had forgotten how well Amos knew her sister. Cami had practically lived at the Monroe house the two years she'd dated Flynn. Gia wasn't sure she wanted to hear what Amos had to say. Apparently, her daughter wasn't sure she wanted to hear what he had to say either.

"How about I get everyone some soup?" Willow said, jumping up from the armchair beside Gia. "Come on, Cami. You can help me serve." She looped her arm through Gia's sister's, guiding her out of the living room.

Gia watched them go, chewing on her bottom lip. It had been almost a year since Cami had come back into their lives and Willow had learned the truth. It should be easier by now.

Once Willow and Cami had disappeared into the kitchen, Flynn reached over, giving her knee a comforting squeeze. "You okay?"

"Now, why would you ask a darn fool question like that? Of course she's not okay. Put yourself in her shoes. She raised Willow on her own for twenty-eight years, and did a damn fine job of it, and now you and Cami come along, taking up all of Willow's time and attention. I'm as much to blame as the two of you, I suppose. My apologies for that, Gia."

"No, please, you have absolutely nothing to apologize for, Amos. I'm thrilled that Willow has you and Flynn in her life. Her brother and sisters too." It was true. She'd never felt a single twinge of jealousy about the time Willow spent with her new family. She was happy for her daughter, and Gia felt bad if she'd given Amos any reason to think otherwise.

"It's just me she'd rather not have in Willow's life, isn't that right, Gia?" Cami said as she walked into the room with a tray for Amos and a challenge in her eyes.

Amos turned in his chair, eyeing her sister with a frown. "What has gotten into you? You haven't been yourself in months."

Finally, Gia thought, relieved that she wasn't the only one who'd noticed something was up with Cami. Then again, maybe the reason Gia had noticed was because she'd been the one on the receiving end of her sister's moods. Gia inwardly rolled her eyes at herself. She bore some responsibility for Cami directing her anger at her. Not that she'd share that with her mother or Eva.

Gia expected her sister to brush aside Amos's question with her usual dazzling smile, but instead Cami stood there with tears rolling down her sun-kissed cheeks. Gia's first thought was, *Why can't I cry like that?* Then she reminded herself that her sister was an Academy Award–winning actress. Of course she'd know how to ensure her mascara and nose didn't run.

Cami sniffed daintily as though to prove Gia's point, but then she did something that caught Gia completely off guard. She made a sound that caused the hair on the back of Gia's neck to stand on end. If she hadn't been sitting right there, Gia would have thought it was an animal howling in pain.

"Mom?" Willow said, as she walked out of the kitchen, looking at Gia as if wondering why she hadn't already gone to her sobbing sister.

Her daughter was right. Their issues with each other didn't

matter at the moment. They were still family. Gia stood at the same time Flynn did. But before either of them could reach for her sister, Cami, sobbing uncontrollably now, dashed to Amos's chair, set the tray on his lap—without spilling a drop—then turned and threw herself into Flynn's arms.

"It's all right. Everything's going to be all right, Cami," he said, his voice as soothing as the way he rubbed her sister's back.

As Gia watched them together, she remembered her prediction of two weeks before when she'd caught a glimpse of them in her rearview mirror. Getting involved with Flynn had been madness. It didn't matter that she woke up with a smile on her face at just the thought of seeing him, that every day with him felt exciting, magical even. There was only one way this would end—her with a broken heart. Even worse would be the fallout with Willow. She'd be torn between her mother and her father.

As Gia looked away from Flynn, she met Amos's steady gaze. "He's always been her security blanket," he said, as if the knowledge would reassure Gia. Her face must be easier to read than she thought.

Flynn glanced from his father to Gia and then gave his head a slight, seemingly frustrated shake. Gia wasn't sure, but she thought his frustration might be directed at her. He took a step back from Cami and guided her to a chair, crouching in front of her.

"Son," Amos said, tossing a box of tissues at Flynn.

He caught it. "Thanks, Dad." After handing several tissues to Cami and waiting for her to finish wiping her face and blowing her nose, he asked, "Are you ready to talk about it?"

Her face hidden behind a tissue, Cami shook her head.

"Too bad," Gia said, her frustration with her sister getting the better of her. It had always been this way, though. It didn't have anything to do with their issues of late.

As the oldest sister, she was used to dealing with Eva's and Cami's over-the-top emotions. The two of them had been drama queens growing up, and they hadn't changed much. Their mother was the same. "You can't just have an epic meltdown and not tell us what it's about."

"Mom!" her daughter said, walking out of the kitchen with a glass of water. "Show a little compassion." She patted Cami on the shoulder and handed her the water.

"Thanks, honey," Cami said, accepting the glass from Willow with a weak smile. "Don't get upset with your mother. She doesn't deal well with people who express their emotions openly. They annoy her. It's not new. She's always been a hard-ass."

"Knock it off, Cami," Flynn said, coming to his feet.

"What? You're taking her side now?" Cami asked Flynn. "This is exactly why I'm upset. Everyone's going to turn on me because of Gia, and it's not my fault!"

Gia had had enough and got up from the chair. "I'll leave you to it then. I have to get back to the restaurant anyway." Despite the ball of emotion caught in her throat, she smiled at Flynn's father. "I hope you enjoy your..."

Gia trailed off as her sister blurted, "I didn't know the reporter was going to track him down, okay? I don't even know how the reporter got an advance reading copy of my book. I haven't even finished revisions."

"Tracked who down, Cami?" Gia asked, feeling like there was a vise clamped on her chest.

"Aaron, okay!" Cami bit her lip, fresh tears welling in her eyes. "I didn't mean for this to happen, Gia. The publisher wanted to track Aaron down to verify parts of my book, but I said no. I said I'd walk away from the deal if they did. And I was serious. They knew I was." She blew her nose. "I'm sorry. I really am. But I'm sure nothing will come of it. It's not like he hasn't known where you are all this time."

"Is Aaron your ex-husband?" Flynn asked.

Gia nodded. "And Sage's father. Although I don't think he qualifies as a father. Sage doesn't remember him; neither of the girls do. He left when they were babies."

"Say it, Gia. Just say it. I know you want to," Cami said.

It was the very last thing she wanted to say in front of Flynn. She didn't know anyone who'd want to look like an idiot in front of the man they were falling in love with.

But of course Cami was only too happy to share the most embarrassing time of Gia's life with Flynn and his father. "Aaron Abbott abandoned his wife and daughter because of me," Cami said, and then burst into tears.

Chapter Eleven

I'm fine," Gia told her daughter and Flynn, both of whom watched her with concerned expressions on their faces as she excused herself to use the washroom. She needed a few minutes on her own to come to terms with her sister's revelation.

Gia wasn't a hard-ass like Cami said. All right, so she could be a bit of a hard-ass, but she wasn't unemotional. Things hurt her as deeply as they hurt her sisters and mother. It's just that she was a private person. She preferred staying in the background, while her sisters and mother loved center stage.

Her mother said Gia was like her father. He'd been an artist and an introvert too. She'd never known him. He'd died not long after Carmen had become pregnant with her, right before their wedding. It had been the same for generations of Rosetti women. They were cursed when it came to love and marriage. So was Gia. Cami too. Her sister had been married three times.

Gia closed the bathroom door on Cami's sobs and then reached for the toilet paper, unraveling a long piece. As she dampened the folded wad of toilet paper under the tap, she looked at herself in the oval mirror framed in seashells. She smiled as she dabbed the damp toilet paper under her eyes. She recognized her daughter's design. She had a similar mirror hanging in her own bathroom. Willow was crafty. Sage not so much.

Gia's smile faded as she thought about Sage, wondering if it was because of her that her daughter was closed off. Sage was more like her than Willow was. Gia briefly closed her eyes. Willow was more like her real . . . her biological mother. And in that moment, Gia realized she needed to work through her issues with her sister before they damaged not only her relationship with Willow but also her daughter's opinion of herself given Gia's negative comments about Cami.

Gia tossed the toilet paper into the garbage pail, pinched some color into her cheeks, tousled her long dark hair, and then opened the door. She walked into a solid wall of male muscle.

Flynn rested his hands on her shoulders, leaning back to search her face. Whatever he saw in her expression had him taking her by the hand. He walked her to the end of the hall. Ignoring her whispered protest, he opened the door to a bedroom of dark wood and a breathtaking view of Sunshine Bay, and gently shoved her inside.

"Flynn, Willow is out there, and so is my sister and your father. We can't do this now."

"I know. It's just that I saw your face when I was comforting Cami, and I didn't like the look in your eyes." He held her gaze. "Don't walk away from what we could have because of my past with your sister, Gia. We were kids. We're friends now, nothing more." He reached for her, drawing her into his arms. "We've got something special here. Don't throw it away because you're scared."

"I'm not scared."

"Yeah, you are, and so am I." A slow smile curved his mouth. "Are you vibrating for me, or do you have a phone in your pocket?"

"Ha-ha." She withdrew her phone from the pocket of her denim skirt. "It's Sage."

"I'll give you some privacy. But this conversation isn't over." He gave her a quick, toe-curling kiss and then walked out of the bedroom.

"What's Mom doing in your bedroom? Is she okay?" she heard Willow ask from behind the closed door.

"Yeah. She just wanted to talk to your sister in private. Let's give her a minute."

Flynn Monroe was everything a woman could ask for in a boyfriend—an incredible kisser, a great listener, respectful, kind, and honest—and most of all, she could be herself with him, and he made her feel special. Except for the facts that he'd dated her sister first and had a baby with her, a baby whom Gia had raised as her daughter, he'd be absolutely perfect. *You couldn't make this stuff up*, she thought as she connected the call. "Hey, honey. How's—"

"Gia, it's Jake Walker. I'm going to preface what I'm about to tell you by saying Sage is okay."

"Oh my God, what happened to my baby?"

The door to Flynn's bedroom swung open, and Willow rushed inside. "Mom, what's wrong? What's wrong with Sage?"

Gia held up a finger. "Jake?"

"Yeah. Sorry, the doctor just came in."

"Is she in the hospital? What hospital is my daughter in, Jake?"

"What do you mean, Sage is in the hospital. Mom, what's going on?"

Flynn walked into the room, closing the door behind him. He stood at Willow's side.

"I'm trying to find out," she told her daughter while holding Flynn's gaze. Just knowing he was there steadied her.

As if sensing she needed him, he stepped closer and placed a hand on her shoulder. "It might be easier if you put him on speaker, Gia."

She nodded and pressed the Speaker button, holding the phone out between her and Willow. Flynn appeared to be waiting for something before he said, "Jake, it's Flynn Monroe. You're on speaker with Gia and Willow."

Okay, so he'd been waiting for her to speak. She wasn't thinking straight. She was usually good in a crisis but not when it involved her children. Then, as she'd clearly proven, she was a basket case.

"Hey, okay. Sorry, they're in out and of here, and I'm trying to get answers for you. At first, they thought she was having a heart attack."

"A heart attack!" she and Willow cried at the same time. "But that's impossible," Gia continued. "She's young and healthy." She heard a familiar voice grumbling in the background. "Is that Sage?"

"Yeah. You can talk to her as soon as they finish up with— Sage, would you do as the nurse says, please?"

Gia raised her voice. "Sage, do what the nurse tells you. She's always hated being told what to do. Hospitals too," she said to no one in particular. "I think it goes back to when she broke her leg."

"Jake, you said they *thought* she had a heart attack. Does that mean they've ruled it out?" Flynn asked.

Gia looked at him, gratitude no doubt shining in her eyes. She was so glad he caught that, which he could obviously tell. He moved his hand from her shoulder and gave her neck a gentle squeeze as they waited for Jake to respond to Flynn's question.

After this was over, and she was positive Sage was okay, Gia was going to have a chat with Jake about ignoring what was going on in the hospital room so he didn't leave them hanging. Then again, from what she could hear, he had his hands full dealing with Sage.

Jake came back on the line. "Pretty much. They have a couple more tests to run but she's bossing everyone around and trying to get out of the bed. I'm sure she'll be fine if she follows doctor's orders." They heard Sage giving him crap in the background. "You don't need a third opinion, Sage. You've already had two. You're burned out. I'm not a doctor, and I could have told you that."

Willow leaned in and yelled into the phone, "I told you last month that you were burned out!"

"Uh, Willow, I don't have you on speaker, so if you don't mind, could you not yell into the phone? You nearly blew out my eardrum. I'm glad you find that amusing, Sage."

Gia frowned. She'd always been keenly interested in holistic healing and had read enough that what Jake was saying didn't make total sense to her. "Jake, how did they confuse burnout with a heart attack?"

"She had a panic attack." He sighed. "Sage, it's nothing to be embarrassed about. People have them all the time, and your burnout probably made you more susceptible."

"Jake, why would my daughter have a panic attack?"

"It might be better if I let her tell you. Hang on." There was a long pause. "They're taking her down to CT. She'll call you when she's back in the room."

"Are they keeping her in the hospital?" The phone went silent for several minutes. "Jake?"

"Sorry, I wanted to wait until they'd wheeled Sage out of the room. She's dehydrated and her blood pressure was high, so the doctor is admitting her overnight. She's at Mass General if you'd like to come."

⌣

Gia stood in line at the hospital cafeteria with her sister Eva. Amos had called her family. Apparently, Flynn's father and Gia's mother had exchanged numbers at one of the many joint family celebrations they'd attended this past year.

"Okay, so now that we've escaped the fam and know that Sage is going to be fine—"

"You were in her hospital room with me, weren't you? She's hardly fine, Eva. She's devastated that she's been suspended indefinitely. You know how she feels about her clients."

"I do, but it's like you used to say to me when you were

my cool, *chill* older sister: *Everything happens for a reason.*" Eva nudged her with her tray. "She's suspended with pay, and you heard the doctor, she needs time to rest and recover."

"I know. And it's not like we could ever convince her to take time off." She smiled. "It'll be nice having her home for a while."

"Are you going to tell her about Aaron?"

"Did you have to bring him up? I've got enough on my plate without thinking about him," Gia said as she grabbed a yogurt, a bottle of raspberry kombucha, and a salad for Sage. Beside her, Eva loaded her tray with doughnuts, cookies, chocolate cake, and two cartons of chocolate milk.

"That better not be for my daughter."

Eva grinned. "Which one?"

"The one lying in a hospital bed."

"A little sugar never hurt anyone. Besides, she's exhausted. A sugar rush will do her good." Covering her ears, Eva moved her tray along the counter with her hip. "I can't hear you so don't bother lecturing me on the evils of white sugar."

Gia grabbed a chocolate chip cookie and put it on her own tray, shrugging when her sister looked at her. "Don't judge. I could use a sugar rush too. It's been a day."

"Okay, don't get mad at me, but you realize the Aaron thing isn't Cami's fault, right?"

"Of course it is. If she hadn't written her memoir, there wouldn't have been a reporter out there hunting Aaron down."

"You're right, and I understand how it must feel thinking about that time of your life being splashed across tabloids and on the big screen. But it's in the past. The very distant past. And Cami's right. It's not like Aaron is suddenly going to show up in Sunshine Bay. Besides, if he did, there is a gorgeous six-foot-four man who would happily beat him up for you."

"As much as I'd appreciate your husband's willingness to go all macho man for me, I can take care of myself."

"My husband is a beautiful, protective beast of a man, but James wasn't who I was talking about, so let's try this again. And remember, while you are my sister, you are also my best friend, and best friends don't lie to each other. So, what is really going on between you and the fabulous Flynn?"

Her sister was her person. She shared everything with her—the good, the bad, and the ugly—and Eva did the same. It hadn't felt right keeping her relationship with Flynn from her sister, and Gia could use a sounding board.

She glanced around for any family members who might have come in search of her and Eva. When she didn't see anyone, she raised her hand. "Pinkie swear you won't tell a single soul."

"In case you hadn't noticed, we're not kids anymore. I promise I'll take your secret to my grave."

Gia wiggled her baby finger.

Eva rolled her eyes but then latched on to Gia's pinkie with hers. "I swear I will not tell a single soul that you are in love with Flynn Monroe."

"Eva!" Gia squeezed her sister's pinkie with her own while once again looking around the cafeteria. Thankfully, her family and Flynn were still in the waiting room on Sage's floor. She had a feeling the nurses weren't as grateful as she was. Carmen had been standing at the nurses' station, grilling them about her granddaughter's *condition* when Eva and Gia had sneaked away. "I'm not in love with him."

Her sister tilted her head to the side, her eyes narrowed on Gia's face. Then she straightened her head and nodded. "Yes, you are. You just don't want to admit it to yourself."

"We've only been dating for two weeks."

"You're dating!"

"Why don't you tell the entire hospital while you're at it?"

"Sorry. I didn't mean to yell. You took me by surprise, that's all."

"How? You just told me I'm in love with him."

"Never mind that." Eva waggled her dark eyebrows. "Tell me everything, and I mean everything. Is he good in bed? Because he looks liked he'd be amazing."

"What does that even mean?" She waved her hand. "Never mind. I don't want to know, and no, we haven't slept together."

"I guess I shouldn't be surprised. You rarely broke your no-sex-until-nine-dates rule, but you've had such a long dry spell, I thought you might have skipped the waiting period. Especially because it's *Flynn Monroe*."

"You better not let your husband hear you talking about Flynn that way. You sound like you have a crush on him."

Eva held up her thumb and forefinger. "I might have a teensy one." She nudged her. "You have to admit the man is off-the-charts gorgeous and just an all-around great guy."

She sighed. "He is. But come on. He's six years younger than me, he was in love with our baby sister for at least two years, and he's the father of my daughter."

"Don't worry, I've seen how this played out, and it's epic. You'll get your happily-ever-after and then some."

Gia rolled her eyes. "Yeah, and I can guess where you saw it play out. *The Young and the Restless.*"

"No. *Days of Our Lives.*" Eva laughed and paid the cashier, who was staring at her.

"Has anyone ever told you you look like JLo?" they asked.

"No, but thank you," Eva said, looking anything but grateful. She got told that all the time.

"It's a compliment, you know," Gia said after paying and walking back to the elevator.

"No, people telling you you look like Eva Mendes is a compliment. She's five years younger than you are. But JLo is five years older than me."

Gia laughed "Eva, you do know time didn't stop the day you turned fifty?" She hip-checked her sister as the elevator doors slid open and they walked on. "You're fifty-two."

They went back and forth teasing each other. After months of arguing over Cami, it was a nice change. But the reprieve ended as soon as the elevator doors slid open on Sage's floor.

"Is that Ma?" Eva asked.

"If you're referring to the woman yelling in Italian, I think we can safely assume it's our mother," Gia said as she fast-walked to her daughter's room. "Ma, what's going on?"

Jake inched his way around the far side of the room as if hoping Carmen wouldn't notice him trying to make his escape. Gia could have told him it wouldn't work.

"This is your fault." Carmen stabbed her finger at him. "You tell her that she has to stay with her mother."

He held up his hands. "I'm sorry, Ms. Rosetti, but this has nothing to do with me."

"Ha! Are you staying at the farm or not?"

"I am," he said, looking at Sage as if seeking support.

Sage smiled as if enjoying a little payback.

"You tell her she can't stay with you. You tell her to come home with her family." Carmen waved her hand at Sage. "Look at her. She looks..." She shuddered, and Sage scowled. "She needs us to look after her, to make sure she sleeps and eats. And you, all you'll want is to keep her up all night having sex."

"Nonna!"

Jake rubbed the back of his head. "Ms. Rosetti, you know as well as I do that no one tells your granddaughter what to do."

"Si, but that's—"

"Ma, stop," Gia said, walking to the hospital bed and putting her cafeteria purchases on Sage's tray. Her daughter wrinkled her nose but smiled when Eva unloaded her contribution.

"You talk to him then. He's convinced our Sage to stay with him at the farm instead of coming home with her family."

"You're not coming home with us?" Gia asked, trying to hide her disappointment but obviously failing. She'd been positive Carmen had misunderstood.

"Mom, it's not a big deal. I'm just a few miles from you. I'll see you all the time."

"You'd see us all the time if you stayed at the apartment." She tucked the blankets around Sage's legs. "We want to look after you."

"I'm not sick. I'm just...tired." She patted the side of the hospital bed. "Sit. We have something we need to talk about."

Out of the corner of her eye, Gia saw her mother sneaking out of the room. "I'm going to strangle her."

Jake looked relieved that she'd leveled the threat against her mother and not him. He headed out the door, with Eva following close behind.

"Don't be mad at Nonna. She was using the situation with my, uh, Aaron, to convince me to stay at the apartment in your time of need."

"She's too much. I'm fine, honey. Am I thrilled that your aunt wrote a book airing our family's dirty laundry, a lot of it sadly mine? No, I'm not. To be honest, I'm mad as hell about it, but there's nothing I can do. What's done is done. And as both your aunts pointed out to me, it's not like he's going to show up in Sunshine Bay." She caught Sage's wince before she could hide it and took her hand. "I'm sorry. That was thoughtless of me. We've never really talked about your father. Would you like to see him?"

"No, of course not. It's just…" She shook her head. "No. I'm good, and I know you're probably hurt about me staying with Jake at the farm, but we've got a lot to do to settle Alice's estate."

"And that's what worries me. You won't take the time you need to heal your body and your mind."

"Pot, kettle."

"What do you mean?"

"How's your body and mind, Mom?"

"They're fine, thank you very much." Heat climbed from her chest to her cheeks at the thought Sage had somehow found out about her and Flynn.

"Uh, Mom. You're looking flushed, and I know for a fact that you've gone through menopause, so would you like to share what's got you all worked up?"

Her daughter was an exceptional lawyer, and Gia didn't feel like being on this side of the witness stand. She leaned over, stroking Sage's hair from her forehead. "I love you, and I want you to get better." She stood up and turned off the overhead light. "Get some sleep."

Chapter Twelve

Sage woke up soaking wet in the middle of the night. It took a moment for her to get her bearings. Despite her family's concerted efforts to get her to change her mind, they'd dropped her at the farm yesterday afternoon and hadn't left until they'd tucked her into the waterbed last night with a glass of warm milk.

She was about to raise her hand to her forehead and check if she had a temperature but the fact that her hand was floating in a puddle of water ruled out a fever.

She rolled over and nearly drowned herself. "Jake, the waterbed sprang a leak!" She tried to lever herself up to pound on the wall to wake him up but couldn't reach around the headboard. "Help!"

The bedroom light came on. It took a moment for her eyes to adjust to the brightness. Once they did, her gaze found Jake, who was standing in the doorway. He had on a pair of black boxers, but he might as well have been naked for how she responded to him. She tried dragging her gaze from all that muscular, bronzed beauty, but her eyes ignored her.

"Sorry. I'm not objectifying you. My eyes are ignoring my brain. It's possibly a side effect of burnout." She raised her hand. "I need help." She frowned. "Jake?"

"Huh?"

"What do you mean, *huh*? Is this payback for my family hanging out here half the day and night?" Her eyes widened. "Wait! Did my grandmother pay you to sabotage the waterbed so I'd leave?"

He scrubbed his hands over his face, then turned and walked away.

"Jake! This is not funny. I seriously cannot get out of the bed. You can't just leave me—" She broke off when he walked into the room with her robe, which she'd left in the bathroom last night. "Why would you—" She glanced down at herself and knew exactly why he'd brought her robe.

It had been hot last night, and she'd worn a white V-neck camisole and ruffle shorts to bed. The sleep set was soaked and see-through, as in *she* might as well be naked.

He threw the robe at her. It landed on her head but also covered everything down to her knees. Jake didn't wait for her to put it on. He simply scooped her up and out of the bed with the robe still on her head. He didn't set her on her feet as she expected but carried her down the hall, depositing her in the bathroom.

"Take a hot shower," he said, then walked out, closing the bathroom door behind him.

"It wasn't my fault!"

Seconds later, he opened the door and tossed her flannel sleep pants and a sweatshirt onto the counter. "I didn't say it was."

"Then why are you acting like you're mad at me? I mean,

besides me waking you up in the middle of the night and flooding the bedroom."

"I'm not mad at you," he said, holding her gaze.

Noting his slightly flushed cheeks, she said, "Oh." Then she caught a glimpse of his tented boxers. "*Oh.*"

"Yeah, *oh.*" He shook his head and walked out of the bathroom.

She wasn't sure what she was supposed to do with that or how she was supposed to feel about it. She imagined Jake felt like she did about her reaction to his mostly naked body. Except she wasn't letting herself think too closely about her feelings for a mostly naked Jake. It was a strategy she decided to stick with. She also considered having a cold shower but went with hot instead. She had no idea how long she'd been lying in the bed's stagnant water. She stayed in the shower longer than was necessary and walked out of the bathroom to a loud, high-pitched whine.

She followed the sound to her bedroom. Jake glanced over as he sucked up water from the hardwood floor with a shop vac. He'd changed into sleep pants and a sweatshirt too. It looked like they'd be cranking up the air conditioner for however long they lived together.

He turned off the shop vac. "Exactly how long were you lying in the water before you called me?"

"Seconds, why?"

"Are you serious?"

"Yeah. It's not something I'd lie about."

"You must sleep the sleep of the dead. It's most likely been leaking all night."

She looked at the blue liner lying flat in the wooden frame. "So that's it. The bed is done?"

"Afraid so." He looked up from wrapping the cord around the shop vac. "Why do you look like you just lost your best friend?"

She lowered herself onto the chair in the corner. "I can't kick Max off the couch, and I can't kick you out of the other bed, so my family wins. I'll have to move into my aunt's apartment." She could move back into her condo, but the idea of doing so and not going in to work every day made her sick to her stomach. Granted, she pretty much felt sick to her stomach whenever she thought about her suspension.

"You don't have to move into your aunt's apartment. There's another bed at Alice's place. I've gotta pack up the last of her stuff today and move it in here anyway."

"Right. I forgot the closing on the house is tomorrow. But FYI, you're not doing it by yourself. I'm helping you pack up the rest of the house."

"FYI, you're under doctor's orders to rest. Carmen's orders too. So that's what you're going to do, because your grand-mother scares me." He carried the shop vac across the room and shut off the light. "What are you doing?"

"Sleeping on the chair."

"You can't sleep on the chair, Sage."

"Trust me, I can. I sleep at my desk at least three times a week."

"And you wonder why you're burned out." He walked back and took her by the hand. "Come on. You're sleeping in my bed."

"Um, I don't think that's a good idea, Jake." She dug in her heels to slow his forward motion.

He tightened his grip on her hand, left the shop vac in the office, and then walked with her to his bedroom. "I didn't say you're sleeping with me in my bed. I said you're sleeping in my bed. I'm sleeping on the couch. Max doesn't mind bunking with me."

He walked into the room and held back the covers for her. The mattress was still warm from his body. It smelled like him too. "This isn't the same bed you slept in as a teenager at Alice's, is it?"

"No. She ordered it for me last month."

"Why would she order you a new bed?"

"Go to sleep, Sage."

She sat up. "No. You're keeping something from me, and I want to know what it is."

"You need your sleep. I'll tell you tomorrow."

"I can't go to sleep now."

He snorted. "You're not going to blackmail me into telling you."

"No. I mean I actually won't be able to get to sleep now. I already got my allotted"—she glanced at the digital clock on the nightstand—"four hours."

"Are you telling me you only sleep four hours a night?"

"Not when you're looking at me like that, I'm not." She patted the pillow beside her. "Lie down. It'll be like you're telling me a bedtime story. Who knows, I might fall asleep."

She shouldn't be encouraging him to lie in bed with her after the last time, but they'd been drunk and sad and had turned to each other for comfort. She ignored the voice in her head pointing out she was sad and looking for comfort tonight too.

The warning voice had a point. Sage hated waking up at night alone in her bed. It had gotten worse since she'd left home. Her insomnia had kicked in then.

He turned off the light and walked to the bed. "Are you saying my story will be so boring it'll put you to sleep?" he asked as he stretched out beside her.

"Probably."

He grinned. "I'll tell you mine if you'll tell me yours."

"I don't have a story."

"Yeah, you do. You're going to tell me what keeps you up at night. I don't think it's only work."

No wonder the man was such a good investigator. She turned on her side, facing him. "Fine."

"I'm holding you to it, you know. And my story will take all of a minute." The moonlight coming through the window illuminated the amusement in his eyes and the chiseled angles of his handsome face. "You know how you always call me a slacker for working part-time as an investigator at the law firm?"

"I didn't call you a slacker."

"But that's what you thought. Admit it."

"Okay, maybe I did. But come on, Jake. You have to admit working a few hours a night when you're young and healthy and smart is a little slackerish."

He laughed. "That's not a word. And it's a little judgy too. I admire the guy you thought I was. Free-spirited, hitting the road whenever the spirit moved him, living life in the slow lane."

"Are you saying the guy I think you are isn't who you are?"

He smiled. "I worked part-time because I was going to

school, Sage. I got my law degree. And I didn't come here to mooch off Alice like I know you thought I did. She asked me to move here and join her practice."

Sage opened and closed her mouth, the shock rendering her speechless, but then it hit her that Alice had known and kept it from her. She felt like an idiot and launched herself at him. "You jerk! All this time you've been laughing at me."

He rolled her under him, holding her hands above her head. "I wasn't laughing at you, and I asked Alice not to tell you."

"Why? Why would you do that?"

"Because I wasn't sure I could do it. Actually, I'd pretty much convinced myself I couldn't. I wasn't exactly an honor roll student."

He'd been lucky to graduate from high school at all. But it hadn't been because he was a slacker or thought he was too cool for school. He was dyslexic and had ADHD. At Alice's behest, Sage had tutored him, so she knew how difficult law school must have been for him.

"I know I could be a brat when we were growing up. Don't raise your eyebrow at me. You were a jerk too. But did you really think I'd be anything but supportive, Jake? We're not kids anymore."

"It wasn't about you. It was about me." He shrugged. "Your opinion mattered to me, I guess. I was okay with Alice knowing if I tried and failed, but not you."

"Alice must have been so proud of you," she whispered, then raised her gaze to his, barely able to see him through the shimmer of her tears. "Don't take this the wrong way. I'm not being condescending. But I...I'm proud of you too." She raised her head off the pillow to kiss his cheek but pressed her lips to his mouth instead. She tasted her tears on his lips, but maybe they were his too. It wasn't fair that he'd worked so hard, achieved so much, only to have Alice die before they made their dream of working together come true.

She freed her hands from his and brought them to his face, kissing him softly before pulling back. "We're not selling the practice." Last week, she'd told him to sell everything. She'd been too overwhelmed to even think about keeping the practice and the farm, and Jake hadn't said a word. "I want you to have it, Jake. It's what Alice would want."

He wiped her tears away with his thumbs. "We'll talk about it in the morning. Things look different in the cold light of day."

"I won't change my mind. I want this for you. It makes me happy thinking of you carrying on Alice's legacy."

"Thank you." He pressed a warm kiss to her lips. "But I still want you to sleep on it." He rolled off her, and she shivered, missing the weight and the heat of his hard, muscular body. He folded his arms behind his head. "Okay, now it's your turn."

"I can't follow that. It was epic. Mine is just..." She shrugged. "Stuff from a long time ago that I should have gotten over but haven't. It's actually a little embarrassing."

"It was embarrassing telling you that your opinion mattered so much to me that I didn't want you to know I was in law school in case I failed. You owe me." He rolled onto his side, facing her. "Spill."

She sighed. "Fine. If I wake up in the middle of the night at my condo, or I guess I should say *when* because it happens all the time, I can't go back to sleep. I've tried everything, but nothing works, so that's what I do, get up and work. Or I work so late that I fall asleep at two or three in the morning."

"You said it's because of something that happened a long time ago. What happened?"

"Ugh, I don't want to tell you. I've never told anyone this."

"Not even your mom or Willow?"

She shook her head.

"I'm surprised. You guys seem really close."

"We are, and that's the problem, I guess. I didn't tell them when the Big Bad happened, and it would just upset them if they knew."

"The Big Bad?"

"This has to stay between us, Jake. You can't . . ." She sighed. "I think I know how my mom feels now. Anyway, you'll hear about it all when Cami's book comes out." She gave him the shorthand version of her family's history and then said, "Cami took Willow when she was four. I was five at the time, and we'd shared a room since we were babies. Cami ran away with her and kept her for three weeks. It was awful, and it was hard, and I missed her so much, especially at night. No one talked about it with me. I'd overhear things but I really didn't know why my sister had suddenly disappeared or if she'd died or why everyone was so angry and so sad."

"No one told you what happened?"

"No. I'm sure they were trying to protect me. And I didn't ask because I didn't want to upset them any more than they already were."

"What about when Willow came back? They didn't talk about it with you then?"

She saw the look in his eyes, and she shook her head. "It wasn't their fault, Jake. They had no idea that I was struggling."

"Yeah, but I imagine they talked about it with Willow. Couldn't they have included you in the conversations?"

"My mom took Willow to a family therapist, but other than that, the subject was closed in our family. And when I say closed, I mean closed. Willow and I had no idea Cami was her mother until last summer. They kept the secret for a quarter of a century. Which tells you how deeply I repressed the memory, because I hadn't made the connection between Willow going missing and my insomnia until last year. I'd completely blocked it."

"That is seriously messed up," he said, then drew her into his arms. "Thank you for telling me. It explains a few things."

She leaned back. "What do you mean by that?"

"Nothing." His lips twitched and he kissed her forehead. "Now let's try to get some sleep. We have a busy day tomorrow. Or I should say later today."

"Uh, Jake, you're supposed to be sleeping on the couch with Max."

"You think I'm going to let you sleep alone after you told me your story? Not a chance," he said, resting his chin on the top of her head.

"That's really sweet of you. But I don't think it's a good idea that we sleep together again. Remember what happened last time?"

"It's not the same. We'd just lost Alice, and we were emotional and drunk." He snuggled her closer. "Now go to sleep."

Chapter Thirteen

Sage carried a large plastic container to Jake, who was loading boxes into the rental van to move the last of Alice's things out of her home on Ocean View Drive.

He had a serious case of bedhead and looked all sweaty and hot—hot as in all muscly and gorgeous in a gray Linkin Park T-shirt and faded blue jeans—and she was doing her best not to look at him or catch his eye. Which meant she was looking at a bed of blue hydrangeas bordering Alice's walkway as she handed him the plastic container. "This can go in the women's shelter pile. It's filled with Alice's collection of rubber boots."

He was standing right in front of her, she knew he was, but he made absolutely no move to take the container from her.

She sighed and went to walk around him. He stepped in front of her. "Are you kidding me right now? We have an hour before the cleaners get here, Jake."

It was ridiculous that he'd booked cleaners when they could easily clean the house themselves, but unless she'd agreed to go back to the farm and rest, he wouldn't give in.

"So stop acting as if what happened last night was a big deal. It wasn't. We're consenting—"

A woman walking her dog across the road glanced back at them.

"Seriously? My aunt and uncle live up the street and you're going to announce to all and sundry that we slept together?" She went up on her toes, shoving the container at him. "I told you it was a bad idea."

"We didn't *sleep together*, sleep together. We fooled around."

She pushed the container into his rock-hard abs. Of course he didn't move an inch. All he did was laugh. "It's not funny!"

"It kind of is. How can you be such a prude? You're a Rosetti."

"You did not just say that to me."

"I'm pretty sure that I did. What's the big deal? I wasn't dissing your family. I think it's great."

Sage's mother, her aunt Eva, and her grandmother had been well known for their love of food, wine, and partying. They hadn't been looking for a man to complete them or make them happy. They enjoyed male companionship on their terms and dated extensively but not exclusively. As fabulous as the three of them were, they'd broken a lot of hearts. It was why they'd been known as the Heartbreakers of Sunshine Bay.

"Of course you do. You're a man." He didn't have to live down the teasing at school. As much as she adored her mother, aunt, and grandmother, and as an adult fully supported the choices they made, their bohemian lifestyles had made growing up in Sunshine Bay difficult at times for Sage, Willow, and their cousin.

"You're right. I'm sorry. I shouldn't have said that. But you don't have to be embarrassed about what happened. You were hot. I was hot. And we got rid of some clothes." He shrugged. "There was a little too much bare skin, and we got carried away. But look at the bright side—you fell asleep and got four more hours of z's."

"Shut up, Jake," she said, shoving the box at him, and this time she let it go. She should have known he'd catch it. She stomped back inside the house.

He followed after her.

"I don't want to talk—" She frowned. "What's wrong?" He'd lost all the color in his face.

He put down the box and linked his fingers on the top of his head, rubbing his hair.

"Jake, what's going on? Are you thinking about Alice?" She knew what it was like when the memories came out of the blue.

"I know you're in there, boy. You can't hide from me," a woman called out.

Jake swore, and so did Sage. Then she gave his bicep a comforting squeeze. "I've got this. You grab a glass of water in the kitchen, and I'll take care of your—"

A raspy laugh cut her off, and she and Jake turned to see his mother leaning against the doorframe. She'd once been a beautiful woman, but booze, drugs, and living rough had taken a toll. "Well, look at you, son. You've moved up in the world. Got yourself hooked up with a Rosetti, have you? The smart one too. Heard you were a big-shot lawyer, bringing in the big bucks," she said to Sage, giving her an up-and-down look. "So, what's someone like you doing with my boy? He's got the looks, I'll give him—"

"Is there something we can do for you, Ms. Walker? We're a little busy here, as you can see."

"Yeah, I can see all right." Her brows lowered, and her upper lip curled. "I hear that bitch left—"

"Alice Espinoza was one of the most beautiful and loving women I've ever known, and she adored your . . . Jake." She didn't deserve to be acknowledged as his mother.

"Oh yeah, I know just how much she adored my boy. Took him from me, and took my husband too. He's dead gone on two years now. It's her fault. He was supposed to get out years ago, but she made sure he didn't. Always at his parole hearings." The eyes she turned on Jake weren't filled with tears or sorrow; they were filled with bitterness and contempt. "You got money now, and you'll be paying for what you and that bitch cost me."

"Alice would roll over in her grave if Jake gave you one red cent, and I, for one, will make sure that he doesn't. So I suggest you get out of this house before I have you charged with trespassing and harassment," Sage said.

"You don't scare me, bitch. I—"

Jake stepped between Sage and his mother. "Leave. Now."

His mother's bravado faded in the face of her son's anger. He'd never stood up to her, never said a single word while she'd hurled abuse at him in the first few months after he'd moved out of their double-wide trailer. Alice had told Sage it had broken her heart to see him shrinking in on himself with every verbal blow his mother landed, as if he deserved each and every one.

His mother ignored her, taking a step closer to her son, her face softening, her eyes pleading. "You got everything. I got nothing. Can't you spare a little something for me? I'm not asking for much. Please, Jakie."

Sage glanced at Jake and wanted to shake him. His mother was getting to him, and that made her livid. "Why? What did you ever do for him?"

"He's my boy," she snarled. "He left me high and dry."

"Don't blame the choices you made on him. You're just angry that he's made a life for himself. You didn't deserve him then, and you don't deserve him now."

"Sage, don't." He shoved his hands in the pockets of his jeans. "It doesn't matter."

But it did. His mother hadn't just verbally abused him; she'd also stood by while his father beat him, and she'd stood by when his father had him steal for their addictions. She'd made him feel worthless, and that was her biggest sin. "Alice deserved him. She loved him like a son. She knew he was good, and loyal, loving, caring, and smart."

His mother rolled her eyes, and Sage growled, stepping around Jake to get in his mother's face.

Jake put a hand on her arm. "Sage—"

She shook him off, her entire focus on the woman before her, hoping to land a few verbal blows of her own. If Jake wouldn't stand up for himself, she'd stand up for him and, in doing so, prove to him that he'd deserved Alice's love and everything she'd given to him. "He's a lawyer now. Did you know that? He's got a law practice, a farm, money in the bank, and people who love him. What do you have?"

A mean right hook.

⌒

Sage wrapped some ice in a kitchen towel and handed it to Jake. "You didn't have to jump in front of me. I was putting up my arm to block her punch."

"Right, because that worked out so well with Winthrop." He gently pressed the ice-filled towel to her eye. "You need it more than I do."

"It's been two days. My eye's hardly swollen, just a lovely shade of purple." She pushed on Jake's arm, trying to guide the ice-filled towel to his eye.

"I'm fine, okay? She barely clipped me." He tossed the towel and ice into the kitchen sink.

"Are you fine, though? That was a lot, Jake. I know she's your mother, but you should have called the police. You still could?" she said, framing it as a question so he'd hopefully reconsider pressing charges.

"It was a lot." His lips twitched. "But I had you to protect—"

"Are you making fun of me?"

"No." He took her hand and drew her close, putting his arms around her. "I appreciated you standing up for me even if I didn't need or want you to."

"But you weren't doing anything. You weren't standing up for yourself, and I hated it. I hated seeing you standing there taking everything she said as if you believed—"

"Hey, look at me." He framed her face with his hands. "Just because I didn't want or need you to stand up for me doesn't mean I didn't appreciate it. I did. I do. It meant a lot, you defending me."

"Why didn't you stand up to her? Let her know what a shitty mother she was and—"

"Because it wouldn't matter what I said. She had an agenda, and until she got to say what she said, she wasn't going anywhere. It ends faster if I just stay quiet."

"You can't tell me you weren't upset, Jake. I saw your face when you walked in here."

"You're right, I was." He lifted his hand, tracing the faded outline of the bruise around her eye with the tip of his finger, then tucking her hair behind her ear. "I didn't want you to be reminded of the kid I used to be or where I came from."

"Jake, it didn't matter to me who your parents were or where you lived or even that you were on the fast road to a life of crime."

He tapped her nose lightly with his finger. "Liar. You had a list of statistics on the likelihood I'd end up in jail that you quoted every time you got ticked at me, and you got ticked at me a lot."

She groaned, bringing her forehead to his chest. "Don't remind me."

He laughed. "Don't feel too guilty. I gave as good as I got."

"Yeah, you did." She looked around the kitchen, the memories flooding in. "I don't know how Alice put up with us. You were always teasing her."

"She loved it." He smiled as if remembering the fun they'd had, and then his smile faded.

"What's wrong?"

"With everything that went down on Friday, I forgot I hadn't shared the results of the coroner's report with you. That's why I'd come to see you."

"You said I had to sign papers for the sale."

"I lied. I wanted to tell you face-to-face. I kept waiting for you to tell me just to scan them."

"I did wonder why you had to bring them to me, but then I got distracted by something else." She searched his face. "What did the coroner say?"

"Alice had cancer. I talked to her doctor after I got the report. Alice got the diagnosis about twelve years ago."

"I can't believe she didn't tell us."

"It was around the time you got into Harvard and I got into the military. You know Alice, she wouldn't have wanted to upset us. She wouldn't want to disrupt our lives. Plus her prognosis was good at the time."

"Did she opt out of traditional treatments?"

"No, not initially. She did everything the doctors recommended, and she went into remission a couple of times. But when it came back the third time, about eighteen months ago, she told her doctor she was done."

Sage's eyes filled. "Why did she keep it to herself? We could have been there for her, spent more time with her. Dammit, I would have come to see her. I would have called her. I would have been there for her."

He cupped the back of her head, bringing her cheek to his chest. "Her doctor said she was doing well. There was no reason to think she wouldn't be around for another year or more."

"It's why she updated her will recently."

"Yeah, and I have a feeling once I'd settled in, she would have had the both of us for dinner and broken the news. The last time we spoke, she mentioned that she was going to call you, get you to come and stay for a few days at the farm. She was worried about your caseload. She thought you'd taken on too much."

"It's not an issue now that I'm suspended." She felt like she couldn't breathe and stepped away from Jake. She walked to the patio door, sliding it open and letting in the warm ocean breeze.

She felt the press of Jake's chest against her back. He moved his hands up and down her arms in comforting strokes. She leaned against him. "I still can't believe they basically fired me after the business I've brought to them, the number of cases I've won, and the amount of time I've given to them . . . I've given them the past five years of my life, Jake. I sacrificed relationships, time with my family, with Alice." She choked back a sob. "And they let me go as if I don't matter, as if I'm disposable. They didn't even give me the opportunity to defend myself."

"They're entitled assholes, and they don't deserve you. Don't you dare doubt yourself because of them. You're a brilliant lawyer. Your clients love you, and so do your colleagues."

Sage snorted. "Thank you, but other than Brenda, my coworkers barely knew me until I started bringing Max to work."

"Then why did forty-five of them, including Bill in security, tell the firm that they wouldn't be in on Monday unless you were reinstated?"

She turned to stare at him. "They did?"

"They did."

"I'm, I'm kind of speechless, and touched. Really touched." She wrapped her arms around her waist. "It won't matter, though. The founding partners never budge on a decision. They'll wait them out." She pulled out her phone. "Brenda has to tell them to go to work tomorrow. I don't want anyone to lose their job because of me. Bill and his wife have a baby on the way, and—"

"Don't worry. No one is losing their job, including you. I had a talk with the founding partners yesterday. I played your recording for them and made a few threats of my own."

"When did you—" She made a face. Her grandmother had informed Jake that her family were bringing her home and sent him on his way. "My nonna was a brat yesterday. I can't remember if I apologized for her. Did I?"

"You did, and so did your mother and your aunt and your sister. They also tried to get your grandmother to apologize, but she ignored them." He grinned. "You and your grandmother have that in common."

"Ha. Now tell me, what did you threaten the founding partners with?"

"I told them you were suing for illegal dismissal, and that we'd jointly be filing suit against Robert for conspiring to catnap Max, animal cruelty, and also conspiring to cause irreparable damage to your reputation, as well as conspiring to injure you. I paid a visit to the congressman too."

"Nice. What is your specialty, by the way?"

"Family and criminal law."

She blinked her eyes in an effort to keep tears at bay. "You want to help kids like you, don't you?"

"I do."

She hugged him tight. "I really am proud of you. Which

is why I'm not giving you hell for handling Robert and the congressman for me."

"Great. So seeing that you're really, really proud of me, you won't give me hell when I tell you that, once they'd rescinded your suspension, I told Forbes, Poole, and Russell that you'd be taking the vacation time they owe you starting now."

"Are you insane? I can't take time off work. I have clients who are counting on me."

He looked like he wanted to shake her until her teeth rattled. "You're just out of the hospital. The doctor told you to take six weeks off. At the very least, you need a month off work, Sage. You shouldn't even be here helping me."

There was a part of her that knew she couldn't keep going the way she had been. "I promise I'll do better. I won't do any more all-nighters. I'll try to take off some time on the weekend. Don't look at me like that. I can't let my clients down."

"Eventually you will, though. But more important, you're letting yourself down. Just because the founding partners backtracked on this doesn't make them good guys. You deserve to be treated better. You all do. And as far as your clients go, Renata and Brenda will take care of them. I'm sure you have everything prepared for them anyway."

"I do, but it's not just my clients at the firm. It's the women I represent at Chrysalis House."

"I can help you with that." He put his hands on her shoulders. "Please, just think about it, okay?"

Her phone rang, and she nodded, glancing at the screen.

"It's my nonna." She looked up at him and knew exactly what he was thinking. "Not one word to her about this."

He pressed his hand to his chest. "You think I'd out you to your grandmother? I told you, the woman scares me. There's no way I'm going to tell her you're thinking about going back to work tomorrow."

Chapter Fourteen

I don't know if this is a good idea," Jake said as Sage drove into the parking lot of her family's restaurant. La Dolce Vita had been as much her home as the apartment beside it.

She backed into a parking space. "It was either come here or they'd bring dinner to us, and trust me, we wouldn't get rid of them for hours. This way, we grab something to eat, and we have an excuse to leave. We have to lock up after the cleaners are done anyway."

"All right, but don't tell them I let you spend the day helping me at Alice's."

"You didn't *let* me help, Jake. I'm a thirty-year-old woman who does what she wants, when she wants."

"I know that, and you know that, but your grandmother is another story. I'm already in her bad book because your autonomous self decided to stay at the farm with me."

She laughed. "Don't worry, I'll protect you from Carmen."

"I don't need your protection," he said as he got out of the car and joined her on the walkway. "I just—" At the sound of a woman yelling in rapid-fire Italian, he broke off and leaned back, looking at the side of the restaurant where the kitchen windows were open, wincing when the yelling was followed by the crashing of pans. "Is that your grandmother?"

She nodded. "Don't ask me what she's yelling about. Other than swear words and the restaurant's menu, I don't speak Italian, but she's always yelling in the kitchen. My aunt and my mother are the same. Half the time, I don't think they realize they're yelling. It's just their thing. When they cook together, tempers flare, and words and dishes fly."

"Has anyone ever called the cops?"

"They used to, but then Bruno, my grandmother's fiancé, suggested they put a warning on the menu."

"I take it back. Maybe I do need your protection," Jake said as he opened the restaurant door for her, the smells of garlic, tomato sauce, and fresh-baked bread greeting them. "If the food tastes half as good as it smells in here, the women in your family can yell at me all they want. It'll totally be worth it."

She inhaled deeply and smiled. "The smells of my childhood."

As soon as the words were out of her mouth, she felt guilty for saying them so soon after the altercation with Jake's mother. Sage could only imagine what his childhood had been like. But it wasn't as if she could explain the guilty look he'd no doubt noticed on her face without making everything worse, so instead, she said, "You and Alice must have come here to eat, didn't you?"

"Are you kidding me? You worked here. You would have dumped a bowl of pasta on my head."

"I wasn't that bad." She grimaced. "Was I?"

"You were the worst. You made me feel about this small." He held his hand to his knee.

Now it was her turn to feel small. "I'm sorry. I wish I could take back every mean thing I said to you. I was jealous of your relationship with Alice. I admired her so much, and you know how great everyone in my family is—they really are, even with the yelling—but there were six of us, all women, and that meant drama and not always getting a lot of one-on-one attention, and Alice was—well, you know, she was so calm and even-tempered and..." She trailed off at the expression on Jake's face. "What?"

He motioned for her to follow as he stepped back onto the walkway, letting the restaurant door close behind them. "I was teasing you. You never made me feel small. We both gave as good as we got. We were hormonal teenagers, and"—he shrugged—"I had a crush on you."

"You did?"

"Oh come on, you had to know that I did."

"No! I thought you hated me. You completely ignored me at school and had a new girlfriend every other month." To this day, she could name every one of them. They were always the most popular girls at school.

"You were too good for me. I didn't think I had a chance with you, and Alice basically told me hands off."

"Don't say that. I wasn't too good for you, and you stood more than a chance with me. I had a crush on you too."

He shook his head with a laugh. "You don't have to say that to make me feel better." The amusement faded from his voice, and he stuffed his hands in his jeans pockets. "I saw your face when you made the comment about your child-hood. It's one of the reasons I didn't want you to see or hear what you did today. I don't want your sympathy, Sage. I don't want you to feel guilty about how good you had it compared with me."

"Me, sympathetic? I think you're confusing me with my sister. But I'm curious. Just how big a crush did you have on me?" she asked, not only because she wanted to know but because she thought lightening the mood before Jake had to face her family might be a good idea.

Jake opened the restaurant door, but just as it looked like he'd respond, a handsome older man with silver hair rushed over, greeting Sage as if she'd just returned from war.

"Bella!" Bruno wrapped his arms around her, lifting her off her feet. He'd been her surrogate grandfather long before Carmen had let him put a ring on her finger. "It feels like you haven't been home in forever. We've missed you." He set her on her feet and patted her cheek. Then his eyes narrowed and his jaw clenched, no doubt in response to her black eye. His gaze slid to Jake.

"Sir, I had nothing to do with her black eye."

"Were you with her when she got popped?"

"Bruno," Sage said. "He wasn't there. You remember Jake, don't you? He lives in San Diego now. He's Alice's . . . son." She ignored the look Jake gave her. She knew it was exactly how both he and Alice had felt, and she thought it was about time he heard the words out loud, especially after today. "He left Sunshine Bay to join the military when he was eighteen. He was special forces," she added for Jake's benefit. Bruno had a deep regard for those who served in the military.

He nodded, looking at Jake with new respect. "Thank you for your service, and my condolences on Alice's passing. She was a good woman."

"Thank you, sir. She was one of the best."

"Who gave you the shiner?" he asked Jake.

"I did." She didn't want Jake to have to admit his mother punched him. But noting Bruno's lowered brow, she realized she might have made matters worse. Bruno had probably thought of several reasons why she'd punch Jake, none of them good. "It was an accident. I hit him with a buck—hammer," she corrected, thinking a bucket probably wouldn't have given him a black eye.

Jake bowed his head.

"A hammer! You're lucky you didn't take his eye out or break his skull." Bruno frowned. "But what were you doing swinging a hammer? You're supposed to be taking it easy."

Several people sitting at the tables toward the front of the restaurant called out their greetings to Sage, reminding Bruno they had an audience and customers waiting, and no doubt saving Jake from a lecture.

"We'll talk about this later. Everyone's waiting for you at the family table," Bruno said.

"I'm winning over your family left and right, aren't I?" Jake said, then reached for her hand. "Hold up a sec. What did he mean by *everyone* is waiting? I thought we were having dinner with your mother and grandmother."

"Shake a leg, babe," Willow called out. "We're all starved, and Nonna won't serve the food until you're seated."

Jake's gaze shot to where her sister sat with nearly their entire extended family at the back table.

"It'll be fine. You've met Flynn." Sage nodded to where Flynn sat beside his father at the end of the table. "His dad, Amos, is great, and so is my uncle James. He's seated across from Willow and her fiancé, Noah, who is super nice too," she said.

"So it's just the Rosetti women I have to watch out for. And Bruno."

She held back a laugh. "Pretty much."

Introductions were made, and everyone said their hellos as she and Jake sat at the table, commenting on her shiner and his. Jake must have wanted to avoid another repeat of what happened with Bruno, because he told the group he'd been fixing one of the doorknobs when Max pushed the door open, and the knob hit him in the eye. It would have been believable if she hadn't decided to give her new, improved version of her previous story at the same time and said she'd accidentally hit him with a bucket. Since their stories basically ran over each other, she had no idea what her family heard, but they were looking at them as if something fishy was going on. Jake must have thought the same thing and opened his mouth.

She was positive he was going to tell the truth, and there was no way she wanted him to have to say his mother punched him. "Crazy, isn't it? The poor guy got hit in the eye twice in one day. Okay, so where's the food? We're starving, and we only have an hour."

"What do you mean, an hour? This is a celebration," her grandmother said, setting down a beautifully arranged antipasto platter of smoked meats, hard cheeses, marinated peppers, artichokes, and sun-dried tomatoes. Sage's mother followed behind, depositing a bowl of bruschetta and a basket of toasted bread on the table, while her aunt Eva placed a platter piled high with cherry tomatoes, fresh basil leaves, and mozzarella balls threaded on skewers.

"We have to—" Sage began.

Jake cut her off. "We're here for however long dinner lasts, Ms. Rosetti." He lowered his hand onto Sage's knee and gave it a warning squeeze.

"There's no way you'd tell her I'm going back to work tomorrow," she said under her breath.

"Try me," he said out of the side of his mouth.

Carmen's eyes narrowed at them, and they both smiled. They must not have been very convincing, though, because several more pairs of eyes narrowed at them.

"So, what are we celebrating?" Sage asked in the hope of distracting their audience.

"You being back in Sunshine Bay, for one." Carmen looked at Jake, her full lips flattening before she continued. "And now that all my family is finally home where they belong, we can go back to our tradition of Sunday family dinners."

Sage's phone pinged, and she looked at the screen. Jake had texted her. **I don't think now would be a good time to tell them you're going back to Boston in the morning.**

She rolled her eyes.

"Lila sends her apologies, Ma. She's got a bug but promises they'll be here next Sunday. She's excited you're starting the tradition up again."

"Me too," Willow said, looking at Sage and nudging her head at their grandmother.

Sage mouthed, *What?*

"Sage, you're not getting texts from work, are you?" her mother asked, taking a seat across from her.

"No, just a friend texting me," she said, and saw her family exchanging glances. "I do have friends other than my family, you know."

"Of course you do, honey."

"I do," she reiterated firmly at her mother's obvious attempt to pacify her. "And, Nonna, I promise, I'm turning over a new leaf. I'll make sure I'm here every Sunday for family dinner. Well, mostly every Sunday."

"You're here for at least the next six weeks, just like the doctor ordered. We'll talk in August about what happens when you go back to work in the fall. But tonight, we're talking about your new leaf. Yours and your mother's."

"I'm not the one who's burned out," Gia said.

"No, you're just—" her grandmother began, but Cami cut her off.

"Let's raise a glass to Sage being home for the next six weeks."

"Home until the fall," her grandmother muttered, but she followed suit when everyone passed the wine and filled their glasses and then lifted them in Sage's direction.

"Thanks. It's nice to be home, and I've missed our Sunday dinners, but—" she began, a part of her wishing she could put it off, but if she was going back to work tomorrow...

Her phone pinged with another text from Jake. **You regretted the time you lost with Alice, don't make the same mistake with your grandmother.**

Her gaze shot to Carmen. "Are you sick? Is this what rein-stating Sunday dinners is really about?"

"What are you talking about?" Her grandmother made a *gimme* gesture with her fingers. "Give me your phone. I want to know who's putting these foolish ideas into your head."

"It wasn't a person. Just one of those alerts telling me my screentime was up this week." She looked at her grandmother. "You'd tell us if anything was wrong, wouldn't you? You'd tell us if you were sick, right?"

"Honey, what's this about?" her mother asked.

"Nothing. I was—"

Jake nudged her. "Tell them."

"Make up your mind. One minute you want me to tell them, and the next you—"

"We got the coroner's report back," Jake said, and told them everything they'd learned. "Sage was upset that Alice hadn't shared her diagnosis with us. We would have spent more time with her had we known."

Her grandmother waved her skewer at them. "You both learned a hard lesson. There's nothing more important in life than spending time with those you love. None of us knows how long we have. But we'll have these six weeks together. They will be a gift to you, me, and your mother. You'll remember how to live your life the Rossetti way, and knowing you both have the tools to live la dolce vita, the sweet life, will allow me to die happy..." She paused for effect. "...twenty years from now." She held Sage's gaze. "Si*?*"

If Alice's death had taught her anything, it was that Jake and her grandmother were right. "Si, Nonna. I'll be here long enough to learn how to live la dolce vita."

But knowing they were right didn't make it any easier for Sage to actually take six weeks off work. It was as if her heart thought she was running the hundred-yard dash, the way it was galloping in her chest. She took a couple of deep, calming breaths, reminding herself that Brenda and Renata were more than qualified to take care of her clients, and they'd have her notes. It wasn't as if they couldn't reach her if they needed her. They could talk every day. A couple of times a day if need be.

Under the table, Jake took her fisted hand in his. She turned her head, and he gave her one of his heart-stopping smiles. It helped slow her racing heart, and she couldn't help but think there was another benefit to sticking around.

⌐

"I didn't think this would be so hard," Sage said to Jake as they did a final walk-through of Alice's house, checking on the cleaning crew's job. She reached for his hand. "It must be worse for you."

He nodded at the door of his old bedroom. "I remember my first night here. Alice had told me I could stay with her if I wanted to, and I went to bed feeling like I'd won the lottery. At the same time, I was terrified that I'd screw it up or that my mother would ruin it for me. It took almost a year of me waiting for the shoe to drop to finally realize that even if I messed up, Alice wasn't giving up on me. My mom's threats and bullshit didn't scare her off either." He gave Sage's hand a squeeze. "Some of my best memories were here in this house, and some of them even included you." He grinned as they walked through the living room to the front door. "At least the you in my fantasies."

The sob she'd been holding back turned into a snort. "Yeah, right."

It didn't take long for her emotions to get the better of her again as they took one last look around the house. Then Jake reached for the light switch.

She cleared her throat. "It's not too late, you know. If you want to keep the house, we can back out of the deal."

He turned to her, his gaze searching her face. "You'd do that for me?"

"Of course I would. This is your home."

He looked around, a half smile on his face, his eyes shiny when they came back to her. "Thank you. I appreciate the offer. But Alice made it my home, and she's not here anymore. Besides, she knew she was dying and chose to sell the house. We need to honor her wishes."

"You're right," she said as she followed him out the front door. "I just don't understand why she bought a lavender farm and left it for us."

"I have a feeling we'll find out. You know Alice—she never did anything without a reason."

"No, she didn't." She touched the blue door in a silent good-bye as Jake locked up one last time. "Nonna sent me home with a nice bottle of Cabernet and a chocolate cake. I think we should drink to a fresh start for you and me."

"She gave you the bottle of Cabernet and the chocolate cake because you lied and told her we were celebrating me getting my law degree and taking over Alice's practice."

"Hey, you haven't tried Nonna's chocolate cake. You'd say

whatever you had to to get just a slice, and I got us the whole cake." She linked her arm through his as they walked down the crushed-shell driveway to her car. "But we *should* celebrate you getting your law degree and taking over Alice's practice."

"And our fresh start."

"And our fresh start," she agreed.

Chapter Fifteen

As they closed up the restaurant for the night, Gia asked her mother, who was wiping down the bar, "Why didn't you tell everyone the real reason for the celebration tonight?"

Eva stopped restocking the wine to share a glance with their mother.

"I don't believe you two. You're keeping another secret from me, aren't you? Let me guess, Cami has convinced Willow to move to LA? No?" Gia said when they rolled their eyes. "Then what is it? Because I know you two, and you're definitely keeping something from me."

"Come sit. We'll have a digestif." Her mother motioned for her to take a seat at the bar. Eva retrieved a bottle of sambuca and the coffee beans.

"This should be good if I need a drink before you tell me," Gia grumbled as she left the cloth on the table she'd been wiping down and walked to the bar.

They closed at nine p.m. on Sundays, so it was still relatively early. Flynn wanted to get together later tonight for the talk she'd been putting off. It looked like this would be the night for her to hear things she didn't want to hear. She had a feeling Flynn was going to give her an ultimatum—either they date out in the open or it was over.

No matter that just thinking about ending things with him made her cry, she couldn't date him openly. Even if he agreed to keep their relationship a secret, it might be best if they end it anyway, before someone got hurt. She was almost positive that someone would be her.

"You knew I was going to announce I was reinstating Sunday family dinners tonight," her mother said.

"I did," Gia agreed, "and I'm as happy about it as everyone else."

Eva poured them each a glass of sambuca, adding three coffee beans to the top of each drink to symbolize health, happiness, and prosperity.

Carmen pulled out the barstool beside Gia. "I know you even better than you know me, cara, and how you felt about your sister joining us for dinner every Sunday was written all over your beautiful face."

"Eva has dinner with us almost every night." They typically shared a plate of the night's special mid-dinner-service, but Gia knew Eva wasn't the sister her mother was referring to. She'd hoped they could go a few hours without talking about Cami. Just because Gia knew she had to figure out a way to make peace with her baby sister didn't mean she wanted to think or talk about it now. She needed time to work herself up to it.

Eva snorted and lifted her glass. "Salut."

It sounded more like *good luck*. Their mother continued looking at Gia with an eyebrow raised.

"All right, so the idea of breaking bread with Cami once a week doesn't exactly give me the warm fuzzies. But you'll be happy to know that I'm prepared to work on my issues with her."

"Bene, and my la dolce vita reminders will help with this, I'm sure."

"Me? You seriously think I need to be reminded how to live la dolce vita? Come on, Ma. Who enjoys the simple things in life more than I do? Who loves their wine and food more than me? Who sees the beauty in every moment and captures it on canvas?" She pointed at herself. "Yeah, me. Now, my daughter? I'm not sure six weeks is enough for you to remind her how to live la dolce vita. But I'm here to do my part, because I agree with you. Sage needs to make some big changes in her life, or she'll risk burning out again."

Her mother nodded, carefully swirling the coffee beans in her glass. "I agree, there are some aspects of living la dolce vita that you do very well, but there are some things you've forgotten."

Gia gave Eva a *can you believe this?* look. "And what would they be, Ma?"

"Going out, socializing, having fun, dancing, having sex."

Gia's sambuca went down the wrong way, and she choked. She couldn't meet her sister's eyes. "I've been busy. We all have with our new venture."

Over the past two years, they'd had several business opportunities open up to them thanks to their La Dolce Vita channel and her niece Lila's savvy marketing skills. Last fall, they'd been approached by a number of grocers on Cape Cod who wanted to carry their sauces. Gia had designed the labels, and the three of them had each created their own signature sauce. Carmen's was a traditional marinara, Eva's a spicy tomato cream, and Gia's a basil pesto.

Their sales in the past six months had exceeded their wildest dreams. The news they'd planned to announce tonight— along with reinstating Sunday dinners with the family—was that their specialty sauces were going to be carried by national grocery chains in both the United States and Canada.

Her mother smiled. "Si, and another person will lighten the load. I didn't want to share the news until we agreed so we'll tell everyone at dinner next Sunday. That way Lila and her family will be there to celebrate with us too." She raised her glass. "To your sister joining La Dolce Vita."

Gia stared at her mother, her glass hanging in midair. Her mother clinked it anyway. Obviously, she'd taken Gia's stunned silence as an agreement.

"It's only fair that Cami be a part of our venture," her mother continued. "I want my three daughters represented in La Dolce Vita's brand, so we'll get her working on her sauce this week. This will also help you to mend fences with your sister and go back to the relationship you once had with her. Because you are not truly living la dolce vita if you don't spend time with the ones you love, your family. All your family, Gia, including your sister."

Carmen knocked back her sambuca, set the glass on the bar, leaned across to pat Eva's cheek, and then patted Gia's before sliding off the barstool. "Now I'm going to take my own advice and make love with my handsome fiancé. Ciao, bellas," she said, hips swaying as she strutted to the doors off the deck in her four-inch heels.

Eva sighed. "I want to be just like her when I'm seventy-one."

"She's seventy-four, and you will be."

As the door closed behind Carmen, she practically ran up the stairs to her apartment.

"No wonder Bruno looks happy all the time." Gia made a face. "I shouldn't have gone there."

"I'm not surprised that you did. I caught you sharing hot and sultry looks with Flynn at the dinner tonight. So did James."

"He didn't, did he?"

"Afraid so. And Mr. Observant caught a few other things."

"Such as? Wait. If it's about Cami, don't tell me. I refuse to talk about her tonight, especially after what Ma just sprang on us without even giving us a say." She looked at her sister. "It wouldn't matter, would it? You agree with her."

Eva came around the bar, carrying the bottle of sambuca, and slid onto the barstool beside her. "I do." She topped up Gia's glass. "And a few weeks from now, so will you, and you know why?"

"I have no idea, so please, enlighten me," she said, taking a sip of her drink as she watched the red-and-purple-painted sky begin to darken outside the restaurant's front window. A car slowed and parked alongside the lane. The windows were tinted, and she couldn't make out the driver, but for some reason it gave her an unsettled feeling.

"What's wrong?" Eva asked.

"I don't know, just something about the car parked across from the restaurant. I'm probably overreacting because of the man Sage was telling us about. You know, the one who'd been asking about us at the Smoke Shack the night Alice died."

For the most part, the attention they'd received from La Dolce Vita's social media channels had been positive and fabulous for business, but they'd had a few issues with overzealous male fans this past year. She slid off the barstool and headed for the front door.

"What are you doing?"

Before Gia had a chance to respond, Eva joined her at the door with her phone clutched in her hand. "If you're going to confront them, you don't do it alone."

Gia unlocked the door. "It's not like I plan on chasing them down the road. I just want them to know we're aware they're there and"—she raised her phone—"have their license plate."

Gia opened the door and walked outside. Her sister followed her onto the walkway. "Maybe they're on the phone," Eva said. "Or there's two of them and they're making out."

The window lowered but not enough to see the person inside. They were alone and not on the phone and clearly watching them. "You've got two minutes to move on or I'm calling the cops," Gia yelled, moving down the walkway as she took a photo of whoever was behind the wheel. It had the desired effect. They started the engine and began driving away...but so slowly that it felt like a statement in and of itself.

They didn't care. They wanted them to know they were there. The car stopped halfway down the road. It was the perfect position for Gia to get a photo of the license plate, only it didn't do her any good—the plate was covered. It felt intentional on the driver's part. Like they were laughing at them.

She turned to see her sister on the phone. "Who are you calling?"

"James."

"Do you really think that's necessary? I'll drive you home if you're nervous," she said as they walked back inside the restaurant.

It didn't matter what Gia thought. Her sister's husband clearly thought they were in danger. As they found out five minutes later when an SBPD cruiser pulled up in front of the restaurant with sirens blaring and lights flashing.

"Madonna santa, Eva! This is crazy. We didn't need the police. They're going to wake up the entire neighborhood. What did you tell James?"

Her sister made a face as the inside of the restaurant lit up with swirling red and blue lights. "I might have told him that Spicy Eggplant had found us and was sitting outside the restaurant," her sister said, referring to one of their top fans whose creepy comments had gotten creepier over the past few weeks. They called him Spicy Eggplant because he ended his posts with fire and eggplant emojis.

"How did I survive growing up surrounded by drama queens?" Gia muttered as she headed to the door to let the officers in.

"Remember how I said you would come around to Cami joining our La Dolce Vita partnership? This here, right now, is why. Growing up, you took care of us as much as Ma did. You were always there for us no matter what. No-Drama Gia. The strong one, the diplomatic one, the one we could always count on in a crisis." She joined Gia at the door, placing her hand over hers. "I know you're going through something, just like I know you'll come out the other side, and when you do, you'll remember the good times that you, me, and Cami had. You've always believed in second chances. Give her one, Gia. For your sake, for her sake, but most of all for our family's."

"I'm tired, Eva. I'm tired of being the strong one, the one who always gives in." She lifted a shoulder. "To be honest, I'm not feeling all that strong anymore."

What she'd been feeling, she realized in that moment, was alone. She'd always been close to her daughters. She used to see Willow every day before Noah and Cami came into her life, and up until this year, she could count on talking to Sage at least once a day and seeing her once a week. But now she rarely saw or heard from either of her girls. And as close as she was with her sister and mother—they saw one another every day—they rarely did anything outside of work anymore. Eva had James, and her mother had Bruno, and as much as Gia was happy for them, it didn't make it any less lonely for her. And then Flynn had come into her life. Flynn who she was afraid to open her heart to.

Gia turned the lock and opened the door when the officers reached the walkway. "I'm sorry, Officers. My brother-in-law is overprotective, but we're all good."

"It doesn't hurt to be cautious. You've had issues with stalkers before. Mr. Sinclair said you have a photo of the vehicle?"

Gia nodded, pulling up the photo on her phone. She turned the screen to the officers. They looked at each other and nodded.

"Do you recognize the car?" she asked.

"It fits the description of the vehicle your sister said followed her home from here this evening."

"Is Cami all right?" Gia asked, pressing a hand to her suddenly racing heart.

"She's fine, and she played it smart. When she realized she was being followed, she went to a friend's instead of going home," one of the officers said.

"As a precaution, we suggested she stay with the Monroes for the night. Hopefully we'll have some answers for all of you by the morning. In the meantime, be careful and don't hesitate to call if you see something suspicious," the other officer cautioned.

They thanked them, and then Gia closed the door, ignoring her sister's intent gaze as she turned the lock. "I don't want to talk about it." She walked to the bar, knocked back the sambuca, and then nearly choked to death on one of the coffee beans that she'd inadvertently swallowed. "So much for bringing me good health."

Arms crossed, her foot tapping, Eva asked, "Would you really prefer if the stalker broke in while our sister was alone at the beach house?"

Willow's fiancé, Noah, had given Cami his family's beach house. He'd bought a home for Willow and him closer to town.

Gia got a bottle of water out of the bar fridge. "We don't know that it's a stalker, and even if it is, they're a stalker, not a murderer. I doubt they'd break in—"

"How do you know they're not going to murder Cami in the shower or in her—"

At the sound of a loud *thump* near the door off the deck, Eva whipped around, and Gia grabbed a bottle of wine. Darting out from behind the bar, she positioned herself in front of her sister.

It wasn't a stalker.

"Cara, are you all right?" Bruno crouched at their mother's side, cradling her in his arms.

"Ma!" Gia and Eva rushed to the back of the restaurant.

"What happened?" Eva cried.

"She overheard you talking about someone murdering Cami in the shower!" Gia knelt beside her mother and patted her hand. "Ma, Cami is fine," she said, then explained what had happened and that her sister was spending the night with Flynn—her ex-boyfriend and the father of their child.

Eva returned from the bar with a sheepish look on her face and a glass of water. "Sorry, Ma. I didn't mean to upset you."

Carmen nodded and took a sip of water. "I need to see my baby. I won't sleep unless I know she's all right." Bruno helped their mother to her feet. As he did, Gia realized he was dressed as a firefighter.

She pressed her lips together, refusing to make eye contact with her sister, who was making weird noises in her throat, clearly trying to swallow her laughter. But they lost their battle with laughter when James arrived and said to Bruno, "I didn't know you were a volunteer firefighter."

Chapter Sixteen

Gia sang "Rise Up" into a wine bottle along with Andra Day while vacuuming around the tables at the front of the restaurant.

Her mother had been right about Gia dancing more. She'd forgotten how good it felt to move to the music, belting out the lyrics of some of her favorite songs while finishing up the regular closing routine.

She couldn't remember the last time she'd danced and sung her way through the final cleanup of the day. Her mother or her sister were typically with her and always eager to get done as quickly as possible. They both had someone to go home to. It hadn't always been that way. They used to have fun doing the final cleanup of the day.

Not tonight, though. Eva had taken off with her hot husband, and Carmen was off with her hot firefighter checking on the well-being of her favorite child. No one, it seemed, was worried about leaving Gia on her own.

Because you're the strong one, she thought with a snort. The melancholy from fifteen minutes ago threatened once more. Then the next song on her playlist came on, and she punched the wine bottle in the air. "You hear that, Spicy Eggplant? You don't scare me because..." She turned the vacuum off with her big toe. "I'm on fire!" She danced around the tables, rocking out to "This Girl Is on Fire" with her girl Alicia Keys.

"Yes, I am, Alicia. I am on fire," Gia said, twisting her hair onto the top of her head and clipping it in place while waiting for the next song on her playlist.

An odd sensation slithered up her spine, and her gaze darted to the front window. It was dark now. The outside lights had come on, illuminating the red rosebushes at the front of the restaurant. Shadows chased each other down the road, the summer breeze moving through the trees. Not creepy men with nothing better to do than watch women in their windows, just a warm ocean breeze.

"Fight Song" came on. It took a little longer for the music to beat back her nerves, but once it did, she danced like no one was standing in the shadows watching. In case they were, though, she danced toward the back of the restaurant with her wine mic in hand, rocking out with Rachel Platten.

At least until someone knocked on the glass. Now the words froze in her throat, the wine mic at her mouth, her knees going weak. Her fear made her angry. She wasn't going to let some jerk make her afraid. She spun around with the wine bottle raised. Nerves fluttered in her throat as she took in the man's tall, broad-shouldered, rangy frame.

Her eyes met his through the glass. Her nerves warred with her temper. She wasn't afraid of him, and she didn't know why she was angry at him. That was a lie. She knew why she was mad at him. He was making her feel things she didn't want to feel. It shouldn't bother her that her sister went to him when she was scared or had turned to him for comfort the other day. It wasn't his fault he was easy to love.

She lowered the wine bottle and walked to the back door, opening it for Flynn.

"What are you doing here?" she yelled to make herself heard over Sia singing "Unstoppable."

It was as if the song had come on to remind Gia how much she was hiding from everyone. But she'd do like Sia said and put her armor back on. She wouldn't let anyone hurt her again.

He gently nudged her aside and walked in, closing the door behind him. "Your—" he began and then shook his head. "You mind turning the music down?"

She did mind, actually. She could still see the look in Flynn's eyes when she met his gaze in the glass, still feel the gentle pressure of his hands on her when he moved her out of the doorway. She needed Sia's reminders if she wanted to avoid the temptation of the man standing before her.

He opened his mouth but then closed it, instead following Sia's voice to the phone on the bar. He turned the volume down, the lyrics faint as they trailed off, and then he sat on the stool and reached for her, drawing her between his legs. "Your sister texted that you were on your own here. She didn't think it was a good idea, and neither did I. So here I am."

He smoothed a damp tendril of hair from her cheek. "Do you want to tell me why I had to hear from your mother that the same person who followed Cami was parked outside the restaurant tonight?"

"You already had one Rosetti to protect." Her tone was flippant, cutting. She knew from the look in his eyes she'd gone too far. But that had been her plan for their talk tonight. To push him away. To make it so he was the one to walk away. She was weak, her feelings for him too deep. She wouldn't be able to walk away from him. He had to be the one to walk away from her.

The muscle in his jaw pulsed, and he placed his hands on her hips, setting her aside as he got up from the barstool. He lowered his hands from her hips and stepped away from her.

"I'm not a kid anymore, Gia. I'm forty-nine. I don't play games, and I sure as hell don't play with women's feelings. I understand you've got issues with what happened between your ex and Cami, but I'm not him. To be honest, I don't appreciate being made to feel like I've done something wrong when all I've done is be there for a friend."

"You're right, and I'm sorry I made you feel that way. It was unfair to you. You didn't deserve it. Thank you for coming to check on me. I appreciate it, but I'm honestly fine." She lifted her wine bottle, forcing a smile that probably came off more self-conscious than cocky. "I'm armed and dangerous."

"What are you doing, Gia?"

"What do you mean?"

"Come on, I know a brush-off when I hear it. So, what, I tell you how I feel and call you on your crap, and that's it? We're done?"

"My *crap*?"

"Crap, issues . . . I don't really care what you call them. All I know is I care about you in a way I never thought I'd care about someone again. My wife was the love of my life, and after I lost her, I devoted myself to my family and my career. It was enough. I was happy. I was content. I dated once in a while but had no interest in a long-term relationship. Until the day I walked in here to meet my daughter for the very first time and I saw you, and you smiled at me, and that was it, I was a goner. No matter how hard I tried, I couldn't get you off my mind. I came back to Sunshine Bay so often this past year that my staff and clients thought something must be wrong with my dad. I was pumping Willow and Amos for information about you anytime we talked while trying to play it cool. I used to have game, you know. Until I met you." He shook his head. "If you could see yourself the way I do, you wouldn't doubt my feelings for you." He stroked her cheek with his knuckles. "Take care of yourself, Gia."

I feel the same way about you. Please don't go. The words were right there, on the tip of her tongue. She swallowed them back. This is what she wanted. As painful as it was letting him go, it would be so much worse if she waited any longer. She'd already hurt him.

"You take care of yourself too, Flynn." She managed to get the words past the painful ball stuck in her throat. Saying them hurt. Her heart hurt. Everything hurt.

He nodded. "Lock up after I'm gone." He opened the door off the deck, his eyes meeting hers one last time before he closed it behind him.

She bowed her head and stayed where she was. Afraid she couldn't fight the temptation to call him back if he was still there. She listened to the heavy tread of his footsteps crossing the deck and then taking the stairs to the beach. It was done. It was over.

I'm safe, she thought as she walked to the door, brushing at the tears rolling down her cheeks. But as she turned the lock, she saw him standing at the water's edge, his hair shining golden in the moonlight.

If you saw yourself the way I do, you wouldn't doubt my feelings for you.

His words played over in her mind, and she pressed her face to the glass, closing her eyes. He was a good man, an honest man, a loyal man, and he'd bared his heart to her. The other day in the pantry, he'd known she was afraid of her feelings for him, afraid to get hurt, afraid he'd walk away. But he was scared too. He'd told her he was, and why wouldn't he be? He'd lost the love of his life. But that hadn't stopped him from letting her in, from wanting her, from revealing how he felt about her with no expectations, no demands, just acceptance.

She groaned against the glass. He was everything she needed and wanted, and she was letting him walk away because she was scared. Of what? Being abandoned again? Having her heart broken again? How was that any different from what she was feeling now?

Maybe it was time she fought for what she wanted, and she wanted him. She wanted Flynn Monroe. Her sister's ex and her daughter's father, and dammit, they were going to have to deal with it because she was going to think about herself for a change. She wasn't just a good daughter, a protective big sister, or a loving mother. She was a woman who . . . she opened her eyes . . . wanted the man standing right in front of her with only the glass between them.

Her fingers slipped on the lock, and it felt like an eternity had passed before she finally got it open. "I'm sorry, I—" They both said the words at the same time, and then Flynn said, "You go first."

"No, you go first," she said, opening the door.

He nodded. "Please don't take this the wrong way. I know you're a strong, independent woman who doesn't need a man to protect her—and trust me, I know how dangerous you can be armed with your wine mic. Your dance moves alone could bring a man to his knees." He gave his head a slight shake, looking like he was having a silent conversation with himself and calling himself a dumbass. It was endearing and adorable, and if she didn't want to hear where this was going, she'd jump him and shut him up with a kiss.

He rubbed the back of his head. "It's just that I couldn't live with myself if something happened to you. So would you mind if I sit on the deck until your mother and Bruno come home?"

"I would mind, actually."

He nodded. "Yeah. I figured you might. Sorry. I should know better. My daughters lecture me about toxic masculinity all the time, and you'd think it would sink in, but I'm a man, so—"

She pressed her fingers to his lips, and she thought he might have groaned. "Shut up and kiss me, Flynn," she said, fisting her hands in his shirt and pulling him inside. She closed the door with her hip.

His eyes narrowed on her. "Is this a test?"

She shook her head and pressed her body against his. "No."

"How much have you had to drink?" He placed his hands on her hips.

"No wine, just some sambuca. Kiss me if you don't believe me." She stretched up on her toes and put her arms around his neck; his moved around her waist. "And I want you to stay, just not on the deck. I want you to stay with me tonight."

"I think I might need to sit down," he said, and she led him to a chair.

"Do you need some water?" she asked as he stared up at her.

"No. I need you to tell me what the hell is going on. I feel like I'm having an out-of-body experience. What changed from ten minutes ago?"

"Can I sit here?" She nodded at his lap.

"No. I need to focus on what you're telling me, and I won't be able to do that with you sitting on my lap." He stood up, offering her the chair, and then pulled one out from the table and sat opposite her.

She rubbed her now-sweaty palms on her thighs. "You know, I thought I'd just kiss you, and then I'd take you up to my apartment, and we'd make love, and we'd be good."

"I don't want us to be good for a night, or a week, or a month. I want us to be good for as long as you and I are here on this earth."

"That's a long time." The pressure in her chest made the words come out on a whisper.

"It is, so I need to know why you changed your mind, and I need to know what you want from a relationship with me."

"I just want you." She smiled, thinking that would be enough, but he gave her an encouraging look. He wanted more from her, and she groaned. "You know, Flynn, most men would rather skip the talking-it-out part and get to the good stuff."

"Amateurs. They haven't figured out that the talking-it-out part elevates the making-love part from good to mind blowing."

She sighed. "I didn't want us to end, but given my past history, I knew we would, eventually." She tried to gauge his reaction to what she said, but there was no judgment on his face. He was simply listening. "It wasn't just that my ex abandoned me. I mean it wasn't great, mostly because he left me with two babies and no income, but things hadn't been good between us."

Flynn opened his mouth, and she waved her hand, not wanting to talk about Aaron now.

"But my sister—I loved Cami. I'd practically raised her. I never blamed her. It wasn't her fault that Aaron decided he loved her and followed her to Hollywood when she got her big break. In some way, he probably thought of her as his ticket to the life he'd always wanted. But what did hurt was that she left me and Willow and never looked back. It was like we didn't matter to her. We weren't enough. I understand what she was going through better now. But I'm not sure, even if I knew what I do now, that I could have gotten past her taking Willow from me, from us, the only family she knew."

She shook her head. "I still can't think about it without feeling like I'm going to throw up. I've never been more terrified in my life. When she brought Willow back three weeks later, I said some things I probably shouldn't have. My sister and my mother did too. In that moment, Cami was dead to us. But no word of a lie, if she would have come to us a year, maybe two years later and told us what she'd been dealing with, we would have worked it out. But she didn't until just last year."

She raised a shoulder. "So those are my issues with Cami, and why it makes it a little hard for me to believe the people I love will stick around. Even my sister, my mother, and Willow and Sage are moving on with their lives, and it feels kind of like they've abandoned me too. I know they love me, and I'm happy for them... Okay, so I'm not happy for Sage because she's not happy. But you see, that's how messed up I am." Tears welled in her eyes, and she blinked them back. "I needed you to walk away from me because I couldn't walk away from you. I'm falling in..." She made a face. "I'm in love with you, and when you walked away tonight, it hurt so bad, I thought, how can it get any worse? If you still want me, and honestly, I wouldn't blame you if you—"

"I'll never stop wanting you or loving you," he said, scooping her up and onto his lap while proceeding to kiss her senseless.

"Gia Rosetti!"

Gia pressed a hand to her heart and whipped her head around. Her mother stood by the bar. "Ma, you nearly gave me heart failure."

"You? How do you think I feel when I walk in and see you kissing your sister's boyfriend." Her mother fisted her hands on her hips. "Are you trying to get back at her for Aaron? Because Flynn doesn't deserve that. He's a good man. He—"

"Ma, stop. This..." Gia moved her hand between herself and Flynn. "... has nothing to do with Cami or what happened with Aaron. And Flynn isn't dating her, he's dating me. We've been seeing each other for weeks."

Her mother looked at Flynn, who nodded. "It's true, Ms. Rosetti. Cami and I are just friends."

"Friends who have a daughter together," Carmen said, making a duck face. Gia didn't know why she hadn't seen it before, but it was the same face Cami made when she wanted to tick Gia off.

"That's true, we do. But I'm not in love with Cami. I'm in love with Gia, and lucky me, she's just told me she loves me too." He smiled down at her.

"You do?" her mother asked her.

Despite Carmen's reaction, Gia couldn't keep the smile from her face. "I do, Ma." She took Flynn's hand. "Very much, and I hope you can be happy for me, for us."

Her mother shook her head. "It's too fast. You've been with him for weeks. Cami, she was with him for years. They won't be happy, you know. Your sister and your daughter."

She winced at her mother voicing her own fears, but Gia hid her nerves from the man she loved and the woman who knew her best with a glib smile. "That's their problem, not mine."

Bruno, carrying her mother's purse, joined Carmen at the bar and gave Flynn a grateful smile. "I'm glad you're here, son. I was worried about Gia being on her own."

A guilty expression crossed her mother's face before she replaced it with a judgmental one. It was just as Gia had suspected. Her mother hadn't given a second thought to leaving her on her own. And perhaps to cover her guilt, Carmen said, "You might not be so glad he came to protect her when you hear what they've been up to."

Bruno frowned. "What have they been up to?"

"Okay. We're leaving now," Gia said before her mother filled

Bruno in. He'd been her surrogate father for a quarter century, and she didn't feel like discussing her love life with him. She'd much rather be having sex with Flynn.

"Are you okay?" Flynn asked as he closed the restaurant door behind them.

"I'm good. What about you? Having second thoughts? My mother can be a lot."

"About you and me? I'm good, better than good, actually. I'm happy. But your mother has a point about Willow. We should probably let her know we're together before she hears it secondhand."

"You're right, and what about your kids? Are they going to be okay with us being together?" She hadn't really thought his kids would have an issue with her. She'd asked because they were talking about Willow, and she didn't want to not mention his other children. But from the way he hesitated, she had a sneaking suspicion she was wrong. "Flynn, are they going to have a problem with me?"

"August won't, but you know girls." She couldn't tell in the dim lighting, but she thought he might have grimaced before covering it with a smile. "I'm sure it'll be fine."

"Is this something else we need to talk about before we get to the good stuff?"

He laughed, taking her hand as they walked side by side up the stairs to her apartment. "No. I'm more than ready to blow your mind." Which he proceeded to do before she'd even gotten the door open, and that was just with his kisses.

She dragged her mouth from his. "I need to open the door."

"You do that," he said, his chest pressed to her back. His

arms came around her, and his fingers moved to the buttons of her shirt. He undid one and then two...

"Put the key in the lock," he ordered in her ear.

She shivered, trying to do as he said, but she had a hard time focusing when he undid a third button and lowered her shirt off her shoulders, his fingers sweeping over her collarbones to the lace edging the cups of her bra.

"Madonna santa, grazie," she cried as the key turned in the lock and she opened the door. They practically tripped over each other in their rush to get inside. The remaining buttons popped off Gia's shirt, and she brushed aside Flynn's apologies, moving his hands away to take it off herself. His gaze was heated as it moved over her, standing in her bra, skirt, and heels.

She hummed her appreciation as she helped him take off his shirt. Smoothing her hands over his six-pack, gleaming golden in the moonlight shining through her studio window, she dragged a nail lightly along his skin just above the waistband of his jeans, loving the way his muscles twitched in reaction to her touch, the way he sucked in a breath.

Her phone rang from where she'd dropped it on the floor. She ignored it and went back to teasing him, only this time she undid the top button of his jeans. His phone vibrated in his pocket, and hers started ringing again.

They looked at each other, and the lightbulb went off at the same time for them both. "I'm going to kill her," Gia said, reaching for her phone as Flynn withdrew his from his pocket.

"Where's your bedroom?"

She pointed, and he took her hand, leading the way. "Why are we going to my bedroom?"

"We might as well be comfortable while we spend half the night talking to your sister, Willow, and my kids." He brushed a kiss over her cheek and then whispered in her ear. "And after we talk to them, we're going to finish what we started and blow each other's minds. Over and over again."

Chapter Seventeen

Sage's phone rang on the nightstand. She didn't have to worry about waking anyone up. She was sleeping alone and not happy about it. It was her fault. Last night when Jake suggested they celebrate their fresh start, she'd mistakenly assumed it was a euphemism for them having sex.

And she'd been ready to have sex with him, more than ready, truth be told. And it wasn't just because they'd had fun feeding each other the chocolate cake or she'd laughed more with Jake than she could remember laughing in a very long time.

Yesterday had been a turning point in their relationship. They'd shared things about themselves, important things. Things Sage had never talked about to anyone else. He wasn't who she thought he was. She admired and respected the man he'd become. It didn't hurt that he was gorgeous or that he'd apparently had a crush on her growing up. She'd thought she'd seen signs that he still did, but maybe she'd been wrong.

Her door opened as she reached for the phone. "Who's calling you at this hour of the morning?" Jake asked, coming over and picking up her phone. "Your sister. Do you want me to tell her you're still sleeping?"

"No. If you answer my phone this early, she'll think you're in bed with me." What was wrong with her? She sounded disappointed. Dammit. How early was it? Too early for Jake to notice the subtle whine in her voice, she decided.

He angled his head. "Are you disappointed that I'm not in bed with you?"

"No! Why would you ask a stupid question like that?"

"Uh, maybe because you sounded like you were."

"Of course I'm not." She raised herself up on the bed, puffed up her pillows, and leaned back against them. "You can give me my phone now. Earth to Jake." She made a *gimme* motion with her fingers while following his gaze.

She smirked. "I think you're projecting, Jake Walker. It's you who's disappointed you aren't in bed with me." Assuming they were going to have sex last night, she'd chosen the sexy, siren-red lingerie that she'd never worn but Willow had packed for her when Sage was in the hospital. Come to think of it, her sister had been the one who'd bought the lingerie for her. When it became apparent sex wasn't on the table, Sage couldn't be bothered to hunt down a T-shirt and sleep pants.

"The day's still young," he said, casting her a cocky grin and walking out with his long, loose-limbed stride.

"You can't just say something like that to me and walk away," she called after him, hearing the rumble of his deep, sexy laugh in response.

She glanced at her now-silent phone. It was five in the morning! She called her sister back. "What is so urgent that you couldn't wait until a decent hour to call me?"

"Oh please, you rarely sleep. Besides, this is my normal wake-up time."

"Hello, it's not mine. And I'm supposed to catch up on my sleep while I'm here—or have you forgotten that I'm burned out?"

"No, but I figured you weren't following doctor's orders anyway. You're not really an order follower. But I'm sorry if I woke you up. I really need to talk to you about this, though. I've been up half the night stewing about it. You can thank Noah for me not waking you up at two this morning."

"Thank you, Noah. Now, what are you worked up about this time?" Usually at this point in the conversation, Sage would be going over a brief while listening to her sister vent. It wasn't that she found the things Willow vented about trivial; it was just that it took her sister a while to get to the point.

Sage put the call on speaker and pulled up one of the online newspapers she subscribed to.

"Okay, so I'll give you a little background info first," her sister said.

"Of course you will," Sage said under her breath while reading an article about lane closures in the city. The one benefit of not having to go into work was not fighting traffic. She looked up from the article when her door opened and Jake once again walked in, only this time she smiled. He'd brought her coffee.

Thank you, she mouthed, reaching for the mug.

He frowned. "Is there a reason you're mouthing your words?" he asked at the same time her sister said, "Did Mom ever mention Spicy Eggplant to—Wait, is that Jake? Is Jake in bed with you? What is going on with my family? You're all having sex, and no one tells me!"

"Drama much? I'm not having sex, and Jake just brought me a cup of coffee."

"But you want to have sex with him, don't you? I can hear it in your voice."

"What? Did I moan his name or something? And if there was a moany sound in my voice, it was over the coffee, not Jake. He makes really good coffee, and he's standing right here, by the way, and I have you on speaker, so he's heard everything you just said."

"What's a spicy eggplant?" he asked as he walked around the bed and climbed in with her.

"Uh, what are you doing?"

"You keep talking about me being in bed with you, and I wanted to hear about spicy eggplant." He shrugged, propping a couple of pillows behind his head. "Two birds, one stone."

Before she could object, he pulled the comforter over her chest and tucked her in, rendering her speechless. Once she'd recovered, she was about to make a suggestive comment just to show him how blasé she was about him being in bed with her, but he beat her to it.

He winked. "You looked cold."

It took Willow approximately fifteen minutes to fill them in on Spicy Eggplant and his online comments.

"She's very detailed," Jake whispered, and Sage had to work to keep from laughing out loud.

But then Willow told them about Spicy Eggplant stalking her mother and Aunt Eva and Cami, and Sage's amusement dried up.

She sensed the change in Jake right away. It was no longer

fun and games. He was hyper-alert. "Willow, do you have a make and model on the car?" he asked.

"Mom took a photo. The police have a copy. She couldn't get the license plate, though. It was blacked out. Hang on. Honey, can you send Sage the photo Mom took of the creeper's car?"

A moment later, Sage said, "Got it," and pulled up the photo. She turned the screen to Jake.

He nodded, his expression grim. "I recognize the car. It was parked outside the restaurant last night for about half an hour."

He'd gone out front to take a call just before dessert was served. She hadn't asked him about it. She thought it might have something to do with his mother and figured he'd tell her if he wanted her to know.

"They drove by Alice's place too."

"Really?" Sage asked.

"Yeah. When we went back to lock up. They slowed to a crawl as they drove by, but I thought it was related to something else." He held her gaze.

His mother. She nodded her understanding.

"You or your cousin notice the car around your places?" Jake asked Willow.

"No, and we've all been more vigilant since Sage told us about the guy at the Smoke Shack asking about the family."

"That's good." He got off the bed. "I'm going to talk to SBPD, add my information to your family's. I want a timeline too. I'll drive over to Alice's. A couple of her neighbors have doorbell cams."

"Jake, it's just after five in the morning," Sage reminded him.

"By the time I head out, it'll be closer to eight. I'll wait until Kendra shows before I go."

"I don't need a babysitter."

"Didn't say you did."

"You didn't say it, you implied it."

Willow interrupted their staring contest. "Uncle James has a doorbell cam, and he goes for a run every morning around six."

"Good to know. Thanks, Willow," Jake said, and left the room.

"No problem." There was a long pause and then her sister said, "He's left the room, right? 'Cause just to say, he totes thinks you need a babysitter, and he's totes into you."

"I heard that," he yelled from down the hall.

Nothing got past the guy. He had the hearing of a bat. She thought it had something to do with his special forces training, and she had a feeling that if anyone found creeper guy, it would be Jake. It was nice to know she could let that worry go and leave it to him. Which reminded her . . .

"So, if Spicy Eggplant, also known as creeper guy but could be creeper gal, was the background info, what kept you up all night?"

"Okay, so obviously major excitement with the police arriving at the restaurant, sirens blaring and lights flashing, and this will make you laugh . . ."

Sage sighed and pulled up the *Boston Globe*, half listening to her sister as she gave her a play-by-play of the night's events.

It wasn't until Willow said, "I can tell I've shocked you. I was stunned too. I can't believe Mom would do this. Without even talking to me. It's no wonder I couldn't sleep last night. What are we going to do?"

Crap. At least Sage knew it had something to do with her mother. She tried to come up with a leading question without giving herself away, but Willow kept talking. Prolonged silence was one of Sage's favorite interview techniques; clients were typically unable to resist filling the silence. She realized then that she'd probably learned the technique from dealing with Willow.

"You have to talk to her, Sage. I'm too close to the situation." Willow groaned. "Can you imagine me sitting down with Mom and talking about her having sex with my dad?"

Sage sent Jake a text. You win. My mom and Flynn are romantically involved. To her sister, she said, "Honestly, I don't know what the big deal is. You've never had an issue talking about sex with anyone. You recently did a segment on *Good Morning, Sunshine!* about sex positivity and the importance of open and honest conversations about sex, didn't you?"

"Wow, you really do watch my show. But this is different. Put yourself in my position. How would you like to talk to your parents...Okay, so it's not like you can put yourself in my position, but you know what I mean."

Her sister's comment stung. But maybe she was being overly sensitive because Willow had a great father who was involved in her life and Sage's father had abandoned his family and had no interest in knowing her. Or was that gnawing little ache just a symptom of burnout? She went with the latter.

Let me know when you're off the phone, and I'll come collect, Jake texted, adding a fire and an eggplant emoji.

She laughed, a warm, little flutter in her stomach offsetting the gnawing little ache in her chest.

"I can't believe you think this is funny, Sage. This is serious. And I'm not the only one who's unhappy about this. Cami thinks Mom's using Flynn as payback for your father abandoning you both to be with her."

It was funny how Willow's perspective had changed, and not ha-ha funny, at least not to Sage. She'd had company in her abandonment when she and Willow had believed they were biological sisters. Somehow, it had made it easier to bear knowing her father hadn't abandoned just her but Willow too.

Sage scrubbed a hand over her face. She'd thought more about her father in the past couple of days than she had in years, and she blamed Cami and her damn memoir. Which might have been why Sage's response was sharper than she'd intended.

"That's a pile of crap and you know it, Will. Maybe you should be spending more time with Mom than Cami, if you're buying into her bullshit."

"Sage!" Willow gasped.

"What? I'm not going to let you parrot Cami's narcissistic crap about our mother and not call you on it. Do you honestly believe Mom would stoop so low, be so unkind and vindictive, as to use Flynn to get back at Cami?"

"No! I'm just repeating what Cami said."

"Maybe instead of repeating what she said, you should call her on her lies. How do you think Mom would feel if she heard this kind of crap? Or Flynn, for that matter?"

"I'm pretty sure they've already heard it. Cami was calling them both."

"And who told you and Cami about Mom and Flynn?"

"I told you already. Nonna did."

"Of course she did," Sage muttered.

"But it's not just Cami and me who are upset, Sage. My sisters are too."

The gnawing little ache grew, and Sage didn't like that it did. She was happy her sister had bonded with her biological family. It was just that, at the moment, it felt like she was choosing them over Sage and Gia.

"I bet August isn't upset, is he?"

"Please, he's a guy."

"Yeah, a smart guy whose only concern will be that his dad is happy. A smart guy who thinks our mother is the bomb. Did you ever notice how August spends half his time at family celebrations talking to Mom? And that he calls her at least a couple of times a month? And you know why he does, Will? Because she's cool, and kind, and funny, and just all-around awesome. And as much as I think Flynn is a great guy, he'd be damn lucky if our mother loved him."

"Why are you so angry about this? You make it sound like I'm choosing sides. I didn't call you for a lecture, Sage. I called hoping you'd talk some sense into Mom."

"Then you called the wrong person. Mom doesn't need my opinion on her love life. She also doesn't need yours, Cami's, Flynn's daughters', or Nonna's. And a word of advice, you might want to lower the temperature on this instead of fanning the flames."

"I'm not..." Willow sighed. "I'll let you go. It's obvious I shouldn't have called you so early. Feel better." The line went dead.

Sage stared at the phone, in awe of her sister's ability to blame Sage's reaction on a lack of sleep. Her phone rang in her hand. She glanced at the screen. *Nonna calling.* Sage was in a bad mood now thanks to her sister. No way was she talking to her grandmother. She declined the call and kept declining them as fast as they came in.

"Tap your screen any harder, and you'll damage it," Jake said from where he stood in the doorway.

"Trust me, I won't." She tapped it again.

"It's not work calling you, is it?"

She groaned. "How could I forget. If it weren't for my nonna, I'd be back at my desk right now." She tossed her ringing phone onto the bed. "The way it's looking, it would be a lot less stressful for me to be at work than hanging out in Sunshine Bay."

"What's going on?" he asked as he picked up her ringing phone and turned it off.

"Why didn't I think of that?" she asked, and she wasn't being sarcastic. She honestly hadn't thought about just turning off her phone.

"Did Willow ever get to the reason for her call?" he asked, lying down beside her on the bed.

"Oh yeah, which is probably why I didn't think to just turn off my phone." She repeated her conversation with her sister verbatim, including her side of it. She caught his wince. "Do you think I was too harsh?"

"I wouldn't say harsh. You were standing up for your mom, and really, it's no one's business but hers and Flynn's."

"What aren't you saying?"

"It's none of my business."

"That's just a cop-out."

"You sounded a little defensive, but I'm sure Willow understands how some of the things she said would make you feel."

"Honestly, I don't think she had a clue. It was so weird. We're in our thirties, almost thirties in Willow's case, yet when it comes to family stuff, you revert back to your teenage-self or kid-self."

"I do the same with my mother. Or at least I used to."

"When you saw that car outside the restaurant last night, were you talking to your mom?"

"Yeah. She was blowing up my phone."

"How did she get your number?"

He looked up at the ceiling. "I gave it to her." He glanced at her. "Aren't you going to tell me that was a stupid thing to do?"

"I'm pretty sure you found that out all by yourself."

He gave her hair a gentle tug and smiled. "I did. But it was right after I had learned my father died in prison, and I guess I was feeling guilty and wanted to check on her."

"And obviously you still feel guilty since you haven't gotten a new number." She turned on her side to face him. "I don't know if I'm supposed to say I'm sorry your dad died. He was an abusive alcoholic and didn't deserve a son like you, but he was still your father."

"Yeah, he was, and to be honest, I didn't know how to feel when I learned he died. He'd reached out to me a few times not long before. Said he'd found religion and wanted to make amends. He'd asked me to come see him."

"Did you go?"

"Yeah, I did." He gave his head a slight shake. "His church needed money, and he thought I'd want to write them a big fat check because they'd helped him see the light."

She rubbed his arm. "I'm sorry."

He lifted a shoulder like it didn't matter. "In a way, I'm glad I went. My last memories of him aren't from when I was a kid. He was a lot less scary than I remembered."

"Do you still have nightmares?" She'd stayed over one weekend at Alice's and had woken up to Jake yelling, battling an invisible foe.

"No. I've dealt with my demons a long time ago."

"What are you going to do about your mother? You can't have her showing up here and scaring off your clients."

"I told her I'd pay for her to go into treatment, but that was the only money she'd get from me. I also told her that next time she shows up and threatens you or me, I'm calling the police." His eyes crinkled at the corners with amusement. "What are you going to do about your demons?"

"I don't have——" she began, only to be cut off by her grand-mother banging on the front door. "Sage, I need to talk to you!"

"So much for me collecting on my bet," Jake said, and got out of the bed.

Chapter Eighteen

Sage sat on the porch swing drinking her third cup of coffee of the day. It was only nine in the morning. She'd said good-bye to her grandmother two hours before. Carmen had been unusually mellow by the time she left. Sage had been about to take credit for defusing another Rosetti family feud but her grandmother disabused her of the idea, attributing the beauty of the sun rising over the lavender fields and the sweet, musky fragrance in the air for her relaxed demeanor.

Sage had wondered if Carmen might be drunk on the per-fumed air when, before she drove away, she told Sage she'd find her sweet life on the farm and to let it work its magic. Sage thought her grandmother must have mixed her up with Wil-low. Her sister would thrive on a farm, whereas Sage would shrivel up and die.

Other than the traffic, she loved city life—the sights, the sounds, the fast pace, her job. The job she wouldn't be back to for six weeks. Unless she proved to her family that she'd wholeheartedly embraced living la dolce vita. She drummed her fingers on the arm of the swing, working up a game plan in her mind.

She texted her grandmother. **I need a sweet life list. Like a list of activities I can check off as I complete them.**

Bahahaha, Carmen texted back.

Sage rolled her eyes. Someone needed to show Carmen where the emoji were on her phone.

Dots came and went on her screen, and then another text from her grandmother appeared. **A checklist is the antithesis of living la dolce vita. You must feel it, breathe it, embrace it to truly live the sweet life.**

Great, just great, I'm stuck here for six weeks. She'd have to figure out something more than keeping the peace in her family to keep her busy since she'd semi-solved that problem. She should call her mother, though, because, despite what her grandmother said, Sage believed she'd contributed to her mellow mood, and no doubt her mother could use some of Sage's mediation magic.

But Gia was either on the phone with someone else or not answering it. Sage did manage to get through to Brenda and Renata, but they were too busy to talk for more than five minutes. Lucky them. Sage was bored out of her mind, the entire day stretching out before her.

She didn't think her night would get much better. Jake was on the hunt for creepy car guy or gal and hanging out at the Sunshine Bay Police Department. She considered letting him know how much she wanted him to collect on his bet but didn't want to come across as needy . . . or easy.

The screen door opened, and Kendra joined her on the front

porch. "I hate to bother you, Sage, but I have a problem. Two problems, actually."

Sage inwardly cheered. "Tell me what you need. The bigger the problem, the better. I love problems." To Kendra's credit, she kept a straight face.

"The funeral home called. They want to know if you and Jake have decided what you want to do with Alice."

Bring her back to life. Ask for a second chance to make things right. See her for one last time. Tell her I loved her. Sage cleared her throat. "Tell them Jake will get back to them...next week."

Kendra gave her a sympathetic smile. "They sounded like they expected an answer today."

"Okay. He'll call them by the end of the day. I'll just let him know," she said, and sent him a text. Her phone rang right away. She wondered if he could somehow sense her desperation.

Or maybe he was just as messed up about this as she was, she thought, when instead of saying *hey*, he swore under his breath. "Sorry. They called Saturday, and I put them off. I didn't think you'd be up to it."

And he thought she was up to it now? "Jake, we can't have the funeral yet. It's too fast. I'm not ready. I mean, I'm not ready to host something, and the planning—"

"Alice wanted to be cremated, so we can take some time to figure out what we're going to do. You don't have to come with me, but I want to say goodbye before she's cremated."

Sage closed her eyes. She didn't know if she could do it, but she wouldn't let Jake go on his own. "Of course I'll go with you."

"Thanks. I'll give the funeral home a call now and get back to you."

Eight hours later, it was over. They'd said their goodbyes to Alice at the funeral home before her body was cremated. Jake would pick up her ashes in two days' time. Alice didn't want a funeral, according to Jake. She'd brought it up the last time she'd visited him in San Diego, saying it was because a friend of a friend hadn't told her family, and Alice wanted to be sure they knew she didn't want a wake or church funeral. Clearly, she'd been ensuring they knew her wishes without having to tell them about her diagnosis just yet.

"This can't be all there is, Jake. Just the two of us at a funeral home saying goodbye." Kendra hadn't wanted to come, and they weren't allowed to bring Max. It had been too fast to search out Alice's friends and acquaintances. Neither Sage nor Jake really knew the people in her life now. "We have to do something to honor her, to celebrate her life."

"We will," he said, continuing past the exit to the farm. She hadn't really been up to driving either to or from the funeral home. Although it hadn't been as difficult as she'd thought it would be. She had a feeling it was because they'd said their goodbyes last night when they'd locked up Alice's house.

"Where are you going?"

"It didn't feel right just going back to the farm. I thought we'd do something in Alice's memory, raise a glass in her honor."

She saw the turnoff up ahead. "Jake, I don't know if I can do it."

"Don't worry. I didn't plan on stopping at the site of the

accident. You can close your eyes. I'll let you know when we get to the Smoke Shack."

She saw a cross up ahead on the side of the road and quickly closed her eyes.

"Sorry. I haven't been down this way since I talked to the couple at the Smoke Shack. I didn't realize someone had put up a roadside memorial." He brought her hand to his thigh, holding it until he slowed the car along the side of the road, parking behind a row of cars. "It looks like everyone had the same idea," he said as he got out of the car and took off the jacket of his black suit, tossing it on the seat. "You might want to take your jacket off too."

She'd worn a black blazer and skirt, pairing it with a ribbed-neck tank top. She hadn't considered that they'd be going out afterward or that she'd be taking off her jacket. But Jake was right. It was too hot to leave it on. She took off her blazer, placing it over the passenger seat. Then she closed the door and joined Jake at the front of the car.

She didn't miss his double take or throat clearing. Nor did she miss the women checking him out as they approached the Smoke Shack. She didn't blame them. He looked amazing in jeans and a T-shirt, but Jake in a suit belonged on the cover of *GQ* magazine. Even without the jacket, she thought when he rolled up his white shirtsleeves.

As they approached the line of people standing at the window of the food truck, Jake nodded at the patio. "Why don't you grab us a table, and I'll put in our order?"

There were only a couple of empty tables left on the crushed-seashell patio. "Sure," she said, thinking they probably should have changed before they came, or she should have at least put on her sneakers. All her shoes had practical heels except the one pair that Willow had packed for her while Sage had been in the hospital, the four-inch black heels she currently had on.

She found them a table, soon realizing why it was still empty. She managed to angle the umbrella to cut out some of the early-evening sunshine. Jake joined her, offering her a bottle of Red from Cape Cod Brewery. He'd chosen a Blonde in honor of Alice, who loved the brewery's pale ale. They toasted their old friend and mentor.

"Do you remember the last time the three of us were here?" Jake asked, leaning back in the chair and stretching out his long legs.

"I do. You told Alice you were thinking about enlisting, and she spent the entire dinner trying to talk you out of it." She smiled, thinking back to that night. "She was proud of you, though."

"She was, and you were as worried about me enlisting as Alice. Except she didn't try to pick a fight with me because of it."

"I didn't . . . okay, fine. I tried to pick a fight with you, but not because I was worried about you. I was trying to distract Alice."

"Sure you were."

She laughed. "I might have been a little worried about you." She sobered at what they now knew. "She'd gotten her diagnosis around then."

"She had. But I don't think that's what she'd want us to focus on. She went on living a great life and making a difference in a lot of other people's lives." He tapped his bottle against hers. "Let's focus on that, okay?"

She knew Jake was right. "We'll have to get Kendra to help us with the list of who we should invite to the celebration of Alice's life." She looked around. "What about having it here?"

"At the Smoke Shack?"

"Yeah, or the beach." She nodded at the path to the beach across the road on their right. "Alice did love it here. We could have the celebration on her birthday. It gives us time to plan." Alice's birthday was July 25. "I'll be back to work by then, but if we have it all organized, it'll be fine."

"You've been off for all of one day, and you're already champing at the bit to get back to work." He shook his head.

"I was bored."

"You're supposed to be bored, and resting."

"I said *was* bored, but then Kendra—"

"Order for Walker," a guy yelled out the food truck window.

"Hang on to that thought. I'll be right back." Jake set his bottle on the table and got up to grab their order.

He was halfway back to the table when the smell of smoky BBQ brisket, jerk chicken, and french fries wafted past her nose. She moaned. Jake looked around as if embarrassed the other diners might have heard her.

She motioned for him to hand her the bag. "You're acting as if none of Smoke Shack's customers have ever moaned over the smell of their food." She opened the bag and moaned again.

"Seriously, Sage, you need to stop moaning like that," he said, sending an apologetic glance at the table behind theirs where a mother sat with her three children as he took a seat.

"Stop moaning like what?"

He leaned across the table and lowered his voice. "Like you're having sex."

She laughed. "I do not sound like..." She caught the mother of three's eye, and the woman nodded as if commiserating with her, pointing at Jake and then shaking her hand in the universal gesture of *that man is hot*.

Sage gave the woman a look while casting a pointed glance at her children. Then she handed Jake his BBQ brisket burger and fries without meeting his gaze.

At his amused snort, she took an aggressive bite of her jerk chicken sandwich. Of course he'd seen her staring down the woman. He didn't miss much. They ate in silence for five minutes with Sage trying to contain her moans, but the fries did her in. She raised a hand to her mouth and uttered a quiet moan.

"Next time we order from Smoke Shack, we're eating on the beach. Better yet, at home. I mean, the farm."

She was embarrassed about her moaning, and Jake seemed embarrassed that he'd referred to the farm as home. She took pity on them both and changed the subject. "So, like I was going to tell you, I think Kendra has cured my boredom problem, and yours too."

"I don't have a boredom problem. I've got plenty to keep me busy."

"Well, unless you want to tell the fifty people who have emailed, and that's not including three senior homes and two day-care centers, that we will not be opening the lavender farm at the end of June, you're going to be even busier." She took another bite of her jerk chicken sandwich, savoring and swallowing before continuing. "We also have twenty-five online orders from the lavender shop that need to be fulfilled, and Kendra has been fielding phone calls too."

"We have a lavender shop?"

She took a sip of her beer and nodded. "We do. You know the cute little weather-beaten shed? That's the physical shop, and there's one online."

"Huh, and what do we sell in our shop?"

"A lot."

"And where do we buy this stuff that we sell?"

She picked up a french fry and shook it at him. "You're adorable."

"Thank you."

"I was being facetious."

"I figured. So you're telling me we're supposed to make the stuff we sell in the shop?"

"Unless we want to disappoint hundreds of people and have our bottom line look bottomless when we put the farm on the market, I am. But don't worry, I've figured out a way to deal with our lavender-product problem and my family-feud problem."

"I thought you said your visit with your grandmother went well."

"It did, and she credited the smell of lavender for making her chillmellow."

"Chillmellow?"

"Chill and mellow. I'll invite my family over this weekend. They'll spend the day making our line of products with us and bonding, and then we'll end the day with a Sunday family dinner."

"We have a *line* of lavender products?"

Interesting. She'd thought he'd focus on the Sunday family

dinner part, but maybe he thought she'd learned to cook in the intervening years. "We do, but we'll cut down to just a few items. Kendra found a book of recipes and a box of ingredients to make the products. We'll go with the easiest ones. Plus there's always YouTube. And my mom. She knows a ton about aromatherapy and the benefits of lavender. So we're all good."

"You sound more hopeful than positive. Are your sister and aunt still upset about your mom and Flynn?"

"According to my mom, they are, and she's still mad at them too. At least she was this afternoon. She'd planned to stop by to give me an update, but we had Alice's thing. She'll stop by tomorrow to give me the lay of the land."

"Do you really think it's a good idea having them all under the same roof?"

"I checked the weather. It's supposed to be nice Sunday. Well, according to my sister it is. I'll call Amos and ask him." Willow's grandfather was a weather whiz. "I thought we'd set up tables under the trees in the back. It will be all nice and—"

"Chillmellow?" he asked, a rumble of laughter in his voice.

"Why are you laughing?"

"You're the least chillmellow person I . . ." His voice trailed off, his eyes narrowing on something behind her. Then he smiled at her—but it seemed a little forced, and she didn't understand why.

"Don't look over your shoulder. We—" He reached over the table, placing his hands on either side of her face, preventing her from looking behind her. "I should have told you to look over your shoulder." He groaned when her head automatically started turning.

"I can't help it. I'm a curious person," she said, her eyes straining to look behind her.

He stood and leaned across the table and kissed her, hard. She had a feeling he was putting on a performance for whoever he didn't want her to look at, but then the kiss changed. His lips softened, and the kiss felt all too real and good and deep and hot, and she wished they weren't sitting on the Smoke Shack's patio with the mother and her three kids looking on. That reminder alone was enough for Sage to break the kiss, which had the added benefit of her synapses snapping into place.

"Is it Spicy Eggplant?" she whispered, so close she could count his eyelashes. She hadn't realized how long they were.

"No. Spicy Eggplant is a seventy-year-old woman who lives in a retirement home in Iowa."

"You talked to her?"

He nodded, his eyes on something behind her. "Just as I was leaving to pick you up to go to the funeral home. I got distracted and forgot about it until now. She's a nice woman who's having fun with her online persona. She loves Carmen, Eva, and Gia and didn't realize her comments might be crossing the line or causing them concern. She promises to rein it in." He trailed his lips across her cheek and brought his mouth to her ear. "We need to get this guy out of the vehicle so I can get a look at him. Let's go."

"Where are we going?"

"For a romantic walk along the beach, and you're not going to look behind you. Right?" He laughed when her head started turning, and he gently nipped her earlobe. "Do you ever do as you're told?"

She held his gaze. "Rarely, but I've been known to make exceptions."

He cleared his throat. "Maybe we should save that conversation for later." He straightened, gathering up their empty containers and putting them in the bag. "What are you doing?"

"Taking a selfie." She smiled at her phone, fluffing her hair while angling the screen to get a look at the cars lining the road. She spotted creepy guy's vehicle two down from her BMW. "You're right. Let's go for a walk."

She took off her heels when they reached the sandy path bordered by seagrass. "Can you see him?" she murmured to Jake, who was walking backward, pretending to take a photo of her.

"You need to pose or smile so this looks real," he said quietly, laughing when she did a series of what she thought of as runway poses. "He's getting out of the car."

They walked across the warm white sand to the shoreline. Jake took off his shoes and rolled up his pant legs. Then he took her hand, and they walked along the water's edge. The white foam topping the waves covered their feet as they kicked water in the air, the sun shining on the water droplets giving it a magical quality.

"That's a great picture," Jake said, and jogged ahead. He turned to face her, smiling at her, encouraging her to kick the waves higher, shaking his head when she got him wet.

She laughed, forgetting for a minute that this was for show. Not really surprised to discover there was a part of her that wanted it to be real. It was a silly thought. She and Jake wouldn't work long-term. They wanted different things in life. For one, he wanted to live in Sunshine Bay, and she wanted to live in Boston.

"Did you get him in the shot?" she whispered when Jake rejoined her, reclaiming her hand.

"No, but I got a great picture of you," he said, holding up the screen. "You look beautiful."

She frowned, wondering if he meant it or was acting for their audience of one. She thought she had her answer when he put his arm around her shoulders, drawing her against him, resting his head on hers. He raised his phone. "Smile."

He took several more, then let her go to look through the photos. "Gotcha. Now to figure out who you are." He turned the screen to her. "He fits the description of the guy Alice was seen talking to. And see that right there." He drew his finger along the man's jaw. "He knows we've made him, which means he'll either go to ground for a while or make his approach in the next twenty-four to forty-eight hours. I have the feeling it will be the latter."

"Do you think he's dangerous?"

"My gut says no, but I'll have my friend run photo recognition on him and see what pops. You can send the photo to your family. Maybe someone will recognize him." He glanced over his shoulder. "We can take off now. He's gone."

"Great," she said, hoping he didn't catch the hint of disappointment in her voice. So much for a romantic sunset walk. It really had been all for creeper guy's benefit.

"Just say the word if you want to keep walking. I don't mind. It's a nice night."

She needed to be more careful around him, or a much better

actress. Maybe Cami could give her some tips. "No. I'm good, thanks."

"You sure? You sounded disappointed."

"It's just that I really wanted to try one of those smoked-bacon-wrapped Oreos the woman behind us was eating." It was as good a cover for her disappointment as she could come up with on short notice. And they had looked really good. She smiled, remembering his reaction to her moaning.

"Sure. I'll run ahead and get you some. I'll meet you at the car."

Sage sighed as he took off across the beach. It was as if he couldn't wait to get away from her. She decided he must have picked up on her romantic feelings and vowed to do a better job keeping them in check, reminding herself why romance and men sucked as she walked back to the car.

Okay, so Jake didn't suck, she thought as she sat in the car, watching him walk toward her fifteen minutes later. He'd stood in the long line with the hot sun beating down on him while she waited in the air-conditioned car.

"Thanks," she said when he tossed her the bag.

"You're welcome. They said they were one of Alice's favorites." He smiled as he put on his seat belt.

She held one up. "Do you want one?"

"Sure. I'll save it for when we get home, though," he said as he pulled back onto the road and headed in the direction of the farm.

Sage bit into the bacon-wrapped Oreo. It was so good that she'd describe it as orgasmic, and that's exactly what her moan sounded like. She smiled around the cookie. And this time she only had an audience of one.

Jake swore, jerking the wheel. "Sage, you almost made me drive off the road."

"How? All I'm doing is eating my cookie." She wiped crumbs from her chest. "I finished mine. Can I have yours?"

"No."

Chapter Nineteen

Sage glanced at Jake as he drove up the road to the farm. It was narrow and winding but that didn't really explain why he seemed to be on high alert. Then again, they were surrounded by dense forest, which meant that a deer, coyote, or fox could dart onto the road at any moment. Her mind traveled to the woodland trail where Alice's body had been found almost three weeks before.

It was about a mile and half from where they were. Jake had made a small stone memorial for Alice there. More apropos than the roadside memorial, she thought, wondering if she would one day be able to make that long walk to where Alice had died.

Jake pulled into the driveway. "Stay in the car for a minute. I want to check something out."

She looked around. "Why? What do you see that I don't?"

He scrubbed his hand along his jaw, the scratch of his beard on his palm audible. It shouldn't have been sexy, but for some reason, it turned her on. Or maybe it was Jake and his protective instincts, the knowledge that he could kick the ass of whoever was out there. No, that couldn't be it. She was a Rosetti. They'd been raised to look after themselves. The Oreo cookies and her orgasmic moaning must have put her in the mood.

"A light where there shouldn't be one. I saw it through the trees as I made the last turn." He got out of the car, shaking his head when she followed suit. "I don't believe you."

"Did you really think you could pull that..." She lowered her voice several octaves. "*Stay in the car, woman, while I catch the bad guy?* I took self-defense classes, you know. I bet I could—" Something hissed, and then a raccoon appeared out of the shadows, lunging in her direction. She screamed and jumped back into the car, closing the door and locking it. She crossed her arms, refusing to give Jake the satisfaction of meeting his amused gaze.

She heard him laughing as he rounded the farmhouse. She could handle his laughter. It was better than him mocking her with a reenactment of her performance.

In the distance, a coyote howled. *Maybe it wasn't that far away*, she thought when the raccoon ran past the car and down the road with its babies, big babies, chasing after her. Good to know it had a reason to be overly aggressive that didn't involve rabies.

At the sound of a text, she glanced at her phone. It was from Jake. It's safe to get out of the car. I'm at the store. Dots came and went. Unless you're still afraid of the scary raccoons.

"Ass," she muttered and went to open the passenger-side door. In case the raccoons had left some of their friends behind in their hidey hole, she crawled over the console and got out the driver-side door.

Fast-walking around the farmhouse while watching for signs of wildlife, she hurried to the shed—also known as the store—as fast as her heels would allow, which wasn't fast at all. But she refused to walk barefoot through the lavender fields on account of the meadow voles. She shuddered at the thought of the rodents and the raccoons and every other mammal, reptile, and insect that the farm seemed to attract.

Jake turned, lighting the way for her with his flashlight. Then he stepped back, and she saw the outer wall of the shed. Its dull gray, wooden exterior had been replaced with a painted field of vibrant lavender, swaying on a gentle breeze. In the middle of the field, a beautiful silver-haired woman wearing a familiar straw sun hat and carrying a basket of lavender on her arm smiled at something in the field. Sage followed the direction of her gaze and spotted a black tabby cat hiding among the lavender.

"It's Alice and Max," she whispered, reaching out with the tips of her fingers, pulling back before she touched her old friend's face and smeared the paint. "It looks so real."

"Your mother is incredibly talented. It's beautiful."

"You think my mother..." Sage picked up the lantern, inspecting the painting more closely. "It does look like her style, but look at the signature. *J.R.*"

"J.R. is the street artist who's been painting murals around Sunshine Bay."

"The one Carmen was complaining about the other night? The artist who painted a mural on Surfside?"

"One and the same."

"My mother wouldn't..." Then again, maybe she would. She'd streaked her hair purple, bought a red Camaro with racing stripes, and was having sex with her sister's ex-boyfriend, so hey, turning into Sunshine Bay's Banksy wasn't that big a stretch.

"The timing fits. You told her Alice was being cremated today, and then this appears. It's her gift to you."

"A gift to both of us," she said, her heart bursting with pride and love for her mother. She took her phone from her pocket.

"What are you doing?"

"Calling my mother to thank her for the painting and to tell her how much we love it, of course."

"You might want to hold off and think about it before you do. For whatever reason, your mom obviously wants to remain anonymous."

"But why? Look how incredible this is."

"I don't know. Possibly because your grandmother is trying to have her arrested for destruction of public property."

"I hate when you're right."

"I love hearing you admit that I am."

She rolled her eyes. "The last thing we need is to give my family something else to fight about. I'll just pretend we have no idea it was her. It doesn't mean I can't let everyone know about this incredible piece of art the street artist J.R. gifted us with and how much we love it, though."

"It doesn't, and it sounds like you plan on rubbing your grandmother's nose in it."

"You know it. I just wish I could rub my sister's and my aunt's noses in it too. All you have to do is look at this to see how much love and thought my mom put into it. How Cami can believe that same person could do anything as despicable as what she accused my mom of doing is beyond me. I think I'll start a campaign to have J.R. given a community achievement award in recognition of their art beautifying Sunshine Bay."

Jake smiled. "There you go. Something else to add to your keep-busy list."

"How did you know I have a list? Were you snooping on my phone?"

"Your phone won't open with my face, but I didn't have to snoop. You made lists for everything as a teenager, and you haven't changed much."

"I guess you're not always right, because I don't make lists for everything anymore." Just for important things, and she had a lot of important things going on in her life, including defending street artist J.R. to her grandmother and her mother to Cami and Willow. It was just a happy coincidence that they would both fit nicely on her What to Do While in Six Weeks of Purgatory list.

His lips twitched. "Do you know that when you lie, you scratch the right side of your nose?"

"I do not," she said, surreptitiously lowering her hand back to her side.

"Okay, prove it. Show me your phone."

"I wish I could, but I can't. I have highly confidential emails on my phone."

"Like what?" he said.

"Lawyer-client types of things," she said, and glanced at her screen. "Oh wow, I didn't realize it's getting so late. Poor Max. He must be lonely with us gone for so long. You should take him for a walk," she said, and with one last look at the mural, she headed for the farmhouse.

"Are you trying to get rid of me?"

"No." Dammit, she moved her finger from the side of her nose to her ear and then realized he wouldn't see. Her back was to him. "I'm just thinking about Max. Look, you see, he's waiting for us." She nodded at the window as they reached the front porch.

"He's lying across the back of the couch like he does every day. The way you're trying to distract me has me curious, though. You must have some interesting stuff on your lists." He reached around her to unlock the door, his warm breath caressing her neck.

She shivered. "What are you doing?"

"Key seems to be stuck."

She pressed her lips together and put her hand over his, turning the key and then the knob. "Would you look at that," she said as she walked inside, moving to the couch when Max lifted his head instead of immediately turning it when he saw her the way he usually did. She tentatively reached out, stroking his beautiful coat.

"Jake, he's letting me pet him," she whispered, slowly lowering herself onto the couch in an effort not to scare him away.

"Maybe you should take him for a walk then."

"Are you crazy? Did you see the size of those raccoons?"

"Do you hear that, Max? She'll risk your safety just to get rid of me." He sat on the other side of the cat, scratching behind Max's ears, receiving a contented purr for his efforts.

"Don't go for a walk then." She nudged Jake's fingers away as she tried eliciting a contented purr of her own. "I just thought it would be nice for you and Max."

"You're happy right where you are, aren't you, buddy?" Jake toed off his dress shoes, looking as content as Max as he relaxed on the couch, stretching out his long legs. "Come on, tell me the truth. How many lists do you have on your phone?"

"You have a one-track mind. I have *a* list." She kept her fingers busy removing her heels instead of scratching the side of her nose. "I'm never wearing heels again."

Now, that was the truth. Although given the way Jake's gaze had moved over her legs when she'd walked out of the bedroom in her heels earlier that day, she might make an exception on occasion. His gaze was just as intent as he watched her take off her shoes now. She released a teasing moan.

She was rewarded by the heat in the gaze that met hers. "I bet you a lifetime supply of smoked-bacon-wrapped Oreos that you have more than one list on your phone," he said.

She swore he'd moved closer to her on the couch. She could feel the heat from his body, smell his cologne. The scent should be illegal. It had her thinking of doing things that . . . she'd been thinking of doing to him on their fake romantic beach walk that she'd wished had been real. Which might have been why her voice came out low and husky when she said, "Those cookies were orgasmic, but that's not enough to entice me to risk the identity of my new celebrity client."

"What if I promise not to look at anything other than your lists?"

"Sorry, no can do."

He leaned in and whispered in her ear, "What would entice you?"

She knew what would happen as soon as she said the words dancing on the tip of her tongue, and still, despite the consequences and complications, she said them. "Whatever you were going to collect from our bet?"

"Are you absolutely sure that's what you want?"

"Yes," she said, her voice breathless and needy, but she couldn't bring herself to care. Well, not until he lunged for her and began tickling her like he used to. And just like she used to, she laughed. She sounded like a seal in heat, and that made him laugh, and then she could hardly breathe, too weak to tickle him back or yank his hand from just above her knee.

"Our bet was you get to tickle me?" she cried when he finally relented. "What kind of bet is that? We're not seventeen."

He grinned, pushing her hair out of her face. "No, but I got to hear your weird laugh again, and I got to touch you."

"You wanted to touch me?"

"I did. I do. I want to touch." He trailed his finger down her neck to her collarbone. "And kiss." He pressed his lips just below his finger. "And lick." He swirled his tongue just above her cleavage. "Every inch of you. But you have to be sure—"

"I'm sure, very, very sure," she interrupted him.

"You didn't let me finish. I don't want to be just roommates with benefits, Sage. I want more with you, from you."

She wanted him. She wanted this. She wanted more with him too. But... "I can't leave my job, Jake. I've worked too hard to get where I am."

"I'm not asking you to. I'm not even asking you to live in Sunshine Bay full-time. I want to explore the possibility of us, together, in a long-term relationship. I don't want it to be just about sex."

"It would never be just about sex between us. But just to say, I'd really like it to be about sex for the next twelve hours at least."

⸺

Sage woke up the next morning in Jake's bed. He had his phone in his hand and an apprehensive expression on his face that made her groan. "You are not the one who is supposed to have morning-after regrets. I am!"

He kissed her shoulder, his mouth curving in a smile against her skin. "I don't have regrets. Do you?"

"I probably should, but I don't." She circled her own face with her finger. "What was with the look on your face then?"

He held up his phone. "The friend I had looking into creeper guy got a hit."

"He's in the system? Exactly how dangerous is he?" Her eyes went wide, and she reached for her phone. She'd forgotten to send her family the photo last night. She'd planned to do it when she got back to the farmhouse, but Jake had pushed thoughts about anything other than him and what they were doing in her bed—and in the shower, and in his bed—out of her head. Several times.

"He's not dangerous in the way you're thinking." Jake propped himself up on the pillow and put his arm around her shoulders. "You know how you said your sister was fanning the flames on the situation with your aunt and mom?"

She slowly nodded, not liking where this was going.

"This guy's the match." His arm tightened around her shoulders. "He's your father, sweetheart."

Chapter Twenty

The drapes in Gia's studio danced in the early-morning breeze, and the sun—a mellow yellow against the azure sky—warmed the floor where she was finishing up her yoga session in a reclined goddess pose.

After so many months of being unable to think about striking one simple pose, let alone completing one, being able to run through an entire routine felt like a major achievement. She'd needed this more than she'd realized. She remained in the pose, basking in the relaxed state of her body and mind. She considered staying right where she was for the entire day. And just like a worm, that tiny thought burrowed into her brain and obliterated her Zen state of mind.

Her mother had decided it was time to introduce their followers to the newest member of their brand—her golden child, award-winning actress Camilla Monroe. Carmen had been teasing the news on social media for the past two days. Gia had no idea how her mother had convinced herself that this was a good idea. But no matter how hard she'd fought against today's Instagram Live, it was going ahead. With or without her, according to her mother.

It would be without her, Gia had informed Carmen yesterday afternoon. She'd wanted no part of it after the vile accusations Cami had hurled at her the other night. How her mother expected them to get along on camera after everything that had been said was beyond her.

Someone knocked on Gia's apartment's door. Her mother coming to convince her to appear with them on Instagram, no doubt. Gia came slowly to her feet. She'd make her mother squirm a little, Gia decided as she walked to the door. It wasn't fair Carmen hadn't taken her feelings into consideration, but Gia didn't intend to let them push her aside. As many people tuned in for her vegan options as they did for Carmen's and Eva's more traditional Italian fare, and she had no intention of letting her followers down. Besides, the three of them were equal partners in both the restaurant and their latest venture. She had as much at stake as they did, especially now that they'd made the decision to invest in an industrial kitchen and warehouse.

But it wasn't her mother standing on the other side of the door. It was Flynn. He handed her an Americano from Fair Trade, her favorite organic coffee shop on Main Street. "I won't stay long. I promise. I just needed to see you."

She opened the door wider, peeking outside to see if anyone saw him.

"I told you I don't care what anyone says about us."

"You did the other night." Neither of them had been prepared for the backlash they'd received from their families. "I didn't see you rushing over here yesterday either." She closed her eyes. Could she sound any needier? "Sorry. I had a bad day yesterday. I shouldn't take it out on you." She held the door open for him.

He closed it behind him, following her into her studio. She hoped some of those mellow vibes still lingered in the room.

"The girls arrived on my doorstep shortly after I got home from here," he said, taking a seat on the stool in front of her canvas. Nothing had come of his heated promise that night. Neither of them had felt much like making love after their families had gotten through with them.

"It sounds like your day wasn't much better than mine," she said from where she'd curled up on her favorite chair. "How did your girls find out about us anyway? And that fast? Please tell me my sister didn't call them to spread her special brand of cheer."

"No. It was Willow, but she hadn't meant to blurt it out. She'd been talking to August when your mother texted her with the news."

"And August told his sisters?" Flynn's son was his dad's mini-me, an old soul and a sweet boy. At the last few family gatherings, she'd gotten the distinct impression he'd been trying to set her up with his dad, so she was surprised and a little hurt by his reaction to their relationship.

Honestly, it made her wonder if she and Flynn were missing something. But more than that, she wouldn't be the cause of a rift between Flynn and his children. He adored his kids and was an amazing father. It was just a matter of time before he'd come to the conclusion that she wasn't worth ruining his relationship with his kids anyway. Or maybe he already had, she thought, taking in his tired eyes and beard-shadowed jaw. "It's okay. I understand, Flynn."

"Understand what?"

"Why you want to end it with me." The backs of her eyes burned, and she stood up, determined not to cry in front of him. She didn't want him feeling guilty about choosing his kids over her. They'd lost their mother. They were still young, and they needed him.

"How did we go from me telling you I didn't care what anyone says about us to you thinking I'd want to throw away my chance of having a life with you?"

"Flynn, we've only been together a few weeks. I'm not worth throwing away your relationship with your kids."

He stood up, put his coffee on the stool, and then closed the distance between them. He raised a hand as if to touch her but instead shoved them both in the pockets of his jeans. "I know we haven't been together that long, but I feel like I've been waiting years for you, and I'm not about to give up on us just because some members of our families are having a problem with us being together. Besides, Sage is in our corner, and so is August. Between the two of them, they'll talk some sense into the others."

"I'm confused. I thought August was unhappy about us too. You said he was the one who told his sisters."

"He did. He thought they'd be as happy about the news as he was." He smiled. "I can see my son's opinion carries a lot of weight with you."

"I don't really know your daughters. Other than Willow, I mean. I just met them when you brought them for dinner over the Christmas holidays." They seemed like nice girls but definitely daddy's girls now that she thought about it. Flynn clearly doted on them, and unlike their brother, they hadn't been happy sharing his attention with their newfound sister. But Willow, being Willow, had won them over, and now they adored their big sister as much as August did.

"You mean when I brought them to the restaurant because we'd missed the party, and I'd wanted to see you, even if you were at work."

She moved closer, placing a hand on his chest. "You ate a lot at La Dolce Vita over the holidays. I thought you just hated cooking and loved our food."

"It was a little of that and a whole lot of wanting to see you." He took his hands out of his pockets and placed them on her hips. "I wanted to see you yesterday too. I called late afternoon, but you weren't picking up. I came by to check on you. I even risked the wrath of Carmen and ventured into the restaurant looking for you. She was upset. Something about you not appearing on today's Instagram Live segment?"

She told him why she'd been going to bail today and how she felt about Cami being part of their new venture. He stayed quiet and listened, his thumbs stroking her sides in a relaxing up-and-down motion.

She couldn't tell if he thought she was right or wrong, but she'd learned over the last couple of weeks that, while Flynn validated her feelings, he didn't give her advice or try to fix things for her.

"I've decided to go despite my feelings about Cami."

"I'm sure that will make Carmen happy."

"I'm glad one of us will be." She sighed, slipping her arms around his waist. "I was at the lavender farm when you stopped by. I'd turned off my phone so I wouldn't have to listen to another member of my family tell me I'm selfish or I'm jealous or I'm vindictive or just a plain rotten human being."

She felt the rumble of his laughter against her cheek, his right hand moving to her neck, kneading the tension from her muscles.

"Anyway, I painted, or J.R. painted, a mural of Alice in the lavender fields with her cat Max for Sage and Jake. Alice was cremated yesterday, and I knew how difficult it would be for Sage and Jake to say goodbye."

He leaned back. "Wow, your family's right. You're the worst." He kissed the top of her head. "I'm sure Sage and Jake loved it."

"I hope so. I haven't heard from Sage. I left one of my lanterns there so they'd see the mural, but maybe they didn't notice. It's not like they'd know I'm J.R. anyway." Her phone rang with Sage's ringtone. "Speak of the devil." She smiled and moved away from Flynn to answer. "Hey, honey. How are you? Are you and Jake okay?"

"Um, yeah, it's..." Sage trailed off, obviously listening to whatever Jake was saying in the background. Then her daughter murmured *Right* to whatever he said before returning to Gia. "Mom, are you going to be home for a bit?"

"I'm actually heading to your zia's shortly. We're doing an Instagram Live today. Why don't you meet me there? We have a big announcement. Lila is still under the weather, so your sister is taking over the filming." She made a face. "Cami will be there too."

"Uh, I don't know..." Sage trailed off again, only this time she was repeating what Gia had said to Jake. Then she heard

Sage say to him, "Do you think I should do it then? They're all going to be there."

Apparently, Jake thought it was a good idea, because Sage said, "Okay. I'll meet you at Zia Eva's. We'll talk then."

"You don't sound like yourself. Are you sure you don't want to talk to me about whatever this is now?"

"No. This isn't a conversation you have over the phone. I need to talk to you face-to-face."

"Honey, are you . . . are you and Jake engaged?"

"No! Why would you think that?"

"Madonna santa! Are you pregnant? Am I going to be a nonna?"

"Seriously, Mom? If you're going to be a nonna, it has nothing to do with me."

"Willow isn't pregnant, is she?"

Sage groaned. "How did this conversation get so out of control?" Jake said something in the background, and her daughter laughed.

"Did he just say because it involved the Rosettis?"

"Of course he didn't," her daughter said, but Gia could tell by the amusement in Sage's voice that that was exactly what Jake had said.

"You tell him no more pizza from me, and I'll see you at your zia's." She went to end the call.

"Mom, wait!"

"What is it?"

"You know that street artist J.R.?"

"J.R.? I think I've heard of them." She met Flynn's warm, smiling eyes.

"They painted a mural for us, and you're talented, Mom,

but this J.R. is just wow, amazing. The painting is so beautiful and so lifelike, it almost felt like Alice was here with us." Sage sniffed, and Gia pressed a hand to her heart, her eyes filling with tears. "It was exactly what Jake and I needed to come home to. I wish there was a way we could thank them. You wouldn't happen to know who they are, would you?"

For a minute, Gia thought about telling Sage the truth, but she didn't need something else to fight about with her mother, and she was afraid that once everyone knew who she was, it would rob her of the renewed joy she'd gotten from painting.

"I don't, honey. But I can ask around."

"Okay. I'll send you a photo of the mural." They said their goodbyes and then Gia disconnected.

"They loved it, didn't they?"

"They did." Her phone dinged with an incoming text, and she turned the screen to Flynn.

He studied the painting. "I knew you were an incredible artist, but this painting . . . I'm in awe of your talent. I'm in awe of you." He kissed her long and slow and then broke the kiss. She was about to pull his mouth back to hers when he asked, "Exactly how much time do we have before you have to be at your sister's?"

⌐

Gia had been walking on air since making love with Flynn. Buoyed by the happy, contented feeling of being loved by Flynn Monroe, she'd been determined to be her best self at the filming. She was in such a state of bliss that she was immune to the shots Cami lobbed her way, and to comments from Carmen that made Gia feel like the favorite child's hand-maiden. Or so she'd thought. Now she was hanging on to her good intentions by a thread.

Gia placed the two dishes she'd made with her pesto sauce on the island. At her niece Lila's suggestion, they'd begun creating dishes around their signature sauces. Cami didn't have a recipe to share, but she'd introduced her four-cheese sauce. She'd gone over her allotted time introducing herself and her sauce and her partnership with the family at the beginning of the segment. Gia couldn't lay the blame entirely at her sister's feet. Carmen had used so many superlatives introducing her golden child that Gia had begun to think she was making them up.

Then Cami provided the shtick for Carmen as their mother prepared calzones with her marinara sauce, adding an extra ten minutes to her segment. Eva had tried speeding things up, but Cami had insisted they sing "Ti Amo" together while Eva created spicy creamy chicken pasta with her signature sauce. The lyrics made Gia think about Flynn, so she was able to brush off the fact she now had approximately three minutes to share her recipes.

She smiled at the camera. "It was great to read in the comments how many of you tried my pesto shrimp pasta recipe last week and how many of you bought our signature sauces. I hope you know how much we appreciate all your support. It's because of all of you that these products from my mother, my sister, and me have gone national. Grazie, grazie, grazie."

Her mother and sister joined in, sharing their thanks.

Cami nudged Gia out of the way with her hip and, pressing her hands to her chest, beamed at the camera. "And I can't thank you enough for your excitement about the introduction of my four-cheese sauce, Maryann. You too, Sophie, Raeanne, Tina..."

Gia squinted at the comments coming up on the screen, wondering if there was something wrong with her eyesight, because nowhere did she see any comments about Cami's four-cheese sauce from the women her sister had named, or from anyone else for that matter.

Gia glanced at Eva, who was studiously avoiding her gaze. So she wasn't wrong. Cami was making it all up and hogging all the attention for herself.

Stay calm. Think of Flynn and his promise for tonight. Good, that worked, she thought as she gently nudged Cami out of the way. Or at least tried to. Her sister had a freakishly strong core.

Gia smiled, pushing her way in front of Cami and displaying her dishes for the camera. "We're excited for the introduction of Cami's sauce too. Now today I've got recipes for my quinoa pesto salad and pesto flatbread. Both would be perfect to serve—"

Cami's booming laugh cut her off. "You guys! I can't keep up with all your comments. But I promise, on my next—"

The music signaling the end of their segment came on, and Gia pushed Cami out of the way, determined to share her recipes with their audience.

"Do you mind? I'm talking to my fans. The oldest in a family are always the bossiest, aren't they?" Cami said to the camera, rolling her eyes.

And that was when the thread to Gia's good intentions didn't just break, it snapped. "And the youngest are attention-seeking narcissists," she said, and dumped her quinoa pesto salad on her sister's head.

Cami, with quinoa pesto salad dripping down her face, looked at the camera. "I'm sorry you had to witness that, but this is what you'll get when you tune in to my show, real, raw emotion."

Gia turned to her mother and sister, wondering if they were hearing Cami take over their show, but they were both wincing as Cami slid a finger down her face, licked off Gia's salad, and made a face. "And recipes with my four-cheese sauce that will put this one to shame."

Fighting against her mother and Eva's hold, Gia tried to reach her sister, swearing at her in Italian. She managed to get hold of her pesto flatbread and fling it at Cami, who fired a calzone at Gia's head, nailing Eva instead. Eva let go of Gia to wipe sauce from her eyes, and that's when the food fight began in earnest.

"Stop! Stop this right now," Sage said, running into the kitchen and putting herself between Cami and Gia. "This is my fault. I should have told you before you got here. I'm sorry."

Cami lowered a ladle of spicy creamy chicken pasta, and Gia lowered a calzone, staring at her daughter in confusion. "It's not your fault, honey."

"It is, but in my defense, I didn't think there was any way you'd find out my father was in Sunshine Bay before I told you."

Chapter Twenty-One

Jake looped the last of the fairy lights from one tree branch to another above the tables they'd set out in the backyard. According to Sage, the fairy lights were more for the aesthetic than for actual light. It seemed a very un-Sage-like thing to say or even think, but she'd been investigating natural methods to level out emotions in stressful situations. Jake voted for alcohol and lots of it, but Sage had vetoed his suggestion.

He glanced to where she was placing battery-operated lanterns on the tables in case her family didn't finish up the body scrubs, body butters, and massage oils before it got dark. The three products were apparently the farm's most popular items.

Jake climbed down from the ladder and was rewarded with a kiss on his cheek when he joined Sage at the table. "Thanks for all your help."

"We're a team, remember," he said, then decided he had to give it one last try. "Are you sure this is a good idea? There's still time to cancel, you know."

"Why would I cancel? We need the products, and my

family needs to figure out how we're going to deal with my fath—I mean Aaron."

His chest tightened at her attempt to cover her slip. No matter how much Sage denied it, she wanted to meet her father, and that worried him. There was no excuse for Aaron Abbott not having contacted his daughter in all those years. He was a deadbeat, and Sage deserved so much better. Jake didn't want her hurt but knew he couldn't protect her. She'd have to find out for herself.

"You know your family better than I do, sweetheart, but less than twenty-four hours ago, your mother and aunt were going at it on Instagram Live. It might be better to do it Sunday like you'd originally planned."

"Yes, but you said that in your experience, Aaron would probably contact us within the next twenty-four to forty-eight hours." She put her hands on her hips. "Why are you looking at me like that?"

"Because you actually listened to me—and you think I'm right. Are you surprised I looked shocked?"

He was shocked, just not for the reason he'd given her. He was shocked by the raw hope in her voice, the naked desire on her face. Her need to meet her father was even stronger than he'd first suspected.

He shouldn't be surprised, though. Look how he'd reacted when his own father had called him from prison. After years of abuse, he'd still held out hope that they might have a healthy father-and-son relationship.

"Oh, okay. It didn't look like a shocked expression to me, but whatever. You've proven you're an excellent investigator. I have no reason to doubt you." She tapped her finger on his lips.

"And don't think I missed the lip twitch when you mentioned my mom and aunt going at it on Instagram. You watched it again when I went to the market, didn't you?"

He wrapped his finger around hers and brought it to his lips, giving it a teasing nip before kissing it. "I did, and I gotta say, I don't blame your mom. But I kind of saw Cami's side too."

She crossed her arms over her chest, distracting him. She wore one of his white shirts tied at her waist and a pair of worn denim shorts with her sneakers. She looked gorgeous and relaxed. These past few days away from work had done her a world of good. He only hoped that between him and her family, they could get her to stay the entire six weeks. He didn't fool himself into thinking he could convince her to resign from Forbes, Poole, and Russell.

"What are you talking about? I watched it too, remember?"

"Then you heard your mom thank the audience on behalf of her, Carmen, and Eva. She left out Cami, and I think your aunt's feelings were hurt."

"Cami had no part in La Dolce Vita or the new product line."

"Sweetheart, she grew up at the restaurant the same as your mom and aunt. She worked there too, from what I've heard." He shrugged. "I could be completely off base, but she might feel like, if it weren't for your mom, she would have been part of their product line from the beginning. They started it nine months ago, and Cami was back in their lives by then, wasn't she? And it's not like your mom hasn't let her know in myriad ways that she wishes she'd stayed in LA."

"You're very annoying, you know."

He drew her into his arms and nuzzled her neck. "That's not what you told me this morning or last night. I think you said—"

She covered his mouth with her palm. "I don't need you repeating what I said in the heat of the moment in the cold light of day."

"It's pretty cute when you act like a prude." He teased her because she was far from a prude in bed.

"Behave," she murmured, even while she tilted her neck to the side to give him better access.

At the hitch in her breath, he smiled against her warm, fragrant skin. "The body butter smells good on you." He nipped her neck. "And it felt really good rubbing it on you after your shower. We should try the massage oil tonight."

"It's your turn tonight, remember?"

"I definitely vote for the massage oil then." He leaned back. "You know, if you cancel your family, we could get started on that right away."

She smiled up at him. "Too late. I hear a car coming up the road."

He angled his head. She was right. He couldn't believe he'd missed it. It was second nature for him to be attuned to his surroundings. Not just because he'd been special forces. When you were raised by abusive parents, you were always on alert. Maybe his body and mind sensed he no longer needed to be hypervigilant. Or maybe Carmen was right, and there was something magical about this place.

"Let's hope the lavender puts everyone in a relaxed state of mind."

"It would take a miracle for my..." She looked around.

"Jake, Alice's celebration, it has to be here, not at the Smoke Shack or the beach. I don't know why I didn't think of it before."

"Because you don't think of this as Alice's place. You never saw her here. I didn't either."

"It didn't really feel like this was her place. I honestly didn't understand why she'd bought the farm. But now, maybe because of the mural, I can. I wonder if my mom knew that we needed a piece of Alice here."

Sage was talking about the farm as if they were keeping it. It's what he wanted. He'd come to believe Alice wanted it too. The pieces had started falling into place the other day. He just hadn't been sure Sage was ready to hear it. But maybe she was. "You remember when we were trying to figure out why Alice bought the farm, and I said she never did anything without a reason?"

She nodded, her gaze roaming his face. "You've figured out the reason?"

"Not completely, but we'll talk about it later," he said as he took in the number of cars pulling into the driveway. "Just how many people did you invite? Because that looks like way more than your immediate family."

"I invited the Monroe family too. All of them, including Flynn's daughters."

"You invited Flynn?"

She winced, probably at his *are you insane?* expression. "August thought it was a good idea. So did Amos. Willow's friends, the Beaches, are coming too. More hands make lighter work or whatever the saying is." She frowned when he started walking away. "Jake, where are you going? We're partners, remember? You can't leave me alone with all of them," she called after him.

"I won't be long."

"Where are you going?"

"To get alcohol. And lots of it."

⌒

Two hours later, Jake realized the alcohol had been a bad idea. He was hiding a case of wine under the sink when Flynn walked into the farmhouse, carrying several empty bottles. "If it were me, I wouldn't be replacing these, but that's just my opinion."

"And one I support wholeheartedly. Thanks." He took the bottles from Flynn. "I don't know what I was thinking."

Flynn grinned. "I have a fairly good idea what you were thinking. The problem is that the Rosetti women can handle their wine and liquor better than most people I know, including myself. My daughters and the Beaches, not so much."

"But they sure know their body products," Jake said, smiling at the memory of Sage's expression when the women took over from her. She'd looked like she wanted to kiss them. "I think we have enough stock to get us through the season."

"I wouldn't count on it. As fast as the Beaches were making it, they were selling it. Sage just confiscated their phones. You might have ten days' worth of product at most." Flynn looked around the kitchen and living room and spotted Max on the couch. "Gia captured his likeness perfectly—" He swore under his breath. "Pretend you didn't hear that."

"Hear what?"

Flynn nodded. "You'd already guessed, didn't you? Does Sage know?"

"Yeah, but neither of us will say anything to anyone, including Gia. We figure she has her reasons for staying anonymous."

"She does." He smiled, pride lighting up his eyes. "The mural is incredible, isn't it? It looks just like Alice."

"You knew Alice?"

"She was a friend of my dad's. I didn't know her well, but in the last couple of months, we'd spoken quite often. We met for dinner when I was home for Easter to discuss the project. It's a shame she wasn't able to see it through to fruition. It was a great idea and would have helped a lot of people."

"What was the project?"

Flynn frowned. "She didn't talk to you and Sage about it?"

He'd been right. Alice did have a plan that involved them and the farm. "No, but I'm guessing it involved abused women and their children."

"It did. Alice wanted to build a shelter here on the farm. Her passion for the project was contagious."

"She wanted you to design the house?"

He nodded. "I had planned on showing her the preliminary drawings when I came home in May, and then Willow called me about joining the search party for her. It was surreal and incredibly sad. Again, I'm very sorry for your and Sage's loss."

"Appreciate it. Would you mind not sharing this with Sage or Gia? I'd like to tell Sage myself."

"I didn't think to talk about it to anyone after Alice had passed. I figured the project ended with her."

"Maybe. Maybe not. I'll let you know in the next couple of days." He frowned at the sound of upraised voices, sighing as he headed for the door. "I guess it was too much to hope that seating Cami and Gia as far apart as possible would keep the peace for the night."

The two women had surprisingly been on their best behavior when they'd arrived. Jake had a feeling they were both embarrassed that their fight had gone viral on social media. They were each pretending the other didn't exist, and the family had broken into two camps. Eva and her husband were playing Switzerland, and so were Willow's friends, sitting at a table between Cami's and Gia's.

There was also the fact that Sage had laid down the law, and even he had to admit she could be intimidating. Albeit in a sexy kind of way, he thought with a smile.

But his smile disappeared as soon as he opened the screen door. "What the hell do you think you're doing here?" he snapped at Aaron Abbott, walking to where the older man and Sage stood facing each other. He stepped between father and daughter.

He felt the light pressure of Sage's hand on his back. "It's okay. Let him finish. I want to hear what he has to say."

Flynn gave Jake a reassuring nod—he'd have his back if he needed him—and then he walked to Gia, who looked shell-shocked.

Jake crossed his arms. "Talk."

Behind him, Sage blew out a frustrated breath and moved around him. "Aaron, we can talk inside."

"I'd like that, thanks." His leaf-green gaze moved to Jake. Sage had his eyes and hair color, but that's where the similarities ended. "I have no intention of hurting Sage. Ever since I learned I had a daughter"—his gaze searched out Gia—"and a wife, I moved heaven and earth to find them."

"What do you mean, you learned about us?" Sage asked.

"Sage," Jake warned, positive nothing out of this man's mouth was the truth. He'd bet the farm that Aaron Abbott was a con man, and Jake had experience when it came to con men.

"If the reporter hadn't found me, I never would have known about either of you. I suffered a traumatic brain injury back in '95. I've been living in Costa Rica ever since. As I understand it, I'd been doing a photoshoot there when I fell."

Jake scoffed. "Nice story. I think I watched it on Lifetime last week."

"Jake!"

"Come on, Sage. You're smarter than this. Don't let him play you."

Gia had joined them with Flynn at her back. Jake glanced at him. Flynn didn't buy what this guy was selling any more than he did.

"Gia, baby, I don't know what to say. When the reporter told me who I was, and relayed everything that had happened from the book your sister's written—" His voice broke, and he cleared his throat. "It was like he was talking about someone else. Then slowly, my memory came back. I don't understand why I would have left you..." His gaze moved to Cami, and his expression hardened. "For her."

It was the first time Jake bought what he was selling. Aaron Abbott did not like Cami.

"I loved you, babe. You've gotta believe me. I wouldn't have left you." As if he sensed Gia wasn't buying his story, he turned his attention on his daughter. "I never would have walked out the door that day if I had known I'd go almost twenty-nine years without having my daughter in my life. Please, give me a chance to make it up to you, Sage."

Jake silently pleaded for her to look at him, but she had eyes only for her father. He knew before she even said the words that she'd give Aaron Abbott a second chance. Jake met the man's gaze, a silent warning in his own. He didn't miss the glint in Abbott's eyes. It was as if he was issuing a silent challenge.

Back off or he'd make sure Jake lost Sage.

Chapter Twenty-Two

It was surreal standing with the man who Sage had spent her entire life believing had abandoned her only to discover it hadn't been intentional. He hadn't left them because he hadn't loved them enough. He hadn't left them because she'd done something wrong.

It didn't matter that she was thirty and well aware that a child blaming herself was a common psychological effect of divorce. Somehow the belief that it was her fault her father had left had lingered in her subconscious, feeding on the lies she'd told herself. She could finally let it go.

It hadn't been anyone's fault—not hers, his, or her mother's. Sage glanced at Cami. Did her aunt bear some responsibility, as her father seemed to imply? As if she knew what Sage was thinking, Cami's eyes widened, and she slowly shook her head.

Willow, who sat at Cami's side, frowned but then seemed to understand what was going on and made a disbelieving sound. Despite Willow's fiancé trying to convince her to stay out of it, she jumped to her feet, said something to Cami, and then the two of them were headed her way. Make that four, Sage thought, when her grandmother and Aunt Eva got up to follow them.

She wasn't the only one who had noticed. Behind her, Jake swore softly, and her mother groaned. In front of her, Aaron moved nervously from one foot to the other, fidgeting with the collar of his colorful dress shirt.

Sage didn't blame him. Finding yourself in the crosshairs of one Rosetti was bad enough; four of them was terrifying. "Why don't we talk tomorrow?" Sage suggested.

"Yeah, that'd be good." He leaned toward her, then leaned back, raised an arm, then a hand, unsure, it seemed, whether he should kiss her or hug her or shake her hand.

She sympathized with his dilemma. "I'll walk you to your car." She moved to his side, noting Jake taking a step toward her. "Alone," she said, unhappy with how he'd acted toward her father.

Jake was bossy and protective. She didn't need bossy and protective. She needed supportive and understanding.

"I'll join you," her mother said, giving Sage a look that said she wouldn't take no for an answer. Her mother also sent a *back off* look to her own intimidating six-foot-four male but softened it with a smile.

Sage's father caught the exchange and didn't look pleased. Sage ignored the ping of a warning alert going off inside her. It was an understandable reaction from a man who was obviously still very much in love with his wife.

"Your boyfriend?" he asked her mother.

"Yes, it is," Gia said, glancing back at Flynn.

Sage wondered how she felt about him comforting Cami. Apparently, her father wondered the same thing. "You sure?

He looks pretty chummy with your sister." His brow furrowed, and he stopped walking, reaching for Gia's arm. "Willow, your sister's kid—"

"Willow is my sister's biological child, but she is my daughter. What about her?"

"She called that guy *Dad*." He jerked his thumb in Flynn's direction. "Is he your boyfriend or your husband?"

"My boyfriend, but my love life is none of your business, Aaron. You gave up a right to have a say in it a long time ago. In fact, I gave you too much say over me when were together. So why don't you tell me why you're really here?"

Sage filed away the first hint she'd ever had that all hadn't been right in her parents' marriage. It was something they needed to talk about.

Aaron wasn't listening to her mother. His gaze and mind were back with Flynn and Cami and Willow, and Sage knew the moment he'd put it together. He laughed. "Are you shitting me right now? You're dating your sister's ex and your daughter's father? Holy shit, Gia, what the hell are you thinking?" He shook his head. "It's like history repeating itself. You really are a glutton for punishment. I—"

Sage held up her hand. "Enough. You do not get to come to my home and speak to my mother like that." She rubbed Gia's arm. "I've got this, Mom."

"I, uh, I'm sorry. I was out of line." He lifted a shoulder. "It's just, you know, hard seeing you with another man."

"It was hard seeing you fawning all over my sister. It was really hard when you followed her to LA and left me with two babies and no income, but that's in the past, and honestly, I should probably thank you for leaving us. We have a great life, and I don't need you coming here and stirring things up. So I'll repeat, what are you doing here?"

Sage smiled, relieved to see her mother's fiery spirit emerge. It didn't show itself often, but when it did, Sage would bet on her mom every time.

"You sure you've got a great life? I mean, I'm not one to judge, but I caught you and your sister going at it on Instagram. Didn't look like the happy little family you're pretending to be, especially with her cozying up to your boyfriend." He made a face and then held up a hand. "Ignore me. I haven't had my memory back for long. It's been a lot. I don't want to make trouble. I really don't. I understand why you don't want anything to do with me, Gia. I'm sorry for the past. Sorry for how much I hurt you. I'd just like to spend some time with my daughter." He glanced at Sage. "If you'd like to spend some time with me."

She didn't need her mother's permission, but she wouldn't do anything to make things worse for her. "Mom?"

"It's up to you, honey." She gave Sage a hug and whispered in her ear, "I know how much you've wanted to meet your father, but for me, keep your guard up. Don't let him in too quick." She stepped away from Sage, reaching for her hand and giving it a squeeze. "I love you."

"I love you too, Mom." She returned her hand squeeze. "You don't have to worry about me. I'm very good at my job," she said, reminding her mom that she dealt with men who used, abused, and manipulated women all the time. There wasn't anything her father could pull on Sage that she hadn't seen pulled a hundred times before.

Her mother patted Sage's cheek, her eyes sad. "It's different when it's your father." She gave Aaron a warning glare before walking away.

"It looks like I've got a way to go before your mother forgives me."

"Don't waste your time. Rosettis rarely forgive, and they never forget. My mom's moved on. You should too."

He nodded, glancing at her as they walked side by side. "You're tough, a hard-ass like your grandmother. She always hated me, you know."

"I know." He looked taken aback, and she shrugged. "What did you expect? I'm thirty years old. I don't play games, and I don't like them either. So why are you really here? And please, don't say it's because of me. I saw the way you looked at my mother."

"You're a straight shooter. I respect that. And you're right, I'm still in love with your mother." He held her gaze. "I'm dying, Sage. I want to make amends before I do."

⌣

"I can't believe you fell for that. It's the oldest con in the book," Jake said, placing the squat jars of body butter in a box.

"I didn't fall for anything, and be careful with the jars." She glanced at her family. Everyone had left but her mother, sister, aunts, and grandmother, who were boxing up product too. "And would you mind keeping it down?"

"You gave him your car!"

Her family stopped what they were doing to stare at her.

She scowled at Jake. "What part of *keep it down* didn't you understand?"

"Honey, you gave him your car?" her mother asked.

"Okay, guys. Everyone is upset, but come on, I don't care if he is her father, Sage is too smart to fall for a con. If she gave him her car, she had her reasons."

"Thanks, Will." She sent her sister a grateful smile. She appreciated her support. Her sister was always there for her, but lately it hadn't felt that way. She was relieved they were back to normal.

"Look, I know you're worried about me, but Willow's right. Aaron didn't manipulate me," she said as she placed a jar of lavender oil in the box, thinking back to how she'd ended up handing over the keys of her car to a man she didn't know and wondering if maybe he had played on her sympathies. Not that she'd admit that to her family...or Jake. "You saw his rental. It's a piece of crap and doesn't have air-conditioning. But more to the point, it wouldn't start."

"Was that before or after he checked under the hood?" Jake asked.

Dammit, she hadn't thought about that. Aaron said he'd been having issues with the starter and checked under the hood before he even tried starting the car. "You're a very suspicious person, you know."

"I am, and you know why I am."

She sat down and rubbed her face. "I'm tired. I don't want to do this now." She lowered her hands. "I don't ask you guys for much, but it's been a lot with losing Alice, and the stuff with the firm, and then the burnout, and now with my father showing up out of the blue."

Her mother set her box on the table and walked over to Sage, wrapping her arms around her neck from behind. "It's been too much. Tell us what you need from us."

Her sister walked over, pulling out the chair beside her. "Anything you need from us, you've got."

"Willow is right," Carmen said, sitting on the chair on the other side of Sage. "Whatever you need, cara. You only have to ask." She widened her eyes at Eva and Cami, who joined them.

Sage glanced at Jake, who continued packing the product away. He met her gaze, his eyes glinting with amusement. He saw through her, the ass.

"We're here for you, Sage. Always," her aunt Eva said, before glancing at Cami, who'd stayed conspicuously silent.

"Camilla?" Carmen said, an irritated snap in her voice.

"Of course, I'm here for Sage too." She wrung her hands. "I'm worried, that's all. You don't know Aaron like I do. I lived with him."

"Madonna santa! I was married to the man. You don't know him any better than I do, Cami," Gia said.

"You married him. That's the point, Gia. You never saw what I did. I tried to warn you, and you brushed me off."

Carmen raised a shoulder. "Your sister, she might be right. I told you he was bad news, and you ignored me too."

Sage felt her mother pulling away and covered her hands with hers. "This is what I'm talking about. I can't take this right now. I need you guys to get along. I don't care if you have to fake it either." She looked at Cami. "I saw your face. I know you feel guilty about Aaron being here. But—"

"She should. He—"

"Mom, he's here. And I think you and Cami are tied for who doesn't want him to be. But since he is, you have to present a united front. You can't let him drive a wedge between us."

Her mother leaned forward to get a better look at Sage. "You think he's faking?"

"Honestly, I have no idea if he's dying or if he wants to make amends or to build a relationship with me. There could be a part of him that actually wants to do both even if he's not dying. But I've seen too many men in court and across the mediation table not to recognize that he's angry. I just don't know if he's seeking revenge or reparation."

She frowned at Jake, who was staring at her. She mouthed, *What?*

You're hot, he mouthed back and then nodded at her family with a pointed glance at the massage oil in his hand.

Willow laughed. "I think he wants you to get rid of us."

⌒

"I don't believe you," Sage said as she waved goodbye to her family.

"What's not to believe? It's not like I haven't told you you're hot, and smart, and gorgeous, and I haven't hidden the fact that I wanted to pick up where we left off this morning. It's not as if we could do that with your family hanging out here. Besides, as you pointed out to them, you have a lot on your plate. You need your rest."

"You know exactly what I meant, and it wasn't any of that." She walked over to the table and picked up a box.

He took it out of her hands and put it on the table. "Leave it. I'll put everything away later. I want to show you something." He held out his hand.

She put hers in his. "I don't think I can take any more surprises tonight, Jake."

"I have a feeling you're going to hear about this sooner or later, so I want you to hear it from me. It's nothing bad," he said, tightening his grip on her hand. "Trust me."

"I do. I'm just tired." She rested her head on his shoulder. "And confused."

He let go of her hand and put his arm around her. "I'm sorry if I made it harder on you. I was just worried you were too close to the situation, too emotionally involved to see through Abbott. But you're smart and one hell of a good divorce attorney, so I should have known you'd see through him if he tried anything."

She sighed. "The thing is, you were right about the car. He could have played with the wires, and I wouldn't have known."

"Don't worry, I'll check his rental out later and see if he was on the up-and-up. But you were right, Sage. Even if he's got a hidden agenda, it doesn't mean that he doesn't want you in his life. He'd be an idiot not to."

"Don't be sweet. Not tonight. I'm too emotional."

His gaze roamed her face. "You're right." He stepped back and once again took her hand. "Let's go back to the house. We can do this another day."

"Really? You think I'm going to be able to let that go?" She gestured to the one-track road he'd been leading her toward. "Let's go. Show me what you want me to see." She held back. "Wait. You're not taking me to see the stone memorial you made for Alice, are you?"

"No," he said slowly.

"Okay, that wasn't a hard no." She stopped walking and crossed her arms. "Tell me what we're doing out here. At night. In the woods." A bird swooped past them, and she ducked. "I didn't think birds were out this late. Owls are, though, right? It must have been an owl." She narrowed her eyes at him. "Why are you smiling at me like that?"

"It's cute the way you're trying to convince yourself that you saw an owl and not a bat."

"That was a bat?" she asked, from where she crouched on the road with her hands over her head.

"No. I'm pretty sure it was an owl."

"Jake!"

He fit his hands under her arms and lifted her to her feet. Then he drew her close, wrapping her in his arms. "With some help from Flynn, I've figured out why Alice bought the farm."

She tipped her head back. "Flynn knew Alice?"

"He did, and I'll get to that in a sec." He rested his chin on the top of her head. "Alice saw me in Kendra. She comes from an abusive home, and Alice took her under her wing just over a year ago, and you..." He leaned back to look down at her. "Alice saw herself in you. The way you defend women who suffer from abuse and neglect. The work you do pro bono at the shelter. It's why she left the farm to us, and why she asked Flynn to build a home for abused women and children here. She wanted us to continue her work but on a bigger scale. She didn't just want me to take over her legal practice; she wanted us to be partners in all of this."

He wanted it too. She could see it on his face, and she closed her eyes, a tear sliding down her cheek. The last thing she wanted was to disappoint him, or Alice. But her life, her position at the firm...She wouldn't give up her dreams to make someone else happy. She knew all too well how that story ended.

"It's okay." He dried her tears with the backs of his knuckles.

"I'm sorry. I wish——"

He placed a finger on her lips. "Don't apologize. I don't expect you to give up your dreams to make Alice's come true."

She groaned. "Jake!"

"I'm sorry, that came out wrong. But you know Alice would feel the same."

"Obviously not, Jake. You're right. It's exactly what she wanted. You and me doing this together." She gestured to the woods, the pond, and the lavender fields. "It makes so much more sense why she bought the farm now. It would be the perfect place for both women and children to recover and thrive." She searched his face. "Tell me the truth. You want to do it, don't you?"

He stepped back and looked around, and then he nodded. "Yeah, I do. And if you give me some time, I'll buy you out of the farm and the practice." He moved his head from side to side. "Even with my share of the house on Ocean View Drive, it might take me a while to pay you back."

"That's okay. It's not like I need the money." She winced. "I didn't mean that the way it sounded."

"You don't have to be embarrassed that you make good money, Sage. Not with me."

"I know, but it's not just about my paycheck. I lead a simple life. I don't go out, and I have a small apartment and I'm rarely there, so I just bank my money." She narrowed her eyes at him.

"You don't have to look at me like that is the saddest thing you've ever heard."

"Not the saddest thing, but it ranks pretty high."

"You're lucky it's how I live, mister. Otherwise, I wouldn't be able to say, 'Go for it, Jake.' I'll back you a hundred percent."

"Seriously?"

She nodded. "I mean, I can't foot the entire bill by myself. We'll work out a repayment schedule for your portion, but I'll be your silent partner." She placed her hand on his chest. "I know you're disappointed, but I promise, I'll be there for you. I'll be as involved as I can be." She smiled. "Now show me where we're going to build Alice's House."

He lifted her up and spun her around under the moonlit sky, the wind whispering through the trees, his eyes shiny with emotion. He opened his mouth, and she thought that he might tell her he loved her, and she didn't want him to mistake his gratitude for love and regret the words later. So she kissed him instead.

Chapter Twenty-Three

Gia didn't have to worry about Aaron messing with their daughter's head. Sage was too smart to let any man mistreat her, including her own father. Gia wished she didn't have to be, wished for Sage's sake that Aaron really did want a relationship with her. But Aaron wasn't Flynn. He'd never been kind and thoughtful. He'd been broken promises and broken dreams. She'd been so stupid to fall for his lies. She couldn't even blame it on being young and foolish.

Cami and her mother were wrong. Gia hadn't ignored their warnings. They'd just come too late. By then, Gia had been in too deep. She'd been pregnant with Sage when she'd married Aaron. She'd wanted so badly for her daughter to have a father, a so-called normal life, that she'd sacrificed her own happiness for her sweet, innocent child. She wished she could go back in time and have a talk with her younger self.

Since that was impossible, she'd been having words with her current self. She'd tried not to let Aaron get to her, but he had. His words kept playing over in her head.

You're dating your sister's ex and your daughter's father? Holy shit, Gia, what the hell are you thinking? It's like history repeating itself. You really are a glutton for punishment.

"Gia, where's your head at today?" her mother yelled, and Gia dropped the wooden spoon, sauce splattering everywhere.

"Madonna santa, Ma! You don't come up behind someone and yell like that." She sniffed the air. Crap. She'd burned the sauce.

Her mother elbowed her aside. "Go home or go see Flynn. Your mind has been somewhere else all day."

Flynn had called several times and left two messages. With Aaron's words playing over in her head, Gia hadn't been able to bring herself to call him back. Sage had worried that Aaron would drive a wedge in her family's relationships, but Gia was worried the relationship he'd driven a wedge between was hers and Flynn's.

"I'll be okay, Ma. We're full tonight, and Eva took it off to stay with Lila."

"You don't think it's anything serious, do you?" her mother asked in Italian, cognizant of the ears in the kitchen.

"Eva would tell us if it was. Lila's always had a sensitive stomach. It's probably why she's having a hard time shaking the flu," Gia responded in Italian.

They worked in companionable silence in the kitchen, and then Gia worked her section of the restaurant and her sister's. It was busy and Gia was run off her feet, but she loved nights like this. Their customers were loyal and vocal in their appreciation of their food. A handful of them brought up the food fight with Cami on Instagram Live, poking lighthearted fun at Gia. She supposed it didn't bother her because they were on her side and not her sister's.

"I agree," said a familiar voice behind her, and she turned to see Aaron being seated in her section.

She opened her mouth to ask him to leave but then closed it. If she made a big deal about him being here, he'd assume it was because she still cared enough to have feelings for him, good, bad, or indifferent.

"Aaron." She nodded, handing him a menu, searching for any sign he was ill. He'd always been a handsome man, and twenty-nine years hadn't changed that. He had some silver at his temples, but it looked distinguished rather than aging him. Instead of the pallid skin tone of a man at death's door, he had a healthy golden glow. She supposed it was plausible his golden glow was simply a result of living in Costa Rica. "You look remarkably well for someone who is supposedly dying."

Gia wanted to slap herself. That was a horrible, vindictive thing to say. She didn't know what had come over her. It didn't even matter that Aaron deserved it after how he'd treated her and his daughter. She was better than that.

He grinned. "Our daughter comes by her straight talk honestly."

"She's more empathetic than her mother." Gia couldn't help it; she laughed. "She isn't empathetic at all, but still, she wouldn't have said something like that. I'm sorry, Aaron. I didn't mean to make light of your illness."

"I forgot how beautiful you are when you laugh," he said before waving aside her apology. "I deserved it and then some after the way I treated you." He looked around the restaurant. "Place looks great. You're doing well. Big deal your product line going national."

Gia's heart began racing as she considered where he might

be going with this. Sage had mentioned reparation. Was that
why he was here? But how could he demand reparation from
her? He'd abandoned them, left them high and dry. *Cami.* If
he wanted money, he'd go after her sister.

"I'm happy for you, Gia. I really am."

"Thank you." She gave him a faint smile. "Now, what can
I get you?"

He opened the menu and ducked behind it. Gia looked over
her shoulder. Her mother stood outside the kitchen, slapping
her palm with a wooden mallet. Gia rolled her eyes, yelling in
Italian, "Get back in the kitchen, you crazy old lady."

Her mother laughed, and half the restaurant turned to look
her way. Aaron said, "That is a scary fricking laugh. Tell me
the truth, should I leave? She's not going to poison me, is she?
I don't have a lot of time left, and I'd like to get to know my
daughter."

"I'll prepare your order myself, Aaron," she said, feeling
sorry for him despite herself, and for Sage too. She didn't need
to lose someone else so soon after losing Alice. Sometimes life
could be unbearably cruel.

⌢

Aaron leaned back in his chair after finishing his meal. "That
was great, Gia. Really great."

He'd ordered her pesto quinoa salad and flatbread. She
couldn't help but notice he'd practically licked his plate clean.

"I'm glad you enjoyed it. Can I get you anything for dessert?"

"Yeah, yeah, that's a good idea. What was that thing you used
to make for me? It had berries and lemon. Semi-something."

"A lemon semifreddo with berries. I'll get you a piece. And coffee?"

"Sure. Sounds great. Appreciate it. I haven't eaten like this since I was married to you." He patted his stomach. "I've missed your cooking."

She walked into the kitchen, and her mother looked at her. Gia held up her hand. "Don't say it. I'm just trying to keep the peace for my daughter's sake."

"He doesn't look sick to me, but Sage, she's a smart girl. We don't have to worry about her," her mother said in Italian. Then she picked up her favorite butcher knife. "But if he hurts her, I'm gonna whack him."

Gia rolled her eyes. "Have you and Bruno been watching *Goodfellas* again?"

After serving Aaron his dessert and coffee, Gia waited on the rest of her tables. They had another rush, and she got so busy she didn't realize Aaron was still there until she sat a table of four beside him. She got them their drinks orders and then approached his table.

"Anything else I can get for you?" she asked.

He startled, looked up from his phone before setting it screen-side down on the table. "No. I'm going to head out. Thanks for everything, Gia. I'm sorry how I acted last night at the farm. I shouldn't have said what I did. But I was being protective of you. Your sister never deserved your loyalty. It's obvious she hasn't changed. Always has to be the center of attention." He stood up. "I'm thinking of getting an injunction against the book. The stuff she wrote about me is all lies. She's slandering my name. And Gia, pardon my French, but she makes you look like an idiot."

"You read the book?"

"I did." He handed her a card. "My lawyer's number. They'll send you the pages the reporter showed me." He turned the card over. "My number in case you want to talk. You should think about joining my suit. You don't want any bad publicity before your big launch."

After he left, Gia couldn't get Aaron's comments about her sister and her book out of her head. She didn't need him to tell her she'd come across as an idiot. She already knew that. She'd said as much to her mother and sister, but they'd downplayed her fears. Aaron was right, though. They didn't want anything to take away from the national launch of their product line, especially with the cost of the new industrial kitchen and warehouse.

She considered talking to her mother and Eva about it but vetoed the idea almost immediately. Why would this time be any different from the last forty-five times she'd broached the subject this year? Talking to Flynn was her best option.

He was fair and honest, and he cared about her. He'd see things from her perspective...and Cami's, which she supposed was for the best. Maybe it was time he thought about himself too. He'd been a teenager and unaware that Cami was pregnant, but Gia didn't think he'd come out looking like a choirboy, and he also had a reputation to protect. Unless Cami took some creative license with his involvement in her past. Gia wouldn't put it past her sister to make Flynn look good. Just like she didn't put it past Cami to make Gia look worse.

She closed up the restaurant, sending her mother upstairs to bed, and then called Flynn. Her call went to voice mail. She glanced at the time on her phone. It was just going on ten. She debated driving over to see him. He'd probably be happy she did. He'd been concerned about her last night. Besides that, it had been obvious his girls were still holding a grudge. They'd barely said two words to her. She didn't want to know what they thought about the arrival of her estranged husband. They probably hoped Gia and Aaron got back together. She wondered if the thought had crossed Flynn's mind. If nothing else, she needed to see him to put his mind at ease where her feelings for Aaron were concerned.

She didn't bother changing out of her skirt and blouse and put several slices of lemon ricotta cake into a box for Flynn and his dad. She could eat a piece too. She'd only had time to wolf down some salad on the fly. She set the alarm, locked the restaurant door, and then headed for her car. She'd ask Flynn if he wanted to have dessert outside. It was a beautiful night, warm with a light breeze.

She rolled down her windows and turned up Lizzo's "Pink" from the *Barbie* movie. She still hadn't seen it and thought it would be a great pick for a family movie night. The girls in the family, at least. She was startled to realize that, up until the last couple of years, other than Bruno, there had only been girls in the family. *Me and the girls against the world* had been a common refrain when they were growing up. This was better, she thought, thinking about Willow and Noah, Sage and Jake. Sage could deny it all she wanted, but she and Jake were in love.

Gia hadn't missed the little looks the couple exchanged, shoulder brushes when they walked past each other, finger touches, and secret smiles. If anyone had been watching her with Flynn last night, she suspected they would have seen the same. With his girls there and her sister, Gia had been careful not to rub their noses in their relationship.

She was glad she'd decided to go see him instead of talking to him on the phone. It was ridiculous, but she missed him, and they'd only been apart for twenty-four hours. She pulled in beside Flynn's beast of an SUV and noticed Cami's car parked in front of it. She frowned, wondering what her sister was doing here.

She'd moved in with Willow and Noah after she'd learned Gia and Flynn were together and before they'd found out Aaron was their stalker. Gia paused with a hand on the car door handle, wondering exactly how long he'd been stalking them and why. It's something she planned to bring up with Sage and Jake. After Jake's reaction to Aaron last night, she wouldn't put it past him to investigate the man. She'd feel better if he did. She doubted Sage would feel the same, though.

Gia got out of the car and walked up to the side door. She was about to knock when she heard her sister's voice. It sounded like Cami was upset. Gia left the boxed cake on the stairs and walked along the side of the house, past Amos's garden. She smiled at the lone daylily. She had fond memories of the night in Liz's garden, she thought as she rounded the house. Only to freeze at the sight of her sister and Flynn kissing on the dock. The couple were illuminated in the moonlight. They looked beautiful together, just like she'd known they would.

A sob worked its way up her throat, and she pressed her palm to her mouth, spinning on her heel. She didn't know why but she stopped and raised her phone, taking a picture of the couple on the dock. Maybe as a reminder in case she ever had second thoughts. She ran to her car, slid behind the wheel, and closed the door quietly behind her. She wouldn't let them know what she had witnessed. They wouldn't know they'd made a fool of her. They wouldn't know the sight of them together had broken her heart. No one would.

She pulled out of the driveway and headed home. She parked in her spot at La Dolce Vita, wiping her eyes as she got out of her car and closed the door. Then she breathed in the sea air, letting the rhythmic sound of the waves wash over her.

"Aaron, it's me." She repeated the sentence until she was positive that he wouldn't pick up on the emotion in her voice and then punched his number into her phone. He picked up on the first ring.

"Let your lawyer know I'm all in. They can file a petition for an emergency injunction on my behalf too."

Gia hung up from Aaron and got back into her car. She had no idea where she was going. She just knew she couldn't be here when her mother and Eva found out what she had done.

Chapter Twenty-Four

A week, Mom. I had no idea where you were for a week," her daughter said with a pinched look on her face and Max the cat cuddled to her chest.

Gia was beginning to think stopping at the lavender farm on her way home hadn't been such a great idea. "But you did know where I was, honey," she pointed out gently, wondering what had happened to her daughter. This wasn't the woman she knew and loved. Sage was acting like a petulant teenager, and she hadn't even been petulant back then.

Sage dabbed at her eyes with a tissue while nuzzling the cat in her arms. "You're such a sweet boy. You knew Mommy needed some extra love, didn't you?"

Gia looked around the living room for a camera, positive she was being pranked. She didn't find one, though. "Honey, is everything all right?"

"All right? How can it be all right? You were gone for an entire week! And all we got was some cryptic text about you needing time alone and that you were staying at a hotel in Boston. Really, Mom? You don't think you need to call us or send us daily proof of life? Nonna was...is...beside herself. Did you let her know you were home?"

"Uh, no. I stopped here first." Gia was beginning to feel like she was the child and Sage the mother. "Did anything happen while I was away? You seem...overwrought?"

Sage's face crumpled, and she burst into tears. Gia stood there for a moment, stunned, and then she moved closer, about to nudge Max out of the way, but Sage clutched the cat tighter to her chest. "Honey, you need to tell me what's wrong," she said, unable to keep the panic from her voice. "Where's Jake?"

"He's...he's gone," her daughter sobbed.

"Gone where, honey?" Gia didn't care that she liked Jake; she was going to hunt him down and hurt him for putting her daughter in such a state.

The front door opened, and Aaron walked in carrying a bag from the farmers market. "Gia, welcome back. How are you doing, babe? Sagey, you didn't tell me your mom was dropping by." He frowned. "What's gotten into her?"

In her gut, Gia knew. It wasn't Jake she needed to hurt. It was her ex-husband. "What are you doing here, Aaron?"

"What do you think I'm doing here? Me and Sage are bonding, aren't we, honey?" He put the bag on the counter. "You want a coffee, Gia? I think we still have some of that stuff from Fair Trade left, don't we, Sagey?"

Sage lifted her head and held Gia's gaze.

Gia stood up. "Don't worry, I can make my own coffee, Aaron." She brushed past him. "You moved in with Sage as soon as I left town, didn't you?"

"Someone had to look after our daughter. Look at her. She's

a mess." He wagged a bunch of carrots at her. "I'm surprised at you, taking off like that, cutting off all communication with your family." She caught a hint of a smirk when he opened the fridge, and her stomach knotted. He couldn't have known what she'd do, could he?

"When did Jake leave?" She directed her question at Sage, but Aaron answered.

"Not soon enough, if you ask me. I've been telling Sagey I don't get a good feeling about that guy. You must feel the same as me, but I understand why you would have been uncomfortable kicking him out. He's a big SOB."

"There's only one person I don't get a good feeling about, and that's you, Aaron." She turned to her daughter. "Please tell me you didn't kick Jake out of his own home because of something he did." She jabbed her finger at Aaron.

"Hey, wait a damn minute here. It's not my fault he had a problem with me staying at the farm with my daughter."

She shouldn't have left town. She should have known better than to leave her sweet girl at the mercy of this man.

"Any fool knows you don't make your girlfriend choose between you and her family."

She nodded. "You're right. No one should ever choose a man over her family."

His eyes narrowed. "That's not what I said."

He already knew where she was going with this, and he was getting nervous. She could tell by the way he fidgeted with the collar of his shirt. The problem with a nervous or angry Aaron Abbott was that you never knew when or how hard he'd strike back.

"You played me, Aaron, and that's on me, not you. I won't

be party to the emergency injunction, and I'm going to make sure Cami doesn't give you a dime to make your suit go away. Because that's what you really want, don't you? You know you don't have a chance of winning. You just wanted to create enough of a headache that Cami or her publisher would pay you off." She stepped closer, getting into his face. "I want you to pack your bags and get out of Jake and my daughter's home."

"Sagey, are you going to let her talk to me like this?"

Her daughter cast a nervous glance at her father but then met Gia's gaze and nodded. "Mom's right. It's Jake's home too."

"It wouldn't be if you'd listened to me and contested the will." He leaned into Gia. "You haven't changed, have you? You're still a bitch." He backhanded the bag from the market, sending lemons and oranges tumbling onto the floor.

Gia fisted her hands at her sides in an effort to keep from trembling in the face of his fury. He had never hit her. Instead, he'd vented his rage on her personal belongings, her paints and paintings. Then he'd tell her he'd done her a favor—the critics would have torn her exhibition to shreds. She had no talent. She'd never amount to anything anyway.

Sage stood up. Aaron had made a mistake venting his anger in front of his daughter. A woman who spent every waking hour of every day defending her clients from men like him. She was no longer the little girl who'd wished for her daddy to come home when she blew out her candles on her third, fourth, and fifth birthday cakes.

On her sixth birthday, when she'd wished for a new scooter instead, Gia had been relieved, but as she'd seen this morning, her daughter had never given up on that dream. Sadly for her, the father she'd wished for was a nightmare.

There was no emotion in Sage's voice when she said, "Before you go, leave the keys to my car on the counter."

"You don't mean that. I'm not a well man. How do you expect me to get around?"

Gia put her arm around Sage's shoulder. "Walk? It's good for your health."

"I have congestive heart failure!"

"Jake fixed your rental before he left," Sage said, bending down to pick up the oranges and lemons off the floor.

"You know what? He should thank me for you showing him the door. You would have made his life a living hell. You're just like your mother." Aaron snorted. "I bet he's having a real good time in San Diego bonking his ex-wi—"

Sage drilled an orange at Aaron. He crouched down, covering his head, and that's when Max attacked. He leaped off the couch, paws and claws out, looking like a flying carpet. He landed on Aaron's back and took him down.

Once Sage and Gia stopped laughing, they freed Max's impressive claws from Aaron's shirt. He didn't stick around long, rushing to the bedroom to pack his bag and then fast-walking across the living room to get to the front door, keeping an eye on Max the entire way.

"You're going to regret this. You both are," Aaron said, storming out and slamming the door behind him.

"For a guy who is supposedly dying from congestive heart failure, he is surprisingly fast on his feet. He wasn't even breathless." Gia glanced at her daughter and wrapped her arms around her. "I'm sorry. I shouldn't make light of it. He's your father."

Sage hugged her back. "Thank you for rescuing me," she

said, letting go of Gia to walk to the couch. She sat and put her elbows on her knees, burying her face in her hands. "I can't believe I let him drive a wedge between Jake and me. I'm such an idiot."

Gia sat beside her. "Jake's a smart guy. I bet he knew exactly what Aaron was up to, and he'd know how difficult it would be for you to take his side over a man you'd been wanting to meet since you were a little girl." She took Sage's hand in hers. "I should have handled things differently when you were young. I did try to find him after your third birthday, but I couldn't, so I thought it was better to act like he didn't exist."

"I wish I hadn't met him. He could have stayed the fantasy father in my head. I loved that guy. Aaron, I . . ." She looked at her. "He gave me the creeps, Mom. Am I a horrible person?"

"No, just a perceptive one."

"If I was so perceptive, he wouldn't have gotten through the front door, and I wouldn't have had a fight with Jake and asked him to leave."

"Did he go to San Diego?" Gia asked carefully.

"Yeah, he had to pack up his apartment. He's having some of his things sent here, and he's giving away the rest." She chewed on her bottom lip. "You don't think Jake and his ex-wife . . . ?"

"No, of course not."

"That wasn't a very convincing *no*, Mom." Sage leaned back on the couch and lifted Max onto her lap.

"Ignore me. That was just me projecting." She reached out and patted the purring cat. "I'm sure you know by now that I broke up with Flynn."

"In a text. Yeah, I know. That's all I've heard about, that

and you joining Aaron's lawsuit. Willow and I are no longer talking, and honestly, if she keeps talking about you like she has been, I'm never speaking to her again." She swiped at her eyes. "Why did you end it with Flynn? Everyone thinks it's because you and Aaron are getting back together, and trust me, just the thought of that makes me want to throw up in my mouth, but from what I just witnessed, he had nothing to do with it."

Maybe going radio silent hadn't been the smartest idea. Gia took her phone from her purse and showed Sage the picture of Flynn kissing Cami on the dock.

"I'm sadder about this than finding out my father is a creepy con man who doesn't care about me." With her thumb and forefinger, Sage expanded the image. "Maybe it's not what it looks like. Flynn's hands are wrapped around Cami's biceps. You know, like you do when you're moving someone away from you. He doesn't look into it either."

For a split second, Gia let herself see what Sage did and wondered if she'd misread the situation. Then she shook her head. "It doesn't matter. Eventually, we would have split up. And look at the trouble it's caused between you and your sister."

"My cousin," Sage murmured.

Gia's heart plummeted to her feet, and she grabbed Sage by the shoulders. "Don't you ever say that. She's your sister. You've been sisters for twenty-nine years and sisters you'll always be."

"Like you and Cami?"

"It's different. She was gone for twenty-five years." She pulled Max from Sage's lap onto her own and sat there quietly with her feelings about her daughters, about Cami, and about her own mother, understanding finally dawning as she saw the similarities. Her mother hadn't been playing favorites. She'd been trying to bring her daughters back together again. Gia stood up with Max in her arms. "Come on," she said, heading for the door.

"Where are we going? And why are you stealing my cat?"

"We're going to fix our family." She nuzzled her face in Max's fur. "And there's something very calming about this cat. I have a feeling we might need him."

⌒

Gia hadn't only needed Max. She'd needed a whole lot of patience, empathy, and wine to deal with her daughters and her mother. Willow was the hardest to bring around. It had helped that Noah was there. Carmen had come around when Gia promised to make things right with Cami. It probably would have been easier to bring both Willow and Carmen around had Gia showed them the photo of Cami and Flynn kissing on the dock. But she knew it would have just made things worse. She didn't want to create a rift between Willow and Flynn or add another layer to the family drama with Cami. They needed to stand united against Aaron when he came at them again, and Gia knew it was only a matter of time before he did.

By the time she parked the car in La Dolce Vita's parking lot, the sun was setting on the bay. She considered taking a walk on the beach, but she was emotionally drained. She didn't want to walk through the restaurant, so she walked down a worn path along the side to the stairs on the beach.

There were two couples dining on the deck, and she smiled a greeting. Too tired even for polite conversation, she'd put off reaching out to Cami until tomorrow.

Gia frowned as she reached her apartment door, positive the lights had been off when she'd left last week. She pressed her ear against the red-painted door. It sounded like someone was singing.

She unlocked and opened the door and walked into her apartment. It wasn't someone. It was Cami. She was curled up on Gia's favorite chair in her studio, Enya's "Watermark" playing softly in the background. "What are you doing here?"

So much for her good intentions. They flew out the window at the memory of her sister and Flynn kissing on the dock.

Cami lifted her swollen, bloodshot eyes to Gia. "I'm tired. I can't do this anymore. I can't fight with you and do what I need to do."

"Maybe you should have thought about that before you made out with Flynn on the dock." She took her phone from her purse, tossing it onto the chair beside Cami's knee. She didn't want to listen to her sister trying to deny it.

Cami picked up the phone and glanced at the screen. "Is this why you broke up with him?"

"Seemed a good enough reason to me." She lowered herself onto the stool where Flynn had sat just over a week ago.

"It's not what it looks like, Gia."

"I was there, Cami. It's exactly what it looks like."

"No. It looks like Flynn is kissing me, but it's me kissing him." She tossed Gia's phone back to her.

"Is that supposed to make it all better? You threw yourself at my boyfriend without any thought about how I would feel."

"I wasn't thinking about you. I was thinking about me."
She got up from the chair and walked to the window, pressing
her hand against the glass. "Hugh broke up with me about
three hours before you took that picture. I, uh, got drunk, and
I threw myself at Flynn." She lifted a shoulder. "Amos is right.
Flynn is my security blanket. He always made me feel better."
She turned to Gia. "He pushed me away. He was angry I'd
kissed him, angrier still when he realized I've been drinking
again."

The puzzle pieces started clicking into place. "When did
you start drinking again?"

"Last fall."

"When you started writing your memoir."

"Yeah. It brought everything back, and all those feelings
that I thought I'd worked through..." She shook her head
as she returned to sit on the chair, as if she didn't trust her
legs to hold her up. "I was so ashamed of everything I'd done
to you, to Willow, even to myself. And I didn't have my PA
to hold my hand. She'd sort of replaced Flynn as my security
blanket, and without her there, I started sliding. I'd have a
glass of wine every now and then or two bottles of beer, so I
didn't think it was a big deal. But a glass a day became two,
then three and four, until I realized I was drinking more than
a bottle a day. I should have come home to write the book so
I had support."

"We should have realized you were struggling."

"I'm really good at hiding it. I always have been."

"Were you drunk at the Instagram Live filming?"

"Yeah, and I'm sorry. I know I've been a bitch to you the
past few months. I guess I subconsciously blamed you for how

I was feeling because I felt most guilty about what I'd done to you and Willow."

"That makes sense. But I watched you do the same to Hugh. You were pushing him away."

"Part of me was mad at him for pushing me to write my memoir. Indirectly, I guess I blamed him for my drinking. But really, after reliving everything I'd done, I knew that we'd never last. He was too good for me, and one day he'd realize it, and he'd break up with me anyway." She smiled weakly. "I think they call that a self-fulfilling prophecy."

"That or self-sabotage. I'm beginning to think it's hereditary." She took her sister's hand in hers. "I'm sorry I haven't been there for you. In fact, I'm pretty sure I've made things worse. But I'd like us to go back to the way we once were."

"Do you really think we can?"

"A week ago, I would have said no. But I think the problem was, we've been apart for so long, I didn't think of you as my sister anymore."

Cami leaned forward and hugged her. "Thank you. I don't think I deserve a second chance, but I'll take it."

Gia looked at her phone. "Madonna santa!"

"Why are you showing me the picture of me and Flynn again?"

"Crap. That's not what you're supposed to be looking at." She held up her phone, making sure Cami saw her delete the photo of her with Flynn. Then she tapped the screen. "Look at the date."

Cami smiled. "It's the first day of summer."

"Come on." Gia pulled her to her feet. "I'll call Eva."

An hour later, the three of them lay side by side in the sand, looking up at the stars, squabbling over who'd found the North Star first.

"Do you think we should have asked Mom to join us?" Eva asked from where she lay between Gia and Cami.

"No, tonight's just for us," Gia said, tapping a bottle of non-alcoholic craft beer to her sisters. "Drink up, beaches. It's time for our traditional first skinny dip of the season."

They finished off their drinks and then started stripping off their clothes to Eva's rendition of Kelis's "Milkshake" while shaking their booties, and it must be said that the Rosetti women were blessed with generous booties.

There was much laughing and shrieking as they tried to outperform one another. The shrieking and laughter only got louder when the three of them ran into the freezing-cold water, but Gia didn't think they'd been loud enough for their neighbors to call the cops. She was wrong.

"Turn around, boys," she ordered the officers, and then the three of them ran out of the water, grabbing their towels off the sand. "I can't believe, after I painted Ted giving her a bouquet of flowers for her anniversary, that Liz called the police on..." She trailed off as her sisters turned to stare at her. "It might be best if you kept that little tidbit to yourself. United fronts and all that. We don't need any more drama."

Chapter Twenty-Five

You don't have to come stay with me, Will. I'm fine on my own," Sage said as she drove the narrow, winding road to the farm.

"You do know who you're talking to, right? The person who knows you even better than Mom does. Besides, Aaron might come back."

"Trust me, I can handle him."

"But that's the thing: You didn't handle him, babe." Her sister placed her hand over Sage's on the steering wheel. "I get it. I remember how you used to talk about him when we were little. You talked about him like—"

"He was Flynn. It's okay. You can say it. I think part of why I got so mad at you, aside from you being such a brat about Mom, is that I was jealous you got the good dad. I wanted him for me."

"I wanted him for you too. A few days ago, I thought we were going to be sharing him. Do you think there's a chance Mom will change her mind?"

"No." She wasn't about to tell her sister why she wouldn't.

She didn't need to know. Sage still couldn't believe it herself. She was sure there was a reasonable explanation why Flynn had been kissing Cami. But even if there was, she could tell her mom had made up her mind, and she was stubborn. Pot, kettle.

"What are you thinking about? You looked sad all of a sudden."

"Jake. I really messed up, Will. He saw through Aaron right away. He was just trying to protect me from getting hurt, and then I hurt him." She told her sister what Aaron said about Jake and his ex.

"He's such a hateful man!" Willow said, then pulled a face. "Sorry. I don't know if I'm allowed to talk about him like that or not. You know, you can talk smack about a family member or friend, but no one else can."

"Feel free. It's kind of like you're talking smack about your own father anyway."

"Wow, I never thought about it like that but you're right. Two years ago, I would have been right there beside you, as anxious to meet Aaron as you were. I'm really sorry. I didn't realize until now how much it must have hurt when I talked about Flynn, August, and my other sisters." She leaned over and hugged Sage. "I'll always love you best, you know. You're my favorite sister."

"Thanks, I'm glad you feel that way, but can you let go of me now? I'm trying to... Will, what is that?"

"What is..." Her sister winced. "Okay, so you know how excited the Beaches were the night we were making the lavender body products?"

"Uh-huh," she said, staring at the spotlights set up in the lavender field.

"Well," her sister said, "they decided to feature the products on their Instagram channel."

"Uh, yeah, so?"

"They're doing a photo shoot."

"In my lavender field? Without asking?"

"They didn't think you'd mind. And honestly, it's my fault. They asked me to talk to you about it, and then we weren't talking, and I forgot to share that with them. Actually, I didn't want to share it with them because then I'd have to share everything else." She sighed and *thunk*ed the back of her head against the headrest. "Why does our family have to have so much drama? Why can't we be normal like everyone else?"

"Once we figure out what Aaron is up to and send him back to Costa Rica, I think our lives will go back to normal."

"Babe, our family has never been normal."

"Nonna would say normal is boring." They looked at each other and laughed. Then Sage's phone rang. She connected her mother's call on hands-free. "Mom, is that you? I can hardly hear you. Is there something wrong with my connection?" she asked her sister, who shrugged.

"We need you to come bail us out!" At least that's what it sounded like to Sage. Crackles on the line made it difficult to make out.

"You got arrested again?" Sage asked at the same time Willow said, "Who's *we?*"

"Your aunts and me," her mother said, and Sage realized the crackles were actually cackles. The three of them were laughing like loons.

"Did you get arrested for drunk and disorderly?" she asked.

"No! We got arrested for indecent exposure and disorderly conduct."

Both Sage and Willow were more upset about missing their family's skinny-dipping tradition than bailing their mom and aunts out of jail. When they got back to the farmhouse, the Beaches and their spotlights were gone.

As Sage parked the car, Willow turned her phone toward her. "Admit it, the farm looks incredible, doesn't it?"

"It really does." She leaned closer to the screen. "Wait a sec. They're telling people we charge a fee for them to do their wedding and romantic photo shoots at the farm?"

"Yep. Pretty smart. You'll be making money hand over fist."

"We'll also be run off our feet." Then again, Sage thought, it wasn't like the Beaches would have many people following them on social. They were just regular women with regular jobs on Sunshine Bay. "How many followers do they have?"

"One point two million."

⌐

Sage carried her fold-up chair under her arm as she walked Max along the one-track road to the site where Alice's house for abused women would one day sit. Sage didn't remember everything she'd yelled at Jake when they got into the fight over her father, but she thought she might have withdrawn her offer to be his silent partner.

So here she was, popping open her chair at almost midnight and calling Jake on WhatsApp. Willow pushed her to do it. She said it would only make it harder the longer Sage waited.

"Hey," Sage said when he appeared on her screen. He was

outside, sitting on a chair with a patio light shining behind him, the sound of the surf audible.

"Hey." He didn't smile, and his cool blue eyes didn't crinkle at the corners.

"I'm sorry, Jake. Aaron is gone. I'd like to say I came to my senses and kicked him out, but my mom did." She blinked tears away. "You were right. Everything you said about him was true." She chewed on her lip. "Can you forgive me?"

He sat back in his chair, lifting a beer bottle to his lips as his gaze remained locked on hers. He took a drink, then slowly lowered the bottle. "It didn't feel good, you siding with him over me or you telling me to take a hike and then holding the money for Alice's house over me...It didn't feel good at all, Sage." He looked down at the beer bottle, picking at the label. "You're not the only one with issues when it comes to a parent. I've got a fair share of my own."

She pressed her lips together to keep from crying, swallowing the ball of emotion in her throat. "You do, and I should have thought about that before I said what I did. I, uh..." She trailed off. It wasn't the time to tell him she loved him. "I understand if you're done with me. I'm a lot of work. I'm stubborn, and I have a temper, and I'm a workaholic, and I get cranky if I don't get a lot of sleep, which is pretty much most of the time. I'm boring too, especially compared with the rest of my family." She looked at him. "You're supposed to tell me to stop. You always tell me to stop."

"Yeah, but usually I'm not thousands of miles away, and I can take you in my arms and kiss you to shut you up. I'm too far away to do that now."

"I didn't think you'd want to hold me or kiss me ever again, even if only to shut me up. Aaron actually told me you were lucky to have escaped from me. He figured you were in San Diego bonking your ex-wife. You're not, are you?"

He muttered something about how he'd enjoy making her father pay for that before saying to her, "You really believe I'd do something like that?"

"No, but I know the reason why my mom broke off with Flynn now, and I guess I was projecting. There seems to be a lot of that going on in my family. I probably shouldn't have called you. It's been an emotional day. But I really miss you." She held up Max, who'd been sleeping on her lap. "So does Max." She waved his paw at Jake. She saw the softening in his expression and wished it had been for her. She sighed. She had it bad if she was jealous of a cat. "Sorry, Max," she murmured, hugging him close.

"I miss him, and I miss you, a lot, even more than I thought I would."

"So you're not breaking up with me?"

"Are you trying to piss me off again?"

"How? I just asked—"

He held up his hand. "Don't say it. I just told you I missed you, a lot, and then you ask me if I'm breaking up with you? After you also asked me if I'm bonking my ex?"

"I'm sorry if I'm being needy. It wasn't easy learning that the father I'd built up in my mind was a creepy con man who doesn't even like me."

"You're right. I'm sorry for being a jerk. I guess Abbott's comments got to me more than I realized."

He'd told Jake he wasn't good enough for her. He'd obviously been in Sunshine Bay longer than they'd realized. He'd known about Jake's family and juvenile police record and had thrown it in Jake's face. At least she'd shut down that line of Aaron's attack, but apparently, he'd landed the blows he'd wanted. He was smarter than they gave him credit for.

"I'm sorry I gave him the opportunity to hurt you. I . . . Um, Jake, there's a . . ." She raised her finger, pointing at the screen. "A monkey behind you."

"Sweetheart, I've got to go. I'll see you—"

"Don't you dare hang up on me. You're not in San Diego, are you? You're in Costa Rica."

He sighed. "Yeah. I am. Look, I know you told me not to investigate him, but I had to follow my gut, and my gut said we needed whatever we could get on this guy."

"Please tell me you got the goods."

He cocked his head. "You're not mad at me?"

"I'm not thrilled you went without telling me, but if you've got what we need to shut him down, we'll play boss and naughty PA when you get home, and I'll fulfill your deepest desires." Sage didn't know if it was her offer or the monkey jumping on Jake's head that made him drop his phone. Whichever it was, their connection cut out, and the screen went dark.

Half an hour later, as she was crawling into bed beside Willow, she got a text from him. I survived the monkey attack with barely a scratch, but you nearly gave me a heart attack. I'll be home Sunday before noon. Be ready.

She smiled. I'm counting down the hours until you get home and fulfill my deepest desires.

I don't care who does the fulfilling as long as we do it all day long.

⌒

Sunday afternoon, Jake walked into Sage's bedroom to find her in bed with Max and her sister. He sat on the edge of the mattress beside her hip, gently swept her hair aside, and pressed his lips to her shoulder. Her eyelids fluttered open. "This isn't what I was expecting. Are you backing out on your promise already?"

"No. I set my alarm for ten." She pushed herself up, wrapping an arm around his waist and reached out with her other hand to pat around the bedside table. She kissed him and brought her phone to her face. "How is it one in the afternoon?"

"It looks like you shut off your alarm." He leaned back, smoothing her hair from her face. "Have you not gotten any sleep at all while I was away?"

"Not much, and before you give me crap, Brenda and Renata needed my help with a couple of cases, and then I had to prepare a brief for one of my pro bono clients and organize the farm's opening next weekend, and Alice's celebration next month." She snuggled into him. "That's what happens when you leave me on my own. I don't follow doctor's orders."

"We'll start making up for it now. I'll keep you in bed for the next twenty-four hours."

"I don't think the doctor would approve of your plans."

"I promise, I'll let you rest in between." He nuzzled her neck and then brought his mouth to her ear. "I missed you."

A pillow smacked him in the face. "Don't you dare start making out with my sister. You're going to scar Max and me." Willow raised herself up on her elbows, her hair in her face. "Did I hear you say it's one in the afternoon?"

"You did," Sage said.

"You, close your eyes, and you, shake a leg," Willow said first to him and then to Sage. "We told Nonna we'd help cook for tonight's family dinner." The bed bounced, and there was a loud thump.

"Don't use all the hot water," Sage called out.

"Am I good to open my eyes?" Jake asked.

"You are," Sage said, and tugged on his arm. "And you're good to get into bed with me."

"But from the sounds of it, you won't be staying in it with me for long."

"You better make the most of it then," she said, wrapping her arms around his neck as he slid his body on top of hers. Her moan went straight to his groin. "Don't leave me on my own again."

He didn't remind her that it wasn't him going anywhere; it was her leaving him for the city. They made out for all of five minutes before Sage's phone started ringing, and Willow's began vibrating on the other bedside table. "This can't be good," Sage murmured before accepting the call. "Hey, Mom. We'll be at the restaurant at two."

Then Gia must have started talking because Sage bowed her head, greeting whatever Gia said with several *uhmmm*s, *I sees*, *okay*s, and then a reassuring *it'll be fine*. Sage started swearing as soon as she disconnected from her mother.

Willow walked in wearing a robe and a towel wrapped turban-style around her head. "What's—" She slapped a hand over her eyes. "I'll meet you two in the living room, and do me a favor and put some clothes on."

"We have clothes on," Sage said.

"Not enough of them," her sister called back.

Jake decided to stay quiet about the phone call until Sage could tell both her sister and him, instead of having to repeat it. He walked into the kitchen to make a pot of coffee while Sage told them Aaron had figured out his next move.

"Because Aaron abandoned us, my mother assumed it wasn't necessary for her to file for divorce. She didn't worry about him seeking custody, and she knew she didn't have a hope in hell of getting support payments from him. And then there was the small fact that he couldn't be found."

"Because he didn't want to be found," Jake said, unzipping his carry-on. He handed the evidence against Aaron over to Sage. "You should have enough here to have him think twice about going after your mom for his share of their marital assets."

"He couldn't do that, could he?" Willow asked, looking from him to Sage.

"Depends how he spins it. He could make a case for it, but I don't think Mom had much in assets when he left, other than from the sale of the house."

Jake thought about the man and the situation. "Unless he claims he didn't abandon his family. He'd simply gone to do a job in Costa Rica, had an accident, and didn't remember he had a family until he was contacted by the reporter."

"And as soon as he found out about his family, he rushed to see them and make amends," Sage said, nodding. "He might even claim that he and Mom had talked about going into partnership with Nonna and Zia Eva. It would be a case of he said, she said."

"You're not saying he could try to go after part of the restaurant, are you?" Willow asked, sounding panicked.

Jake felt a touch of that same panic at the thought of what this could mean for Sage's family, but she seemed completely unfazed by it, even when she nodded and said, "And their new product line."

"How can you be so calm!" Willow yelled.

"Because I'm very good at my job," she said, looking through the evidence Jake had given her. She smiled up at him. "Jake is too, and so was Alice."

"What has Alice got to do..." He slowly nodded as the final puzzle piece clicked into place. "Your mom would have gone to her seeking advice about divorcing Aaron, and as thorough as Alice was, she would have opened a file whether your mom went through with the divorce or not."

"Yes, she did. After I talked to you, I got to thinking about some of the things that Mom said to Aaron and her expression when he backhanded the bag of groceries off the counter. He scared her, and I'm sure that wasn't the first time he had. It wasn't a big leap to think that the one person Mom would seek out would be Alice, so I spent yesterday and most of the night going through her old case files. I found this in the last box I went through."

Sage handed him a file folder, a shimmer of tears in her beautiful, tired eyes. "This was why she was coming to the farm that night. She was trying to protect my family."

Chapter Twenty-Six

Ma, I think we should cancel tonight's family dinner. Everyone will understand," Gia said, looking at her sisters for support. They were in the restaurant's kitchen, prepping for Sunday night dinner service. Sage and Willow were on their way over. Sage had arranged a meeting with Aaron at La Dolce Vita for four o'clock. The restaurant opened at five.

"No, Ma's right," Eva said. "We go into the talks with Aaron knowing that Sage has everything under control and there's nothing to worry about, and then we'll celebrate getting rid of that odious man once and for all with the rest of the family."

"I know how to get rid of him once and for all," their mother said, slapping the meat mallet against her palm.

Cami, who was sitting on the counter instead of preparing the main entrée for the family dinner, beef braciole, said, "Too messy, Ma." She closed her eyes and then opened them, smiling. "Did you guys see *Practical Magic*? Nicole Kidman and Sandra Bullock starred in it," she added when they didn't respond right away.

"We loved it. They were sisters, and the woman Nicole played was dating an abusive man. Remember now?" Eva asked Gia.

"Uh, yeah, they poisoned him and then did some kind of spell on him and turned him into a zombie." Gia shuddered and then looked at Cami. "You're joking, right?"

Her sister shrugged. "He said he's dying. We'd just be helping him along." Then she laughed. "I'm just messing with you."

"I think Ma missed that part," Gia said, nodding at their mother, who appeared to be seriously considering poison as a means of getting rid of Aaron permanently. Honestly, Gia didn't blame her. She just prayed that Sage could work her own special brand of magic and get rid of him for good.

But the thought of her daughter facing the reality that Aaron only cared about the money he could bleed from their family—the same type of man Sage fought against every day instead of the loving father every little girl deserved—made Gia want to throw her mother's meat mallet at Aaron's head. The anger, the shame, the guilt, all of it was getting to her, and she felt sick to her stomach.

"What's with your face?" Eva asked her. "Do not tell me you're feeling guilty about this."

"How can I not? I'm the one who brought him into this family. I married the man." She turned away and wrapped her arms around her waist. "And he's putting everything we've built together at risk."

Cami got off the counter and came to Gia, putting her arm around her. "We won't let him do that. I won't let him. If Sage can't shut him down, I'll pay him off."

Eva joined them, and they ended up in a group hug. "Cami's right. James said the same thing."

"No," Carmen said, slapping the mallet against her palm. "He does not get a single dime of your hard-earned money, or James's, or any other member of this family's. If Sage can't make him go away with his tail between his legs like the rabid dog he is, I will." She looked at Cami. "I don't remember the movie. Tell me more about how they killed the culo."

Sage and Willow walked into the kitchen. Sage frowned. "What's going on?"

"You got here just in time," Gia said. "Your nonna is plotting to kill Aaron."

"Please do not tell me that. I'm an officer of the court."

Willow covered her sister's ears. "You can tell me. How are we going to get rid of him?"

"Poison," Carmen said, holding up her phone. "I googled. They used belladonna, and we'll need witches too, but ones who actually know what they're doing. This family did not. Do any of you know any witches?"

"Oh, *Practical Magic*. We loved that movie, and the book," Willow said, lowering her hands from Sage's ears. "And there's a coven right here in Sunshine Bay. I've interviewed them for *Good Morning, Sunshine!* I can call them if you... Why are you all looking at me like that?"

"Because this is not a movie or a book. This is real life, honey. We're not murdering anyone," Gia said, making big eyes at Willow in an effort to remind her she was talking about her sister's father. No matter how despicable he'd turned out to be, Aaron was still Sage's dad.

"Sage is totes okay with it, Mom," Willow said, putting an arm around her sister. "Aren't you, babe?"

"No. I'm not okay with you talking about killing Aaron, even if he is a snake," Sage said, her gaze taking in all of them. "No more joking about this."

"I'm not—" Carmen began.

"Yes, you are joking, and it ends now, Nonna. I know you're all upset, and you have every right to be, but I've got this. And Mom, this isn't on you. It's on him. And Willow is right too. Does it suck that Aaron has turned out to be a snake in the grass? It totally does. But I didn't have a father in my life growing up, and I grew up happy and well loved. I don't need one now."

"Sage is right. I didn't have a father either, and we had an awesome childhood." Willow bumped her sister with her hip. "But it's kind of nice having one now, especially a dad as wonderful as Flynn." Willow's gaze moved to her, and Gia wanted the floor to swallow her whole. "You should get on that, Mom."

"About that family dinner," Gia said, her cheeks flushed. "Is it on or not?"

"It's totally on," Cami said.

Gia caught her sisters sharing a grin and groaned. "No way. Flynn and I are over. Don't you dare stick your noses where they don't belong. I mean it." She put her hands on her hips, giving them both her best *older sister* look. "I'm serious. This isn't a joke. People's feelings are involved, including Flynn's other daughters."

Her family completely ignored her, and she knew this because, as soon as Flynn walked into the restaurant with his father three hours later, Cami looped her arm through his and turned to wink at Gia. Flynn must have caught the exchange. He glanced toward the table where she sat with Sage and Aaron and his lawyer, who'd arrived fifty-five minutes late for the meeting. They'd walked through the door just two minutes before Flynn.

Flynn's eyes narrowed at Aaron before coming to rest on her. It was the first time she'd seen him since the night at the farm, and her body came alive with want and need.

But she didn't think he felt the same. His eyes didn't warm with amusement or desire, and his lips didn't curve in a smile. All she got was a polite nod of acknowledgment. She wanted to tell her sister not to waste her time. There was no going back now even if Gia was willing to once again put her heart on the line.

She glanced at Aaron, who met her gaze with a smirk, as if he knew they were over, as if he thought he'd played a part in their breakup. Thinking back, she wondered if he might be partially to blame for how she'd reacted to seeing her sister with Flynn, for her running away to Boston and holing up in a hotel with a mini-bar and movies.

She straightened—sitting tall in the chair with her shoulders squared—and looked Aaron in the eye, hoping he could read her silent message. *You're going down.*

He glanced at their daughter, and Gia saw it, a flicker of doubt in his eyes. She imagined that his lawyer—a man Sage was acquainted with—had shared their daughter's reputation as one of the best divorce attorneys in the state.

They'd already done the introductions. Watching Sage exchange pleasantries with the other lawyer had made Gia smile. This was a side of her daughter she rarely saw, and she was looking forward to seeing her in action. They might not be able to literally murder Aaron, but Gia prayed Sage would figuratively eviscerate the man.

Ten minutes later, Gia was ready to plunge the butter knife into Aaron's heart. "That's a lie! You abandoned your family when you followed my sister to LA. We never discussed going into partnership with my mother and Eva. You hated them, and they hated you!"

"I'd suggest you get your client under control, Ms. Rosetti, or I'll be obligated to call the police to ensure my client's safety. I'm sure you would prefer that we don't file for a restraining order against my client's wife."

"I am not his wife, and if anyone needs a restraining order, it's me! He's been stalking me and my family for months."

Flynn approached the table, placing a heavy hand on Gia's shoulder. "Is there a problem here?" he asked, deftly removing the knife from her hand and pocketing it, earning a grateful smile from Sage.

"We're good, thanks. Aren't we, Mom?" Sage asked, reminding Gia with a pointed stare to keep her cool.

Sage had warned her that Aaron would most likely try claiming he hadn't intentionally abandoned her and that they'd discussed a partnership with her family before he left for LA. But Gia hadn't believed he'd stoop so low or tell the lie with a straight face. He didn't just do it with a straight face. He actually seemed to believe the lies coming out of his mouth.

Flynn moved his hand to her neck, giving it a familiar squeeze. She looked at him through angry, tear-filled eyes, blinking to bring his gorgeous face into focus. There was warmth in his eyes now, concern too, and a tender smile curving his lips. "I'm here if you need me."

She nodded, her chest tight. She hadn't realized how much his cool, detached response to her earlier had hurt or how much she'd hoped he might give her a second chance.

"We'll talk once you're done here," he said, giving her neck another comforting squeeze before walking away.

"How sweet," Aaron said, but Gia didn't miss the gratifying hint of anger in his eyes before he turned to his lawyer, who was frowning over several papers that Sage had handed him.

"So you can see why we'd find Mr. Abbott continuing to reference my mother as his wife confusing when he married two women in Costa Rica. I believe bigamy is still a criminal offense."

"When you can prove intent, which you can't. At the time, my client was unaware he was married as a result of the head injury he had sustained."

"Except these sworn affidavits prove that, while he might have sustained a head injury, he hadn't lost his memory as he's claimed." Sage handed Aaron's lawyer the sworn affidavits from his attending physician, a nurse he'd tried to date, and the first women he'd married in Costa Rica.

"How did you get these?" Aaron asked, flicking them away. "They're fake."

"I'm afraid they're very real. As to who acquired them, Jake did." Sage bared her teeth in a semblance of a smile. "It's too bad he had all that time to kill while you were making yourself at home on our farm. He took a little trip to Costa Rica." She passed his lawyer two more official-looking documents, her eyes hard, her voice knife-sharp when she addressed

Aaron. "Alice must have recognized you that day at the Smoke Shack. She would have seen the resemblance between us, and she knew what you would try to pull. She'd planned to shut you down before you had a chance."

"What are you talking about, honey?" Gia asked.

"When you went to Alice asking for advice about your divorce, she opened a file and began investigating Aaron. She had witness statements from people who lived in your neighborhood."

Gia's face got hot as she thought about what her neighbors would have told Alice. She'd never mentioned the witness statements to her. Maybe she would have if Gia had gone ahead with the divorce, but she'd been afraid to. Afraid to put them on Aaron's radar. She'd hadn't seen or heard from him in over a year by then.

Aaron's lawyer passed him the papers. He paled as he read them over.

"I think we're done here," the lawyer said as he came to his feet, nudging Aaron to do the same.

"Not before your client signs these, we're not," Sage said, passing several more documents and a pen across the table.

Less than fifteen minutes later, they were done, and Aaron was on his way back to Costa Rica. "What were the last papers that you passed to Aaron's lawyer?" Gia asked Sage.

"The divorce papers, along with the witness statements from your old neighbors and the owner of the art gallery where you had your first showing in New York," Sage said. "Your neighbors paid attention to what was going on in your home. They didn't like what they heard or saw Aaron saying and doing to you. The gallery owner testified that the night before your second showing, your work had been destroyed, and you had to withdraw. He pointed the finger at Aaron, relaying several instances of him belittling your talent in his presence." She rubbed Gia's arm. "I'm sorry that he did that to you. That he stole your dream."

Gia shook her head, reaching out her hand to Willow, who'd just joined them. "He didn't. I got my dream right here. The two of you," she said, and hugged her daughters.

Jake joined them. "I gather from the way Aaron and his lawyer slunk out of here that Sage notched another win."

"The win isn't mine alone. It's as much yours and Alice's," Sage said as she came to her feet and kissed Jake's cheek.

"We made a good team." He smiled.

"You make a great team," Gia said, standing up to hug him. "Thanks for everything, Jake."

"Don't mention it. I was happy to help."

"After this, you two deserve a holiday," Willow said.

"Great minds." Sage smiled at Jake. "Now that we've got the Aaron problem taken care of and the Rosettis are one big happy family, I thought you and I could take a one-week vacation before I go back to work."

Sage might have missed it, but Gia caught the subtle shift in Jake's expression. He wasn't a fan of her daughter going back to work this soon. Gia wasn't happy about it either. But she knew her daughter. She just hoped the couple were able to make a go of their relationship with Sage working and living in Boston.

"Great. Where do you want to go?" Jake asked.

"Home." She whispered something in his ear that made him smile.

Gia had a feeling they wouldn't be staying for dessert. On her way to the family table, she greeted several customers who were checking that she was all right. She obviously hadn't been whisper-shouting as she had thought. But the majority of customers on Sunday were locals who were well acquainted with the Rosettis.

She'd noticed a slight uptick in Sunday reservations and had a feeling they were a result of people hearing they were reinstating their Sunday family dinner. They'd be disappointed tonight, she thought as she made her way to the back of the restaurant. They'd witnessed all the Rosetti drama they were going to get for one day.

While accepting her sisters' hugs, she worked at hiding her disappointment that Flynn was noticeably absent from the table. Then her mother appeared with a picnic basket. "Go. He's waiting for you on the beach."

Her family and Flynn's ushered her out the back door with shouts of good luck and some love-life advice. Gia had been wrong about not providing their customers with something else to talk about. But all thoughts about being the subject of tomorrow's gossip emptied from her head when she spotted Flynn sitting on a blanket on the beach. She slipped off her heels, leaving them on the stairs to the family's apartments, and after a quick hello to their customers eating on the deck, she walked down the stairs and across the beach to join him.

He came to his feet and took the picnic basket from her. "Your mom thought we'd like some privacy. Your sisters did too." He gestured for her to sit.

She wondered if he'd gotten the same send-off she had. "I'm sorry I broke up with you over a text, Flynn," she said as she opened the picnic basket. "It wasn't my finest moment. I saw you with Cami on the dock and jumped to the wrong conclusions. I should have given you a chance to explain."

"Yeah, you should have." He set a container of caprese skewers on the blanket. "I found the cake on the stairs. I knew what you'd seen and what you'd think, so I went to talk to you. By the time I got to your place, I'd gotten your text. I sat outside your apartment waiting for you."

"I needed time to think. I needed time by myself."

"Would it have killed you to send an update to your daughters? They were beside themselves with worry."

"So I've been told. Funny how they don't have the same problem keeping me updated with their lives. I'm lucky if I hear from them once a week." She opened a container. It held spinach and Havarti paninis with an olive tapenade.

"You're mad?"

"Yes, I'm mad. Earlier, when you came over to the table, you seemed like we were okay. But it doesn't feel like we are so if you just want to rehash what happened and then break up with me, get it over with." She tossed the container and crossed her arms, looking past the whitecapped waves rolling onto shore. In the distance, against the pink horizon, three sailboats raced across the water. "You didn't call me. You didn't text me."

"No. I didn't. I was angry and worried about you, and then I thought, given the way the girls reacted to us being together, maybe you were right and it was for the best. By day two, I called Jake. He had a friend track you down using your credit cards, so I knew where you were, and I knew you were safe." He picked up a panini. "And then when you came home, you visited with your daughters and your sisters, got yourself arrested, and again, I didn't hear from you." He ate his sandwich while looking out to sea.

"I thought about going to see you. I wanted to see you more than anything, Flynn. But I talked myself out of it. Aaron got into my head." She told him what he'd said. Flynn's eyes came to hers. He was angry, and she thought Aaron was lucky he'd left town. "I was trying to protect my heart."

"A broken heart is the price we pay for living and loving, Gia. Sometimes you have to decide if it's worth loving someone if the alternative was not loving them at all."

"What would you say if I said I wanted to take the risk, with you?" She moved the containers and the picnic basket out of the way.

He lifted her onto his lap. "I'd say I'd do my best to make sure you never regret being brave enough to take a chance on me."

"What would you say if I told you I loved you?"

"I'd say it took you long enough to realize it. I fell in love with you the day I walked into La Dolce Vita and you smiled at me." He glanced over his shoulder and grinned. "Now you better kiss me so they can go and eat."

She looked to see her family and Flynn's standing on the deck, and she shook her head. "Are you sure you're ready for this? I'm a package deal, you know."

"I'm ready for anything as long as I've got you by my side," he said. Then he kissed her to the cheers of their families.

Chapter Twenty-Seven

Seriously, she can't be sleeping. No one could sleep through that noise," a woman said over the loud bleating of a foghorn, ensuring that her prediction came true.

Sage tried waving her hand to get the woman to stop talking and the foghorn to stop bleating but apparently her body parts weren't taking orders from her brain.

"Renata, you know she can sleep through anything."

"I guess I forgot. She rarely does it anymore."

The conversation sounded weirdly familiar, but Sage's entire body was numb, including her eyes, and she couldn't see where she was or who was talking. The name sounded familiar and so did the voices, especially the loud one.

"Jake isn't going to be happy she's falling back into her old pattern of work, work, work."

She knew that voice now. *Work, work, work* gave her away. Renata probably would rat her out to Jake. She had a big, annoying crush on him. Sage understood why. She loved the man, but he was still annoyingly bossy when it came to her work-life balance. If he only knew how much better she was.

"But we're not going to tell him, are we? Repeat after me, Sage is our boss, and we are loyal to her."

"You'd better be loyal to me. I saved your job last week," Sage rasped, lifting her hands to pry her eyelids off her eyeballs. The firm didn't appreciate Renata organizing a petition to have a designated meditation space. Sage raised her head and peeled the keyboard from her face.

"Just FYI, ladies, I wasn't sleeping. I was meditating."

"Please, you can't keep that monkey brain of yours quiet long enough to meditate," Renata said.

"Isn't that the whole point of meditation?" Sage yawned and covered her mouth. "Anyway, I had a good reason for pulling an all-nigher. Alice's celebration of life is tonight, and I promised Jake I'd be home early. I'm leaving before noon." She caught the women's silent exchange. "What? I'm not supposed to be in court. I worked extra hours this week to make sure my schedule was clear."

"Mr. Forbes implemented a new policy. No one is allowed to take off early on Friday, no matter the reason. We got the memo this morning," Brenda said, holding up an official-looking document.

"I've worked till midnight every night this week, except last night, and I worked until four this morning." Sage got up from her chair and headed for the bathroom. "Brenda, do me a favor and get Emilia to squeeze me in with Robert this morning. And once you have a time, ask Nina to meet me there."

"Do you think that's a good idea?" Brenda asked. "Mr. Forbes wasn't happy when you intervened on Renata's behalf." She made big eyes at Sage, reminding her that it wasn't only the meditation space the firm had taken issue with. Renata had received a warning about her billable hours, and Sage had called them out on their unsustainable expectations. "There was that thing with Bill in security too, and Roland in personal injury." Brenda made a face. "You can only push them so far, Sage."

"You're right." She withdrew a small jar of lavender hand cream from her pocket. "I'll slather this on, and I'll be completely chillmellow when I meet with Robert."

"How many times do I have to tell you? That's not a word." Renata sighed. "Don't worry, Brenda. I'll do some breath work with Sage before her meeting with Mr. Forbes, and she'll be completely relaxed."

"Thanks, Renata. That's very thoughtful of you," Sage said.

"A little selfish too," the other woman admitted. "I need next Friday off for my sister's wedding."

"Oh my gosh, I couldn't change my mom's radiation treatments. They're scheduled for late Friday afternoons."

"Don't worry. I've got this, Brenda."

An hour later, Sage sat in Robert's office, thinking she should have done at least two hours of breath work and slathered lavender over her entire body. She gritted her teeth and then repeated the hours she'd put in this week in order to clear her schedule for today.

Robert studied his cookies and picked one up. "That's a shame you'll miss Alice's celebration of life. You should have scheduled your personal activities for Saturday, like every other person at the firm."

"Life happens, Mr. Forbes. You can't always schedule family obligations outside nine to five during the week."

He frowned. "Who at Forbes, Poole, and Russell is working

nine to five?" He pointed his cookie at Nina. "Look into this immediately. It's entirely unacceptable."

"You know what?" Sage said. "The demands you put on your employees are unacceptable. In fact, I'm positive that the firm is breaking several employment labor laws at the federal, state, and local levels."

He looked at her over the top of his bifocals. "Are you threatening me, Ms. Rosetti?"

"Nope, it's not a threat." She ignored Nina's warning squeaks and stood up. "It's a promise. I'll be drafting a list of issues you need to address before I leave in the next hour for the celebration of Alice's life, and you'll have until Monday at nine to respond. If I don't hear from you at that time, I will be contacting every news outlet on the East Coast."

His face got red. "Ms. Rosetti, you're—"

"Save your breath. I wouldn't want you to strain your heart." She nodded at Nina. "In case that wasn't clear enough, I quit. I hope you do too, because life is too short to spend even a second longer at this firm."

"You're right." Nina got up, left her iPad on the chair, and said, "I quit too. And I'll be signing on to head the lawsuit against the firm."

"Nice. I was trying to figure out how I'd have time for that too."

Emilia, Robert's personal assistant, looked up from her desk. "What's going on?"

"We've just quit, and we're filing a lawsuit against the firm for unfair employment practices," Nina said. "And don't bother with the list, Sage. I've been documenting issues for years."

Emilia looked back at Robert's office and got up from her

desk. "I can add to your list." She picked up her purse and joined them. "Let's go."

Three hours later, Sage found Jake in his office at the farmhouse. He leaned back in his chair and smiled. "I should have taken the bet with Kendra. She said you'd get home five minutes before the event started, and I said no way, she'll be here at least an hour before."

"And look at me, I'm seven hours early." She sat on his knee, wound her arms around his neck, and kissed him. "So, I have some good news and some bad news. What do you want first?"

"Bad news."

"I quit my job."

"You're supposed to give me the bad news first, and that's the best news I've heard in weeks." He kissed her, long and deep. "Are you okay, though? Really?"

"A little nervous, but honestly, he gave me no choice." She told him everything that had taken place in Robert's office.

"I'm surprised everyone didn't walk out. I don't know how far you'll get with the lawsuit, though. They do have friends in high places."

"But if we give the story to the media first, those friends in high places might not want to be on the wrong side of the story. Honestly, with the documentation Nina has, I wouldn't be surprised if the founding partners accede to the demands and retire. Nina put together a committee, and they're drawing up a list of the senior partners they'd like to see head up the firm."

"If that happens, what will you do?"

"I gave it a lot of thought on the way home, and as much as I enjoy living in the city and my coworkers, I miss you during the week, and it gets harder and harder to leave here Sunday night. I want to be your partner in life and at work." She smiled. "So what do you say?"

His lips twitched. "Are you asking me to marry you?"

"No." She laughed. "I was asking to be your partner . . . Huh, I guess I was kind of asking that. We haven't been dating—I mean living together—for that long, but—"

"Yes."

"Yes what? Yes, we haven't been living together for that—"

He took her face between his hands. "Yes, I'll marry you. Today, tomorrow, a month from now, a year from now. I'll marry you anytime you want, Sage Rosetti. I adore you."

"Good, because I love you with all my heart, Jake Walker."

He stood with her in his arms. "We have seven hours before the guests arrive. I have some ideas on how we can spend them."

Six hours and fifty-five minutes later, Sage hopped down the hall on one foot while slipping on her other shoe. She heard Kendra say to Jake, "I told you she'd get here five minutes before everyone arrived."

Sage fast-walked to Jake, covering his mouth before he could out them to Kendra. "And the only reason I could be here five minutes before they arrived was because of you. You've done an incredible job, Kendra. Thank you, and I know somewhere up there, Alice is thanking you too."

Jake glanced at her, and Sage nodded. "We have a little something for you," he said, pulling an envelope from the pocket of his white dress shirt. "It's from Alice, Sage, and me. We know this is what she'd want for you. We want it for you too."

Kendra's hand shook as she opened the envelope. She pulled out the check and the offer of admission to Boston University School of Social Work and shook her head. "No, this is too much. I can't take it."

"It's not a handout. You've earned it," Jake said, and Sage remembered how he'd reacted as a teenager when he thought someone saw him as a charity case. "There are some strings attached to it."

"Okay." Kendra nodded, her eyes shiny and bright.

"We're hoping you come work with us at Alice's House once you graduate, and we'd like you to work with us here during the holidays. We'll pay you, of course. And there's always a room for you here if you need it."

Kendra burst into tears, hugging them both. "I was afraid you'd want to get rid of me."

"Of course not. You're part of our family," Sage said. "We couldn't have done any of this without you. Now it sounds like the guests are starting to arrive. We should probably get out there."

Kendra had created a playlist of all of Alice's favorite music with some input from Sage and Jake. At that moment, Robbie Williams's "Angels" was drifting over the rows of deep purple and soft mauve plants on the warm, late-July breeze, carrying with it the sweet, heady scent of lavender. It didn't take long for Sage and Jake to be separated as they greeted their guests, listening to their memories of Alice and the differences she'd made in so many lives.

Over 150 invitations had gone out, and given the crowds of people walking among the rows of lavender and the clusters of guests with their drinks in hand chatting around the pond, it appeared everyone had accepted. Sage's family had insisted on catering the event, and the Beaches and her sister's coworkers at Channel 5 had volunteered to act as their servers and bartenders for the evening. The trees in the backyard and the ones bordering the pond, the lavender fields, and the lavender store were all decorated with fairy lights.

Her mother's mural was the focal point of the celebration, and it took everything Sage had not to announce Gia's secret during her speech. She'd shared it with her sister, though, and now that the tributes to Alice had ended, they stood arm in arm, admiring their mother's mural. Beside it, an easel displayed Flynn's preliminary plans for Alice's House. They were just waiting for the town's approval before breaking ground.

"The plans for Alice's House are truly inspirational. Noah and I've been talking about it, and we'd like to document Alice's legacy in a series," Willow said. "We'd open with an interview with you and Jake. We'd have you talk about working with Alice when you were young and her influence on both of you." Her sister smiled at Jake when he joined them, repeating what he'd missed. "The series would follow you through the planning and building stages, and then wrap up with stories of the women and children who eventually make Alice's House their home. We'd protect their anonymity, of course." She looked from Jake to Sage. "What do you think?"

"I think it could be a great way to raise awareness about gender-based violence and raise money not just for Alice's House but also for all the organizations involved in the cause," Sage said, thinking about Chrysalis House. She'd spoken to Nina about it already and was hopeful that new management at the firm would continue their support. "We'll talk about it and get back to you. When do you need a decision?"

"In the next couple of weeks. I know you two have a lot on your plate but we just need to know if you're on board so we can start planning. We wouldn't begin interviews until the new year."

"You didn't tell her?" Jake asked Sage, but before she could answer, he said, "Sage quit her job. We're going to be partners in business and in life."

Sage laughed. "It really did sound like I was asking you to marry me."

"Hey, I said yes. You can't back out now."

"You're getting married?" Willow squealed. "Everybody, Sage and Jake are getting married!"

Sage sighed as her sister took off in search of the family, sharing their news with anyone who cared to listen. Apparently, everyone did, because they were inundated with congratulations as they joined their guests on the walk to where they would release the sky lantern on the plot of land where Alice's House would eventually stand.

They'd considered doing a group release but had decided that they'd release only one lantern in Alice's honor. Their guests had been invited to write a message to Alice or a word that symbolized what she'd meant to them. Sage and Jake had decided on their message together. *You were and always will be our guiding light.*

Sage's family joined them. "Okay, guys," she said when they began asking for details about their wedding. "It was kind of a spur-of-the-moment thing, so we'll get back to you when we know more."

Jake laughed. "You're such a romantic."

"It's Alice's memorial," she said, a little embarrassed at how unromantic she'd sounded.

"No, it's a celebration of her life, sweetheart. And trust me, nothing would make her happier than you and me getting married."

Together they stood out in the open under a star-littered sky with a half-moon shining down on them surrounded by the people who'd known and loved Alice. They sang "You Raise Me Up" with Josh Groban as she and Jake released the lantern. Watching the flame flicker as it floated up into the night sky, Sage whispered, "Thank you for loving us and for trusting us with your dream, but most of all, thank you for guiding me back to Jake."

Epilogue

One month later

Carmen turned the knob on the stove to low, giving the pot of sauce a quick stir before turning to study her granddaughter. She patted her cheek. "You're pale. Are you sure you're feeling up to doing this?" she asked Lila.

"Don't worry about me, Nonna. I'm fine, and I think this is a great idea. Your followers are going to love it."

"Our customers seem to, so I thought, why not invite our followers to join us for a family dinner at La Dolce Vita? Not all the time, just once in a while, on a special occasion." She gestured out the restaurant's front window at the line of people waiting to get inside. "It's been like this for the past two weeks. Ever since we reinstated our family dinner tradition, the restaurant is packed on Sundays. We're booked solid for the next three months." She nodded at the window. "They're hoping for a cancellation. They've even taken to trying to bribe Bruno. He was accosted at the farmers market yesterday." She shook her head, reaching up to untie her apron.

"They're hoping for some good old-fashioned Rosetti family drama." Lila grinned. "No pressure, but I think your followers are too, after your last Instagram Live. They're still posting memes of Zia Gia and Zia Cami's food fight."

"They might just get some."

"Oh no, don't tell me Gia and Cami are fighting again. Mom will be so disappointed. She says it's just like old times. The three of them have been having so much fun together."

Carmen smiled, thinking about her daughters. Her girls were acting like sisters again, and she couldn't have been happier. About them being close again, si; about what her Gia had been up to, not so much. "Gia and me, we might have some drama." She gestured at the camera in Lila's hands. "Don't tell me when you start filming. We'll let it unfold organically, naturally."

"I, uh, I don't think that's a good idea, Nonna. Instead of live, why don't I film and edit and then post."

"No, I want it happening in real time. Now I'm going to pretend you are just looking at yourself in your phone and not filming. You have a little chat with our followers and tell them what's up." She waved her hand. "Do it now."

"All right, but I'm not taking the rap for this, Nonna. It's all on you."

"Si, si." She walked over to one of the tables in the corner and straightened the silverware, doing the same at several other tables before waving Lila over. The time for the reveal had come. She couldn't put it off any longer. "Come, it's time for Gia's big surprise." She rolled her eyes.

"Why are you acting like that, Nonna? Zia Gia has worked really hard on this."

"I know, I know. But what, do they think when you turn seventy-four, you're suddenly clueless, you don't see and hear what's going on around you? Seventy is the new sixty." She tapped her red-framed glasses. "I also have twenty-twenty vision, but more than that, I know my Gia. I know her brush-strokes, the way she blends her colors... Her heart, it comes through her paintings."

"Um, what are you saying, Nonna?"

"Her big surprise. Her big reveal. *Bah.* I knew she was this street painter, this J.R., from the very beginning."

"Then why did you say all those things? Why did you threaten to have her... J.R. arrested for destruction of public property?"

"Because I wanted her to stop wasting her talent painting for free on the streets of Sunshine Bay!" She opened the door onto the deck, the gentle breeze off the ocean, the rhythmic slap of the waves on the shore doing nothing to ease her temper. "God gave her a gift, and she's squandering it giving it away for free."

"Another way to look at it, Nonna, is that she's sharing God's gift with everyone."

"Bah, sneaking around in the middle of the night? Hiding in the shadows? She should be proud of her talent. She should own it, claim it. Show the world who she is, a beautiful, strong woman who has nothing to hide."

"Nonna." Lila reached for her arm. "I think we should prac-tice how you're going to act when Gia reveals her mural to you." Lila circled her face with her finger. "Show me your sur-prised face? Nonna, that's what Mom would call your consti-pated face."

Carmen raised her hands palms out, widened her eyes, and let her mouth drop open.

"Uh, no, just no." Lila tapped her finger on her lips. "Okay, pretend Bruno has come up behind you and surprised you." She shuddered at Carmen's impression of her surprise. "That's a hard no."

Carmen clutched her chest. "Madonna santa, I'm going to have a heart attack."

"Nonna, what's wrong? Should I get you a glass of water?"

"No! That was me acting surprised."

"No, Nonna, that is what you do whenever you get news that you don't like and want to guilt us into changing it. You're a big faker."

"Sometimes si, sometimes no." She sighed. "Let's go. I can hear them whispering, all excited."

"Do not roll your eyes."

"Okay." She made a face.

"Don't do that either."

"You're so bossy, just like your mother. But I made that face because I remembered you were filming live." She nodded at the camera and whispered, "You were right. I don't want my Gia to hear me talking about her like that. Can we delete it or something?"

"I love you, but you taught us to follow our gut, and my gut said do not, no matter what Nonna says, film her on Instagram Live."

She patted her cheek. "My girls, you've all grown up so smart. I'm proud of you, of all of you."

"That look right there. All you need to do is look at Zia Gia that way, and you'll make her day."

"Okay, I can do that." She rubbed her chest as she walked down the stairs onto the beach, rehearsing what she'd say to her daughter. She wouldn't hurt Gia for the world, so she'd do like Lila said and keep her mouth shut and let her love for her daughter shine from her eyes. Yes, she could manage that, she thought, taking the worn path to where her family stood waiting for her.

A huge black tarp covered the side of the restaurant. Flynn stood with Gia, his arms around her from behind, whispering in her ear, making her smile. Flynn could tell her daughter was nervous, and so could Carmen.

"Are you ready for your big surprise, Ma?" Eva, standing with her husband, James, nudged her head in Gia's direction and mouthed, *Say something.*

"Si, si, that's me, excited." Madonna santa.

Cami was standing with Hugh—Gia and Eva had driven to New York City last weekend and had basically kidnapped the handsome director and the love of her daughter's life. This was the first Carmen had seen of the couple. They'd spent the entire week getting *reacquainted* at the beach house, and Carmen had a good feeling that they would go the distance this time and her daughter would get the happily-ever-after she deserved.

Cami looked at Carmen with a *crapola* expression on her face and took a step in her direction.

Bruno patted Cami's arm. "I've got this, bella." He smiled at Carmen and took her hand in his, leaning in to whisper in her ear, "You don't have to worry, amore mio dolce." My sweet love. "I've got you."

"You do." She stroked his cheek. "I love you."

"And you'll really love me tonight." He waggled his silver eyebrows at her. "Or I should say you'll really love Officer

Bruno. I'm picking up my uniform before we open, so let's get this show on the road."

Carmen laughed, and the tension left her body. She turned her smiling eyes on Gia, who was laughing along with everyone else. Bruno had made sure they'd heard him, even though she knew he had been embarrassed that the girls had discovered they enjoyed a little role-playing. "You are a good, good man," she said, and kissed his cheek.

"I am, otherwise you wouldn't have finally agreed to set a wedding date." He got a *crapola* look on his face, but hey, it served to delay her daughter's big reveal a little longer, as everyone wanted details.

While they were distracted, Carmen tiptoed to the side of the restaurant and reached for the edge of the tarp.

A familiar voice said, "Uh-uh, no peeking."

She turned to see Sage and Jake smiling at her. "You two, you don't miss a thing, do you?"

"We don't." Sage lowered her voice. "Don't be nervous, Nonna."

"What if I don't like it?" she whispered. "I don't want to hurt your mother's feelings."

"Ms. Rosetti, trust me, you're going to love it," Jake said.

"I do trust you. You're a good boy." She glanced to where her daughters were huddled together, no doubt making plans for her wedding. "Now take the tarp down so I can see it without an audience, and you'll be my favorite grandson-in-law."

"Hey, I thought that was me." Lila's husband Luke approached with his twenty-month-old stepdaughter in his arms and a smile on his handsome face.

Carmen held out her arms. "Come to your bisnonna, bella." She cuddled the little girl while sidling closer to the wall, whispering to the baby, "You pull on that for your bisnonna, si?" She wiggled her finger at the edge of the tarp.

"Si." The baby nodded and yanked on the tarp, with a little help from her bisnonna, of course. "Me do!" The baby cheered.

Carmen didn't hear her family's responses. She stood speechless, staring at the beauty her daughter had created for her. Tears rolled down her cheeks as she took in each member of her family sitting at their table at the back of the restaurant below the words *La Dolce Vita—The Sweet Life*.

They were all there, her girls with their partners and their families, happy, laughing, and eating. She pressed her fingers to her lips and looked around for Lila. She was there just behind her—all her girls were, standing together, tears in their eyes and smiles on their beautiful faces, their partners standing behind them.

"A bambina," Carmen said, pointing at Lila's baby bump in the painting.

"Zia guessed it wasn't the flu and asked if she could include the baby-to-be in the painting."

"Bambina*s*," Eva corrected, doing a little shimmy shake. "We're having twins!"

The news brought more tears and more laughter and teasing, and then Carmen saw it and gasped. The family went quiet. The customers who'd joined them did too. She walked to the mural and crouched, reaching out to draw the tip of her finger over her daughter's signature: *Gia Rosetti*. She nodded and stood, walking to Gia. She cupped her daughter's face in her hands. "You are a gift, and I thank God for you every day and for blessing you with a talent such as this."

"You like it, Mama?"

She put an arm around her daughter's shoulders. "How can you ask? It's like you painted my heart on the wall. It's the most beautiful thing I have ever seen."

"Ma, you do know that God blessed your other two daughters too, don't you?" Eva said, linking arms with Cami.

"Yeah, Ma. You're not supposed to have favorites," Cami said, her eyes shining with laughter.

"We need to find out if we're having boys or girls, babe," Luke was whispering to Lila, unaware in his obvious panic that everyone was listening to him. "Because if we're having two more girls, and they're anything like those three together"—his face went slack—"or you and your cousins, I need time to prepare myself."

Everyone broke up laughing, Luke's cheeks becoming flushed as they teased him. Then Eva must have taken pity on him, and in that beautiful strong voice that God had gifted her with, she sang "Sweet Life" by Paul Davis, and Cami joined in.

Soon everyone was singing, everyone but Carmen, whose gaze moved over her family and friends. Her life had not always been easy—she'd faced financial hardships, betrayals, and tragedies—but through it all she'd had her family and friends to lean on. She'd been blessed with a sweet, sweet life.

"Come, we eat now!"

About the Author

USA Today bestselling author **Debbie Mason** writes romantic fiction with humor and heart. The first book in her Christmas, Colorado, series, *The Trouble with Christmas*, was the inspiration for the Hallmark movie *Welcome to Christmas*. When Debbie isn't writing or reading, she enjoys cooking for her family, cuddling with her grandchildren and granddog, and walking in the woods with her husband.

You can learn more at:
AuthorDebbieMason.com
Facebook.com/DebbieMasonBooks
Instagram @AuthorDebMason